DEATH ON THE AISLE

DEATH ON THE AISLE

DEATH ON THE AISLE

FRANCES AND RICHARD LOCKRIDGE

Introduction by Otto Penzler
Foreword by Richard Lockridge

THORNDIKE PRESS
A part of Gale, a Cengage Company

GALE
A Cengage Company

LIBRARY OF CONGRESS CIP DATA ON FILE.
CATALOGUING IN PUBLICATION FOR THIS BOOK
IS AVAILABLE FROM THE LIBRARY OF CONGRESS

ISBN-13: 978-1-4328-7885-6 (hardcover alk. paper)

Published in 2020 by arrangement with Penzler Publishers, LLC

Printed in Mexico
Print Number: 01   Print Year: 2020

INTRODUCTION

Mr. and Mrs. North may well be the most beloved married couple in the history of American detective fiction. A strong case could be made for Nick and Nora Charles, of course, but they appeared in only a single book, *The Thin Man* (1934), and undoubtedly became more and more loved because of the superb acting job of Myrna Loy and William Powell, who portrayed the boozy couple in six motion pictures.

Both couples were crafted in response to trends in mystery novels of the era, many of which feature young women as charismatic as they are scatterbrained. These characters often find themselves in unlikely and somewhat dangerous situations, never quite knowing how they got there, only escaping some horrible fate in the nick of time. While their actions may be exasperating to their husbands, to the police, and often to the reader, their indisputable charm can squeeze sincere affection out of even the grumpiest of those parties.

No character better exemplifies this type of personality than Pam North and her effect on her long-suffering but loving husband, Jerry. Created by Richard Lockridge for a series of vignettes and short stories, published in the *New York Sun* and *The New Yorker,* it was Frances who conceived of a series of mystery novels based on the entertaining couple. Together, with Frances creating the plots and Richard supplying the actual writing, the Lockridge's produced twenty-seven books (twenty-six of which were mysteries) featuring the Norths, the series ending when Frances Lockridge suddenly died in 1963. In addition to those twenty-seven books, Mr. and Mrs. North appeared in a Broadway play, a motion picture, and several radio and television series.

Richard Lockridge was born in St. Joseph, Missouri, in 1898, attended Kansas City Junior College and the University of Missouri, served in the Navy in 1918, and became a reporter for two Kansas City newspapers in 1921 and 1922, the year he married Frances Louise Davis. They moved to New York City's Greenwich Village the same year. He joined the *New York Sun* as a reporter, becoming its drama critic in 1928. His background covering the theatrical world is evident in several books, including *Death on the Aisle,* with its insider and backstage knowledge and portrayal of theaters and the people who work in them.

Richard Lockridge was responsible for four other detective series, three of which he began with Frances and then continued on his own after her death. *Think of Death* (1947) launched a series of twenty-two novels about Lieutenant (later Captain, then Inspector) Merton Heimrich of the New York State Police. Most of the action takes places in the suburban counties of Westchester, Putnam, and Dutchess, where the Lockridges lived after they left New York City. The Norths met Heimrich with their friend Bill Weigand, an NYPD homicide detective who regularly appears in the Mr. and Mrs. North series.

Also in collaboration with Frances, Richard began a series in 1956 with a diffident New York City police detective, Nathan Shapiro, who, when moved up in rank, cannot understand why he received the promotion. He always appears to be depressed. He starred in ten books, beginning with *The Faceless Adversary* in 1956.

The ever-busy Lockridges began a short-

7

lived third detective series with *Night of the Shadows* (1962), a police procedural featuring NYPD detective Paul Lane. Lane and his partner Sergeant, later Lieutenant, John Stein, were later prominently featured in the fourth Lockridge series, this one by Richard alone, focused on New York County Assistant District Attorney Bernard Simmons, that followed that character's first appearance (in a Paul Lane novel), *And Left for Dead* (1962).

Two years after Frances Lockridge's death, Richard married Hildegarde Dolson, also a mystery writer, though they did not collaborate. They moved to Tryon, North Carolina, where Richard died in 1982.

More details about the Norths, and the Lockridges, may be found in a delightful essay written by Richard in 1977 and published the following year in *The Great Detectives,* which I edited; it was published by Little, Brown. It follows as a foreword to *Death on the Aisle.*

— OTTO PENZLER

MR. AND MRS. NORTH

Mr. and Mrs. North had been fictional, or semifictional, characters for several years before they first met murder. I paraphrase the title of the first mystery novel about them — *The Norths Meet Murder.* I had written pieces about them for *The New Yorker* — not short stories, precisely, but what *The New Yorker* then called "casuals." Brief domestic comedies, I suppose they were. And they were based, sometimes closely, on things which had happened to my wife, Frances, and me.

I wrote, and the magazine bought, a good many of those pieces, and eventually they were collected in a book called *Mr. and Mrs. North.* The publisher, rather ill-advisedly, called this collection a "novel." Several reviewers snorted and so, in a mild way, did I. Novels, like short stories, require plots, and I, then, was plotless. And the Norths, in the early *New Yorker* pieces, were without first names.

The surname was easy. It was merely lifted from the somewhat amorphous, and frequently inept, people who played the North hands in bridge problems. In *The New Yorker,* in their early appearances they were merely "Mr." and "Mrs." But midway of one piece, it became necessary for Mr. North to call to his wife in another room of their apartment. It seemed unlikely that he would call out, "Hey, Mrs. North." So, on the spur of the moment, he called for "Fran." I do not remember that I had ever called Frances that, although, among other things, I did call her "Francie."

When proofs — *The New Yorker* always sent proofs — came back the "Fran" stuck out. The spur of the moment had, clearly, struck too close to home. As a one-time printer I could count spaces, so that only one line would have to be reset. (I had been, a few years earlier, the printer in the Kansas City, Missouri, post office. I had learned to set type in a "journalism" course at Kansas City Junior College, where journalism certainly started with the fundamentals. I was taught to run a job press at the office by an elderly man, who really was a printer and was retiring. He lacked two fingers on his right hand, which was conventional for long-time operators of job presses. I did manage to retain mine.)

Anyway, I counted spaces, and "Pam" came close enough, and Mrs. North became Pamela, "Pam" for that line of type. I have no idea how her husband became "Jerry" or, for that matter, how he became a publisher. In *The New Yorker* stories, he had no occupation, so far as I can remember. Except, of course, that of being foil, straight man, to his wife.

Actually, I suppose the Norths did not first appear in *The New Yorker,* although that was the first time they had names.

When we first went to New York to stay, the *New York Sun* devoted that part of its back page not occupied by John Wanamaker to a department called The Sun Rays. It consisted of very short, preferably humorous pieces, and fragments of verse. We were broke; *flat* broke is not excessive. Frances got a job reckoning payments due from people who were buying on time — buying electric generators, as I recall. She was paid twenty-five dollars a week. It was a job for which she was totally unsuited, and which she did very well. We paid twenty dollars a week for a large room with a bath and a gas plate at one end. I, for some months, had no job at all, although I kept applying to all the city's newspapers, which then were numerous. So I started submitting pieces to The Sun Rays.

Most of them were about the "babes in the studio apartment." In retrospect, the "babes" seems to me unbearably cute. It was also inaccurate. We were both experienced newspaper reporters, Frances much more experienced than I. But we *were* babes in Manhattan and had fallen into the habit of eating. The Sun Rays pieces helped us sustain the habit. They also helped me, finally, to get a job on the city staff of the *Sun.*

The "babes" were the Norths in embryo. And the time was fifty years ago. You could buy twenty-five cents' worth of stew meat and make it do for two dinners. If, of course, the stew didn't spoil between meals: we had no refrigeration in the studio.

I kept on writing North stories while I was doing rewrite, and covering murder trials, on the *Sun.* We seemed to spend more than our combined salaries, although by then Frances had found a job more suited to her skills, and somewhat better paying. *The New Yorker* kept on buying. And we both, from time to time, read detective stories — mystery novels, novels of suspense, whatever publishers care to call them. (My own preference is for "detective stories," or the variants which I think of as "chases." Chases are more likely to become one-shots in magazines, or did before general magazines shrank so drastically in size and, of course, in number.)

It was Frances who first decided to write a detective story of her own. For several days her typewriter clicked happily. Then she came to me. There was one point with which she was having a little trouble, and perhaps I could help.

I read the dozen or so pages and it seemed to me to start very well. Then there was a scene, obviously crucial. A rowboat, apparently with nobody in it, was crossing a lake in the moonlight. I recognized the lake; we were renting a summer weekend cabin on just such a lake.

The rowboat came ashore. There was a body lying in it.

"Fine," I said. "Very good scene. Foreboding. Only, with only this dead man in it, what made the boat move? You say it was a still night; no wind to blow it ashore. So?"

"Yes," she said, "that's the point I'm having trouble with. I though maybe you could help. After all, you were in the navy."

I had been. On a battleship which had spent most of 1918 in what was then Brooklyn Navy Yard. New engines were being installed. With new engines she could move herself. In fact, she did move while I was still aboard. Across water in the yard and, with a considerable bang, into a pier. *U.S.S. North Dakota* managed, later, to steam to a drydock for junking.

None of this seemed to have much to do with a rowboat, occupied only by the dead, moving across a quiet lake under a full moon.

Frances was disappointed. I promised her we would work on it.

We did work on it. And we got nowhere. I still think about it now and then. I still get nowhere.

But then we got the idea of collaborating on a mystery, without the magical boat, but with Mr. and Mrs. North, already established characters.

The way we worked together, on that and subsequent books in what became a series, was to have story conferences. Who will we kill this time? Male or female? And who will do the killing, and why?

We would talk things out, making notes, coming up — usually slowly — with ideas, each of us accepting or rejecting the other's notions.

After some hours of this, each of us would

type up a synopsis of the book and of individual scenes in it. We would name the characters, which is often a tricky business. We would, finally, jumble it all together. Then I would write the story, drawing on our outlines and my experience, not very extensive, as a police reporter. And also my experience in covering murder trials, which was much greater. (Hall-Mills, Snyder-Gray and others celebrated in the now-distant past. Newspapers went all out for trials in those days. Some rented houses to lodge their covering staffs. The *Sun* made do with three of us and now and then, as in the Browning separation suit, with only two.)

I did all the writing on all our books. Frances summed it up neatly in one speaking appearance we made together: "I think up interesting characters and Dick kills them off."

(The Norths themselves almost got killed off before, as detectives, they were ever born. Somebody, and I am afraid it was the late George Bye, my agent and close friend, suggested that they be renamed — perhaps become the Souths, or maybe the Wests.)

It would be too much to say that by then the Norths had a following. But they were known to *New Yorker* readers. The suggestion that this perhaps minimal advantage be

15

thrown away was hooted down, mostly by me, but also by the editors.)

When Frances died very suddenly and I kept on writing, several reviewers searched diligently for change in our style. One or two found it, which I thought very astute of them.

I wrote no more North stories after Frances's death, partly because, in my mind, she had always been Pamela North; partly because the spontaneity seemed to be ebbing out of them.

People used to ask me what Pam and Jerry looked like. I could never tell them. I have always avoided detailed physical descriptions of characters. It is better, it seems to me, to let readers form their own conceptions. (This attitude of mine may stem from the days when I was a boy and my mother read Dickens to me. She ready from heavy volumes of an edition set two columns to the page in six-point type. There were sketches of the characters. None of them ever looked remotely like the people I had learned to know so intimately from Dickens's words).

So Inspector Heimrich is a big man, who thinks he looks like a hippopotamus; Lieutenant Shapiro is tall and thin. He wears gray suits which need pressing and has a long sad face. Readers can take it from there.

They have taken Pam North a good many places. Nobody ever seemed to care much about what Jerry looked like. When the collection of North stories was published in England, the publishers decided they needed to be sketched as chapter headings. They were stolid-looking characters. Pam was matronly; Jerry smoked a pipe. Neither was in the least what I had, vaguely, imagined.

I suppose I had thought, insofar as I thought of it at all, that Pam was small and quick and blond. I had no quarrel with the casting of her in either the play or the television series. Either Peggy Conklin in the play or Barbara Britton in the TV series was all right with me. (During rehearsals of Owen Davis's play, Miss Conklin used to crouch in the wings, for all the world like a runner preparing for the hundred-yard dash, and make her entrances at a runner's speed. Which was, to my mind, entirely appropriate.) Gracie Allen, in the movie, seemed to me a triumph of miscasting.

Pam's mind is another matter. It seemed to me to glint. Its logic was darting, now and then bewildering but always acute. The female mind is often like that. Owen Davis once told me that Pam North was what every well-married man likes to think his wife is.

I have been most lucky to be twice married to women with minds like that, which is obviously more than any man deserves. Men plod their ways on paths of logic, and laboriously reach conclusions to find women sitting on them, patient as they wait for laggards.

Men like to call this superior mental alacrity "womanly intuition."

— RICHARD LOCKRIDGE

I
TUESDAY, OCTOBER 28

2:20 P.M. TO 3:10 P.M.

This time, they assured each other, nothing was going to intervene. They agreed to this and nodded confidence over their coffee cups, with the gravity of children, and were for their purposes quite alone in the unchildlike atmosphere of Club 21.

"Absolutely nothing, this time," William Weigand promised himself and her. "Right?"

"Right," Dorian said. "Exactly right."

They nodded again.

"And so," Weigand said, "are we waiting for something?"

Dorian Hunt said she couldn't think what.

"Approved and ready," she said. "That's what we are. Approved for matrimony by the Empire State."

She finished her coffee and put the cup down and looked, turning a little to face him, at Weigand on the seat beside her.

"And who are we," she wanted to know, "to disappoint the Empire State?"

"And ourselves," Weigand said. "Do we want brandies or something?"

Dorian thought they didn't. She said she had no use for people who had to get drunk to get married. She said that Bill would have to marry her cold sober.

"Any time," Bill said, firmly. "Now."

"We'll go find a little minister," Dorian said. "A very quiet little minister."

Bill said, "Right."

"Only," he said, "don't you have to find a little dressmaker and a little milliner first? I thought that was a rule."

Dorian didn't say anything for a moment. She looked at Bill through eyes which always seemed to him to have a glint of green in them, and which now looked darker than they usually did. That might, he thought, be the lighting in the upstairs room at "21." For a moment they looked at each other, slowly, with a kind of care.

"We are right, aren't we, Bill?" Dorian said. Her voice was grave; the question was a real question.

"Yes," Bill said. "For a long time, now. Didn't you know?"

She smiled a little then, quickly.

"Whose fault was it that it was such a long time?" she wanted to know.

"Well," he said, "for a good while, yours.

All that stuff about marrying a cop. And then, I'll grant you —"

"Then," she said, "it was you being a cop, and too busy. What with men in cement. And men without teeth in condemned houses. And such charming incidents."

Bill would, he realized, have risen to that not so long ago; have answered, worried and anxious, and tried to make her see that something had to be done about men who killed other men and, for reasons which rather slowly became apparent, pulled out all their teeth; about men who encased their fellows in cement, and lowered them into rivers. Lieutenant William Weigand of the Homicide Bureau had often argued such matters with Dorian Hunt since that first day, which came so quickly after their first meeting, when they had realized that they were going to have to explain themselves rather fully to each other.

The fact that Weigand was Lieut. Weigand of the police, and that it was his primary duty to pursue, had been the one thing most difficult to explain to Dorian. At first she had said only "why?" and then, which was even more difficult, "why *you*?" It had taken time to explain that last, and a good many words, and in the end, Weigand suspected, it was not really the words that had done it.

Never, he somewhat suspected, had Dorian come to approve his occupation, because she felt strongly, and with a personal bias, on the subject of hunters. His profession had become, in the end, merely a somewhat unfortunate attribute of William Weigand, and Dorian had decided to overlook it. After that, she seemed quite light-hearted about it, and even interested in pursuit as an exercise in logic. But Weigand did not suppose that she had changed essentially on the matter, and, since he was logical and wanted everything thrashed out fully, this sometimes puzzled him. He looked at her now and decided it was not an important puzzlement.

"Well," he said, "I'm off today, if nothing breaks. So why not today? Why not" — he looked at his watch — "three o'clock at some small, and convenient, clergyman's? The Little Church?"

"No," Dorian said, firmly. "Not the Little Church. Just some little preacher's, where nobody's ever gone before — a *new* little minister's, without any tradition."

"Right!" Weigand said, and raised eyebrows at a waiter. He looked at the check, managed not to wince, and laid bills on the tray. The waiter pulled out the table and they wriggled forth and Weigand held Dorian's fitted, furless gray coat. It looked military, he thought, and said "Damn" under his breath. Dorian's eyebrows went up.

"Things," he said. "Your coat looks like part of a uniform."

Her eyes darkened again and she waited until he came beside her. Then she took his arm, suddenly, almost angrily. It was not like Dorian, who seldom took arms.

"Come on," she said. "We've got to hurry, Bill. We've got to hurry — so *fast*! They're taking all our time away, Bill."

Urgency went with them down the stairs. Bill was abrupt, hurried, as he collected hat and coat. He was quick and casual with the doorman who opened the door of his car — parked prominently and conveniently, as became the car of a police lieutenant. Inside the car his fingers moved automatically, hurriedly. The radio switch clicked in response to one familiar gesture; the fingers of the other hand twisted the key in the ignition lock. The motor took hold and the radio said, harshly, indifferently:

"— call your office."

"Bill —" Dorian said. Unconsciously he held up his hand, quieting her as he listened.

"Car 8 call your office," the radio said. "That is all."

It was enough.

"Damn!" Weigand said, not under his breath. "Damn it to hell!"

"Oh — Bill!" Dorian said. *Again?*

The motor died as Weigand cut the switch.

"Maybe it's nothing," he said. He didn't believe it. It was one of those things — when the car radio spoke metallically; when the telephone demanded angrily in the middle of the night; when a police messenger appeared suddenly at his desk, it was always one of those things. A man with his teeth out. A man in cement. One of those things. People, Weigand thought angrily, picked the damnedest times to murder.

"Maybe it's nothing," he repeated. "I'm supposed to be off today. But I'll have to see."

"Of course," Dorian said, in a small voice. "You'll have to see. Oh, Bill — why don't you sell ribbons?"

"Nobody buys ribbons any more," he said, opening the door. "Didn't you know about ribbon clerks, Dor? Technological unemployment — dreadful thing."

He was out, and leaned back in.

"We'll hope," he said. "You wait and hope."

But it was no use hoping. Weigand turned away from the telephone in "21" knowing

24

that. It was murder again, and Bill cursed it. But there was excitement, still, in a new case starting, and excitement ran under his disappointment. And then, half pleased and half perturbed, he contemplated the message he had just received, relayed, as to instructions, from Deputy Chief Inspector Artemus O'Malley and, as to information, from Detective Sergeant Aloysius Clarence Mullins.

The instructions were simple. There was a man dead in a seat in the West 45th Street Theatre, which was against regulations. Lieutenant (Acting Captain) Weigand to investigate and report. The information, added with a touch of amusement in the voice by the patrolman on telephone duty, amplified by one sentence, quoting Mullins:

"Tell the Loot the Norths is here."

To that, Weigand had said, simply, "My God!"

He repeated the gist of it to Dorian. It wasn't nothing; it was a case.

"And," he said, "Jerry and Pam seem to be in it."

Again? said Dorian.

"I know," Weigand said, "it's peculiar. And what do we do with you?"

"We don't get married?" Dorian said. "There isn't going to be any little preacher?"

25

"I know," Weigand said. "But there's a man dead. We'll fix that, and *then* the little preacher." He looked at Dorian. "Damn," he said, "it's a note, Dor."

Dorian admitted, a little drily, that it was inconvenient. She said she had had her afternoon all planned.

"This is leaving me at loose ends," she explained. "You should never leave a fiancée at loose ends, Bill. Didn't you know? So I think I'll just go along."

"But —" Weigand began, getting into the car.

"If the Norths can, I can," Dorian said, making movements of not getting out.

"But —" said Weigand, starting the motor.

"Of course," Dorian said, "our other plan was better. But you would be a detective, and whither thou goest —"

"That," Weigand said, "was said by one woman to another woman. Which nobody seems to remember."

He turned on the siren, and cars scattered like alarmed chickens before a hawk's dive. Cars stopped at Fifth Avenue by the lights surged ahead in answer to commanding whistles and a traffic patrolman's strangely indignant gestures. Weigand's Buick, wailing, turned south on Fifth, and civilian cars

26

hugged the curb obediently.

Dorian grabbed the door handle as the car swerved off Fifth into Forty-fifth and sent more traffic scattering. She gasped as the Buick swerved left and right again to avoid a grinding truck. She shouted something, and Bill leaned toward her.

"— stay dead —" he heard, and said, "What?"

"He'll stay dead," Dorian shouted. "You don't have to —"

"Custom," Weigand shouted back. "Cops always do. Regulations."

They were beyond Broadway when Weigand flicked the siren off and put the brakes on. For a moment the change in sound was one rather of pitch than volume, as the tires shrieked on the pavement. Then the Buick nosed in beside a police radio car which was one of a covey of radio cars. The Homicide Squad car was against the curb in front of a theatre entrance. The marquee of the theatre had a title spelled out in light bulbs, with a word preceding it. The bulbs spelled out:

"Coming: TWO IN THE BUSH."

There was a crowd, held back by patrolmen, so that the sidewalk immediately in front of the theatre was clear except for three lean men with cards in the bands of their hats. They saw the Lieutenant and

27

started for him. Weigand waved at them.

They advanced with modified eagerness, and Weigand shook his head.

"Later," he said. "I don't know myself."

Dorian held on to Bill and the reporters looked at her curiously. They pushed through glass doors and patrolmen inside displayed interest. Weigand said "Homicide" and one of them jerked a directing thumb.

The lobby was long, and Dorian's heels clicked on tile. There were more doors and another lobby, and her heels dug into carpet, scarred with cigarette burns. Then they were in the theatre. The seats were empty under dim lights. Ahead and down, it was lighter and men and women were clustered, some on the flatly lighted stage, others in the rows of seats nearest the orchestra pit. At the head of each of the four aisles a uniformed patrolman stood, waiting and detached. Weigand started left and the patrolman there stiffened when he saw Dorian, and waved them the other way. They went down the right-center aisle and Weigand looked across the house. There was a little knot of men in the left-center aisle, toward the rear of the house, and as he looked a light flared, blindingly, and went out.

"Over there," Dorian said, pointing.

"Right," Weigand said. "Later."

They came into the reflected light from the stage, and Pam North, trim in a yellow dress which had the look of a uniform about the shoulders, stood up from a seat on the aisle.

"Bill!" she called. "Here we are!"

"Hello, Pam," Weigand said, and Pam said, in a tone of pleased surprise: "Dorian!" Then she went on:

"Bill," she said, "he says it's *me*! Did you ever?"

Weigand was conscious of a slight loss of contact with reality.

"Who says what's you, Pam?" he said, slowly and carefully. Then he said: "Just a minute, Mullins."

"O.K., Loot," Mullins said. "The Norths is here."

"He says if it hadn't been that I came he would still be alive," Pam said. "I don't think he means it, but he sounds as if he did. You tell him, Bill."

Bill looked inquiringly at Mr. North, who was still sitting in the seat next that from which his wife had risen. Mr. North was running the fingers of his right hand through his hair.

"Hello, Jerry," Weigand said.

"Probably," Mr. North said, "it is nothing. Of course it is nothing, really." He looked up at Weigand. "But," he said, "you can't help wondering, can you? Wherever we go. I can't even sit up with a sick author."

"Jerry," Bill said. "For God's sake, don't *you*!"

Gerald North stood up and smiled at Dorian and said he was sorry.

"Penfield Smith," he said. "He's the author here. We publish him. He said it was driving him nuts, and would I sit in one afternoon just to see who was crazy. And Pam said she had never seen a rehearsal and wanted to come, and it seemed all right." He paused, and looked around the gloomily lighted auditorium. "At the time," he added darkly. Pam said: "Jerry!" and he reached out and touched her shoulder, gently.

"All right, Pam," he said. "It's just a co-incidence."

He still, Weigand thought, seemed rather haunted by it. And so, a little way under the surface, did Pam North. Her eyes were wide and alarmed, Weigand thought. He could sympathize.

"I know," Pam said, uncannily astep with his thoughts. "Typhoid Mary — Homicide Pam." She stopped and looked at him: "Bill, *you* don't think —"

Weigand shook his head, and told her to

forget it. He said, "All right, Mullins," and Mullins said, "O.K., Loot, back here." Weigand left the Norths and Dorian together and sidled between seats to the other aisle. He walked back up it and a man in white who was bending over a dark huddle in a seat on the right of the aisle stood up.

"Dead," he said. "Stabbed in the back of the neck. Punctured the spinal cord, apparently."

He was a young man, and looked pale.

"Do you know who this is?" he asked suddenly.

"No," Weigand said. "Do you?"

"Sure," the ambulance surgeon said. "I heard him lecture once. Carney Bolton — *the* Carney Bolton." He looked down at the huddle. "Sinus man," he said. "About the best." He looked at Weigand, waiting for comment. It came in a soft whistle.

"Well," Weigand said. "So this is Dr. Carney Bolton! So it caught up with him, finally." The ambulance surgeon looked as if he knew what Weigand meant, and nodded. "Right," Weigand said.

"Nothing for me," the ambulance surgeon said. "He hasn't been dead long; an hour or two. But that's the M.E.'s guess."

"Right," Weigand said, and waved him on his way. The detective watched a moment

31

as the young man in white went up the aisle, nodded to the patrolman at its head, went out through the lobby doors.

"Well," Weigand said, to nobody in particular. "Dr. Carney Bolton. Let's have a light here, one of you."

Dr. Carney Bolton had been a long, thin man and was now a long, thin corpse. The body had folded up in the seat, the head fallen forward and to the left, so that it partially rested on the arm of the orchestra chair which was farthest from the aisle. A plain, wooden handle stuck out of the back of the neck: a handle of unpainted wood. If you wanted to straighten Dr. Bolton up and look at his face the handle would, Weigand thought wryly, be very convenient. The Medical Examiner's man, when he came, would no doubt find it convenient. Now it was hard to see much of what had been Dr. Carney Bolton. Weigand lowered the seat in front and knelt on it and stared at Dr. Bolton without touching anything.

He had been around fifty-five, Weigand guessed — a man almost starkly thin and almost arrestingly tall, with thinning blond hair which did not show the gray that must be there. His face was long and narrow and the staring eyes — staring now at the floor and the back of the seat in front — were set close together. The lips, partly open, were unexpectedly soft, and sensual in the long face, above the long chin.

"He looks," Pam North said from behind Weigand, "as if he had been somebody. If you didn't know, you asked, like Chesterton."

"Look," said Weigand, twisting toward her, "you are supposed to be down with Jerry and Dorian, Pam. Not — this." He gestured toward the corpse, and curiosity overcame him. "What about Chesterton?" he asked.

"I know," Pam said. "It's awful, but I had to see. And Mullins said it wasn't very awful. He said that when he went down the street if people didn't know who he was they asked. Because he was so funny looking, he meant. And this man, because he would look as if he were somebody you ought to know. Was he?"

Weigand sorted out the pronouns, deduced which "he" applied to Chesterton and, belatedly, nodded.

"He was Dr. Carney Bolton," he said. "You know?"

Mrs. North said, "Oh!", and looked at the body with renewed interest.

"Always in the papers," she said. "Lots of women; lots of fingers in lots of pies. At all the first nights. Yes."

That, Weigand told her, was Bolton. Backer of plays and beguiler of women; physician to the theatrical profession at its most solvent; dabbler in motion-picture enterprises. A man who got around and was a good name in gossip columns; a man who frequently had been sued, with one hope or another, by women, and had always seemed to enjoy it. And now —

"Now somebody's stuck an ice-pick in his neck," Mrs. North pointed out. "Not even a very good ice-pick. Just the dime kind, or maybe just given out by ice-men."

Weigand looked at her and then at the wooden handle in the back of Bolton's neck. Obviously, when you looked at it with that in mind, it was the handle of an ice-pick, and a very cheap ice-pick.

"It's funny how seldom you see an ice-pick nowadays," Mrs. North said conversationally. "They've gone out. Only we have them in the country just like that."

Weigand nodded. Somebody, he said, had been bright. Mrs. North made an inquiring sound, and said it seemed very ordinary, somehow. Not ingenious. Weigand nodded in approval and said that that was, of course, precisely it.

"That's the beauty of it," he said. "Nothing complicated to misfire. No special weapon to be traced. Not even a handle which will take fingerprints. Just an ordinary ice-pick from the nearest hardware store: cost, ten cents; traceability, zero. Next to a club on a dark night, the perfect weapon."

Mrs. North said "Um-m-m!" and shivered. She said she didn't like them this way, so much.

"It's too real," she said. "Too close. I think I'll make Jerry get an electric one in the country."

Weigand's mind hesitated almost imperceptibly at the jump. He was, it was gratifying to realize, improving rapidly. He could recall the time when that would have left him flatfooted. He recalled his mind and slid to the floor; he dismissed the flashlight with a gesture and it went out. And where the hell, he asked, was the man from the M.E.'s office? A couple of detectives made low, agreeing sounds.

"Got your pictures?" Weigand wanted to know. The police photographer wanted another shot or two. Weigand said "Right," and that they could get on with the printing, not moving it more than they had to. He pushed Pam North gently in front of him, and went down toward the stage, his eyes flickering over the people on it and in the seats in front. He wriggled through the seats to Mullins and smiled fleetingly at Dorian, and shook his head ruefully. The headshake reported that this one was going to take time and doing; it relegated into the uncertain future the little preacher. Dorian looked resignation at him. Weigand shook his head sadly and went to business. He said, raising his voice for the first time, "Mullins."

The Manual of Procedure specified that "what is desired at the scene of the crime is a dominating mind, exemplified by the Commanding Officer present." It was time, Weigand decided, to exemplify a dominating mind. He wished his felt more like one.

"O.K., Loot," Mullins said. Weigand moved down the aisle toward him. He said, "Let's have it."

"People?" said Mullins. "Or just generally where we are?"

"Where we are," Weigand told him. "Too many people to start with."

Mullins said "O.K." He said the first report came through at 2:11, apparently only a few minutes after the body was found. Weigand interrupted. Who found it?

"Him," Mullins said, pointing. He pointed to a thin young man, almost as tall and thin as Dr. Bolton had been. But this man was

36

twenty years younger, and stooped, and a lock of red hair fell down over his forehead. A gray suit hung on him indifferently, with an air of only casual acquaintanceship, and a blue shirt gaped open at the neck.

"That's —" Mullins said, and consulted a notebook. "Humphrey Kirk. He's a director." There was a slightly rising inflection on "director." Weigand nodded. "Right," he said.

"Well," Mullins said, "this guy Kirk went back and nudged the corpse, wanting to ask it something, and it fell over. He yelled. And after they'd looked at it somebody called Headquarters. So we sent out a call for you and came running."

"Right," Weigand said. "Was he fresh dead?"

Mullins shrugged.

"Sort of, I guess," he said. "And sort of not. Where's this guy from the M.E.'s office?"

Weigand shrugged back.

"As always," he said, "somewhere else. Give me the rest."

"Well," Mullins said, "they all knew this guy Bolton. Seems he backed the show — this show they're getting ready to put on. 'Two in the Bush.' " He paused and considered the title. "A hot one, huh?" he said.

"Two in the bushes."

"I don't know," Weigand said. "We'll review it later. So Bolton was producing it — putting it on?"

Mullins shook his head. He said they made it more complicated than that.

"There's another guy they say is the producer," he said. "A guy named Max Ahlberg. Seems like I've heard of him?" Weigand nodded. Weigand had himself; plenty of people who heard of Broadway heard of Max Ahlberg and more swore by him than at him. "Well," Mullins said, "Ahlberg is putting on the show and Bolton was putting up the money. Angeling. O.K.?"

Weigand nodded.

"They're going to open next week," Mullins said. "Or was. Kirk told me all this; told me more about the show and when it was going to open than anything else. He was sore as hell at Bolton for getting killed; said it messed things up proper. He said" — Mullins consulted his notebook — " 'Something like this always happens when you try to open cold.' Does that mean anything to you, Loot?"

"Without a road tour," Weigand explained. "So —"

"So," Mullins said, "they're rehearsing here, in the set, which it seems they don't usually do, and I gather they're pretty well rehearsed. And Kirk thinks it's the lousiest trick he ever heard of, Bolton's getting bumped off just before they start the previews." Mullins looked at his notebook and shook his head gloomily. "Kirk's something," he said. "Half the time I don't get him. Anyway . . ."

Anyway, they had rehearsed during the morning, with Bolton sitting in. "And making everybody sore, as nearly as I can gather," Mullins said. "He didn't seem to like the way anything went and kept yelling at them." At 12:30 they had knocked off for lunch, early because Kirk had to see somebody, and they started again at 1:15. It was — Mullins consulted his notebook again — "a straight run-through of the second act."

"And Bolton?" Weigand said.

Mullins shrugged. He said that was one of the things they had to find out. Just now it looked as if nobody had seen him alive since just before lunch. Nobody had seen him go out or come back. Just before they knocked off for the morning, Bolton yelled that he couldn't hear a word anybody was saying and said he was going back to the rear of the house and that they had to make him hear there.

"So?" Weigand said.

"So he went, I guess," Mullins said. "Nobody paid much attention, because Kirk was telling somebody on the stage what was wrong with him. He says he heard Bolton say he couldn't hear and waved, but didn't turn around. And the next thing we know about Bolton he's dead. Only it's two hours later. So he could have been killed any time between —"

A voice broke in. It was a woman's voice, low and musical. It said: "Wait a minute, officer. That isn't right."

Weigand turned and looked toward the voice. The woman was slighter than her voice indicated; she was a slender girl with reddish brown hair which hung softly down almost to her shoulders and she had brown eyes which seemed immoderately large. Even after you realized what makeup had done for them, they still seemed immoderately large. And now they were also, Weigand decided, frightened.

"Why isn't it right?" he said.

"Because I had lunch with him," the girl said. "Or coffee, anyway. At the Automat up Eighth Avenue."

"Yes?" Weigand said.

"Yes," she repeated. "He said he only had time for coffee. He said" . . . she paused and looked at Weigand . . . "he said he had to get right back to — to see Mr. Ahlberg."

II
TUESDAY
3:10 P.M. TO 3:45 P.M.

The stage set was a rectangular room with gray walls and bright pictures. Standing with his back to the auditorium, Weigand faced casement windows, curtained and outlined by heavy yellow drapes. At his left, the windows sliced a corner from the room. There were cupboards under the windows and their cushioned tops made a window-seat. Along the left wall, there was a long, modern table. Close down to the footlights at the left was a door.

Weigand let his eyes flicker over the people sitting in chairs in a semicircle in front of him, and continued an examination of the set. He was detached, measuring, and hoped he was dominating the situation, as per instruction. He was giving the men and women in front of him time to get nervous, if they were going to.

The windows ended three-quarters of the way across the rear of the set. Then a railing

42

ran out from the rear wall, bounding a raised platform, two steps up from the floor of the rest of the room. In the rear wall, opening off the platform, was a door. In the right wall, also opening off the platform, was another door. A little down-stage from this second door, another rail jutted from the side wall for a few feet, ending as the steps began. Closer to the footlights on the right wall was a fireplace and over it a modern French painting of a woman sitting by a window and looking out. The woman was rather oddly shaped, and oddly attractive, and engagingly undressed. Weigand thought of other things. He set his feet a little apart on the mauve carpet which covered the stage floor and let his eyes drift slowy over the half-circle of possible murderers.

The girl with the large eyes was named Alberta James, and she sat third in from the left. Weigand, facing everybody — he hoped — who had been in the theatre when Carney Bolton was killed, ticked off her name in his mind. Slender girl with reddish brown hair hanging almost to her shoulders, and big, disturbing eyes — that equaled Alberta James. There were — Weigand counted quickly — exactly seventeen others. "Too damned many," he told himself. He waited while Mullins' eyes plodded around the semicircle; waited for Mullins to turn to him and say it. Mullins obliged.

"Jeeze, Loot," Mullins said. "Why do we *always* get the screwy ones?"

There wasn't any answer. Weigand wondered too.

"Right," he said. "Is everybody on the stage?"

Humphrey Kirk leaned forward in his chair beside Alberta James and appeared to count off. Then he turned to Weigand and nodded.

"All our crowd, I guess," he said. "Plus some of your crowd?"

The last was a question. Weigand looked at Dorian and the Norths, sitting at the opposite point of the semicircle, and a little behind the others, and nodded. Deduct his crowd and he still had fifteen. With luck, he had fourteen innocent persons and a murderer; had fourteen who might be as puzzled as he was at the moment and one who wasn't puzzled at all — one who had stood, or sat, behind Dr. Carney Bolton, drawn an ice-pick — from where? — felt its points for reassurance, perhaps, and stabbed it into the back of Dr. Carney Bolton's neck, having great luck. (Or had Bolton's head been already inclined forward, so that the serra-

44

tions of the vertebrae were visible? Had there been enough light to see the serrations if Bolton's position made them prominent?)

"Right," Weigand said. "Now here is where we stand. Somebody, and I think one of you in front of me, stabbed Dr. Carney Bolton some time within the past two or three hours. Bolton is dead. Whoever did it used an ice-pick. Whoever did it was lucky and killed Bolton, as you say, instantly. I am Lieutenant William Weigand of the Homicide Squad, and I'm in charge here at the moment. This is Detective Sergeant Mullins. That makes everything clear. Right? Now — does anybody want to say something?"

He stopped and looked at them. He looked at them slowly, turning as his eyes picked them out, one by one, in the semicircle. He made it last; made it cold and quiet and challenging. He gave them plenty of time to think it over; gave plenty of time for somebody's nerves to tighten, for peril to scratch along somebody's spine. And nobody said anything. Everybody met his eyes with appropriate expressions of serious regret and innocent bewilderment. Weigand finished his scrutiny with an unsmiling stare at Mrs. North, who raised slender shoulders in response.

45

"Right," Weigand said. "So that's the way you want it."

His tone was level and without expression. The idea they were to get was that this was implacable routine; that a machine had started. He hoped they got that idea.

"All right, Sergeant," Weigand said. "Let's find out who we've got here. We'll take them — we'll take them as they sit, starting here." He returned suddenly and pointed to the man sitting at the extreme left prong of the semicircle. Weigand stood with his back to the footlights, and the flat light from an overhead border above him threw heavy shadows down on his face. Shadows fell across his eyes. The faces of the others, although also shadowed, were clearer in the light.

"You," Weigand said, expressionlessly to the man. "Suppose you stand up so I can look at you. Who are you?"

The man who stood up, Weigand decided, was exactly the kind of man who, multiplied, makes a crowd. He was anybody with the quality of everybody. He was about middle height and his shoulders were middling broad. He had blue eyes and not much light brown hair, and as he stood up he drew glasses from his pocket and began to polish them with a handkerchief he drew slowly from the breast pocket of his jacket. He looked at the glasses, held them up to let the light from the border panel shine through, cleaned off another spot and put the glasses on. Then he looked at Weigand. When he spoke his voice was mild and entirely unexcited.

"My name is Smith," he said. "Penfield Smith, if it makes it any better. I wrote this god-damned thing."

He then stopped and looked at Weigand, without any visible emotion. Weigand waited and Mr. Smith took off his glasses and put them back in his pocket. There was nothing to indicate that he could not now see Weigand quite as well as before. Weigand thought he was going to have to speak, but Smith cleared his throat.

He spoke without heat and deliberately.

"As for Dr. Bolton," he said, "I did not stab him with an ice-pick. It seems to me, however, that it was an excellent idea. I would very much have enjoyed stabbing Dr. Bolton, although I should have preferred something blunt. Was the ice-pick blunt, Lieutenant?"

Weigand stared at him. The detective's face did not display more emotion than that of Penfield Smith. Weigand ignored grumbling noises of surprise from Mullins.

47

"Thank you, Mr. Smith," Weigand said. "We'll have some questions to ask you later." He paused and spoke generally to the men and women before him.

"It won't be necessary," Weigand said, "for each one of you to deny the murder. We'll give you that chance later. Now I want your names, who you are, and a chance to look at you one by one. Right?"

Several nodded. The rest merely stared. Mr. Smith sat down, took out his glasses and held them to the light. He shook his head sadly, took out his handkerchief, and began to polish.

"Right," Weigand said. "Now — you, Mr. Kirk, isn't it?"

Kirk stood up. He pushed back the lock of red hair which fell over his forehead.

"Humphrey Kirk," he said. He spoke nervously. "I'm directing what Penny calls 'this god-damned thing.' This 'thing' is a polite comedy, we hope, and is called 'Two in the Bush.' " He stopped and stared at Weigand. "As an outsider," he said abruptly, "what do you think of that for a title?"

"Very," Weigand said, "provocative. Thank you, Mr. Kirk."

Kirk sat down. Alberta James, who was next, stood up without prompting.

"I'm in the cast," she said. "Sally Bingham." Her voice was low and steady. Weigand felt she was keeping it so with an effort.

"Sally Bingham is the name of the character you play?" Weigand said, "Right. Thank you, Miss James."

Alberta James sat down, the curtain of her reddish hair swinging a little as she moved. Her large eyes remained focused, expectant, on Weigand. Weigand stood for a moment, turning an idea over. He turned back to Kirk.

"Have you got a program handy?" he asked. "I'd like to look at these names as they come up."

"A proof," Kirk said. He raised his voice. "Jimmy!" he yelled. There was no answer. *"Jimmy!"*

"All right," a voice said, muffled, from somewhere behind the fireplace. "Coming up."

Weigand stared hard at Kirk.

"I thought you said everybody was on stage," Weigand said. "Who's this Jimmy?"

"Stage Manager," Kirk told him. "I forgot. I sent him out for something." Kirk paused and looked perplexed. "Now what the hell was it?" he asked himself. The door above the fireplace on Weigand's right opened and a harried-looking young man with scrambled hair entered. He carried a cardboard container.

"Here's your coffee, Humpty," he said. "And what do you want now?"

He looked at the tableau before him.

"What's the matter?" he inquired, as if he was sure something was. "Are we going to have a new third act?"

"Listen," Penfield Smith said suddenly and loudly, standing up and reaching for his glasses. But when he got them he shook them at Jimmy. "Once and for all that last act stands. And to hell with you and Bolton." He stopped suddenly. . . . "Well, to hell with you, anyway," he said. "Bolton has preceded you."

"These men are detectives, Jimmy," Kirk broke in, and waved one hand loosely, restrainingly, at Smith. "Somebody stabbed Bolton. He's dead."

"Good," Jimmy said, matter-of-factly. He looked at Weigand.

"Jimmy Sand," he said. "Stage Manager for Humpty here. I was out."

"Right," Weigand said. "Sit down somewhere."

Sand drew up a chair behind Kirk and leaned forward, looking over the director's shoulder.

"Oh," said Kirk. "I forgot. The inspector

50

wants a proof of the program."

"All right, Humpty," Sand said. "Coming up."

He pulled a roll of paper from his pocket, flicked off a rubber band, and separated a long, smeared sheet. Mullins took it from him and handed it to Weigand. In familiar type, it carried a description of "Two in the Bush." It read:

WEST FORTY-FIFTH STREET THEATRE

Max Ahlberg

presents

TWO IN THE BUSH

A New Comedy
By Penfield Smith

WITH

Ellen Grady and Percy Driscoll
Directed by Humphrey Kirk
Scenery Designed by Arthur Christopher
Costumes Designed by Mary Fowler

51

CAST OF CHARACTERS
(in the order of their appearance)

Wade Bingham .... John Hubbard
Sally Bingham .... Alberta James
Gladys .... Ruthmary Jones
Francis Carter .... Percy Driscoll
Martin Bingham .... F. Lawrence Tilford
Joyce Barber .... Ellen Grady
Douglas Raimondi .... Paul Oliver

SYNOPSIS OF SCENES

Act I. A Sunday afternoon in late fall.
Act II. Immediately following.
Act III. Later that night.

The action takes place in the apartment of Martin Bingham, in the East Sixties.

Weigand said he saw. The next person in the row was a very handsome young man, his features regular and his teeth, as he showed them smiling, miraculously white.

"Hubbard," he said. "First name John. I play Alberta's brother, chap named Wade. Wade Bingham."

Weigand identified Hubbard on the program and said, "Right." Hubbard sat down and turned to Alberta James and smiled, showing the white teeth. Alberta's smile was faint and momentary but it was a smile.

Weigand nodded to the next man in the row. The next man spoke without rising. He was a plump man with pale hair and he wore his glasses all the time. His voice was light and sharp. He said he was Christopher. He stopped saying anything.

"Christopher?" Weigand repeated. "Christopher what? Oh, Arthur Christopher?"

The plump man nodded. He seemed very depressed by everything. Weigand began a nod to the next in the line and Christopher stood up quickly, excitedly.

"Lieutenant," he said, "I simply have to get away from here. Terry Packard will go mad. I mean, she'll go mad. She's over there waiting — *waiting* — for the drawings and I just *sit* here."

Weigand looked at him, and shook his head.

"I'm sorry, Mr. Christopher," he said. "You'll have to wait with the rest. For the time, anyway. Probably we'd all rather be doing something else."

Weigand tried not to look at Dorian. He looked at Dorian. She nodded with animation. Weigand sighed and indicated attention to the short, round man with the heavy face who sat next to Christopher.

53

The round man stood up, as straight as a round man could.

"I am Max Ahlberg," he said. "I am producing this play. It is a beautiful play, Inspector. Whatever they say, it is a beautiful play. They are ruining the theatre with what they say."

"Who?" Weigand asked, involuntarily.

"The god-damn critics," Mr. Ahlberg said. "But they will love this play. Even they will see that it is a beautiful play. And if they like it — um-m-m!"

The "um-m-m!" was ecstatic. A child anticipating the most shining of parties might have sounded so. In spite of himself, Weigand smiled in sympathy with Mr. Ahlberg's anticipatory exultation. Mr. Ahlberg sighed.

"They are smart-alecks, the critics," Mr. Ahlberg said, grimly. "For a laugh they will kill anything."

Mr. Ahlberg made what might have been a little bow toward Weigand and sat down. Kirk spoke from his seat.

"They'll like it, Maxie," he promised, as a parent to a child. "This is the sort of thing they go for, Maxie."

But Maxie seemed sunk beyond recall. Weigand declared a moment of silence over him and then continued.

You would never, Weigand decided, lose Miss Mary Fowler in a crowd. She stood quietly and gave her name and Weigand caught himself trying not to stare. She was a heavy woman with a heavy, chiseled face. Her hair was black and pulled back from a broad, low forehead and a little row of bangs was left behind. There was a thickness about her body which loose, flowered clothing did nothing to ameliorate. When she gave her name her low voice sounded younger than she looked — younger and more vibrant. But it was none of these things which made Weigand stare. He stared because Mary Fowler seemed to be staring outlandishly herself.

It took him only an instant to realize that the stare was physical; that Miss Fowler seemed to be staring because, more alarmingly than any he had ever seen, her eyes protruded from her head. They were not merely prominent; they seemed about to pop out. Weigand decided he had never seen anything quite like them before, and never wanted to again. But there was nothing in his voice as, nodding in acknowledgment of her name and giving Mullins time to write it down, he said:

"You are designing the costumes, Miss Fowler?"

"Yes," she said. If she sensed the revulsion in Weigand she did not notice it by the inflection of her voice. Probably, Weigand thought uneasily, she was used to being stared at. He nodded, dismissingly, and she sat down again.

The man who stood up on her left said he was Percy Driscoll. He looked, Weigand decided at once, like nothing on earth except the successful actor he presumably was. He was, Weigand guessed, in his late forties; he was suave and mannered with the suavity of middle-aged success and the manner of one who lives by manner. And the light, falling from above, accentuated the pouches under his eyes.

"I think," Driscoll said, after he had named himself, "that we're all giving you a wrong impression, Lieutenant Weigand. An impression of flippancy and — animosity toward poor Carney. I'm sure that doesn't really represent our feelings. A regrettable impression."

His intonation was British. Weigand corrected it — stage British. But it fitted like a glove, long worn. Weigand said, "Right."

"I take it you liked Bolton, Mr. Driscoll?" Weigand said.

Driscoll said Bolton had been a fine chap, a very fine chap. And a very dear friend.

56

Weigand waited a minute, heard nothing more, and said, "Thank you." Driscoll sat down. The man next to him stood up and faintly caricatured Driscoll in gesture and inflection.

"F. Lawrence Tilford," the man said. "Actor."

He managed to make the few words rotund. He was, Weigand decided, in his middle sixties. He had . . . Weigand hazarded a guess:

"Didn't you play with Booth?" Weigand asked.

"As a boy, my dear sir," Mr. Tilford told him. "As the merest boy. But I have never forgotten —"

"Thank you," Weigand said. "I was sure you had!"

Tilford stood looking at Weigand.

"Thank you, Mr. Tilford," Weigand repeated. He repeated it with finality. Mr. Tilford sat down. He sat down and sighed deeply.

"And you," Weigand said to the very lovely young woman, in a simple, vividly colored, green dress, who sat next Tilford, "must be Ellen Grady."

It was an easy deduction; the semicircle was running out of women and there was an Ellen Grady featured on the program.

Miss Grady looked as if she would be featured on a program, or know the reason why she wasn't. Looking at her admiringly, Weigand doubted whether there would ever be a good reason why — she was slight and blond and perfect, with a cameo face so clearly cut and so expressive even in repose that the woman who wore it would never have to wonder too much about anything. Miss Grady stood with absolute control and absolute poise.

"I am Ellen Grady," she said. Her voice, lighter than that of Alberta James, had something of the same quality. And she might have been saying, "I am Helen of Troy."

"You play the lead?" Weigand said, politely.

"One of the leads only," Miss Grady corrected him. "Mr. Driscoll plays opposite me."

"Yes," Weigand said. "You and Mr. Driscoll play the leads?"

Miss Grady inclined her head. There was great dignity in the inclination; it was as if Miss Grady were, at the same time, bowing to fate. She would prove to be, Weigand decided, quite a girl. The case was looking up. Involuntarily, he looked at Dorian, and wished he hadn't. Dorian nodded with excessive enthusiasm and made gestures of

58

applause.

"Right," Weigand said. Miss Grady sat down. Weigand ran out the rest. Paul Oliver was a blond young man who looked like a football player and radiated innocence, Weigand decided. Ruthmary Jones was ample and white-toothed and black of face, and it was disconcerting to have her answer with a British intonation more pronounced than that of Driscoll. She was West Indian, Weigand gathered, and very superior; then he remembered the broad, bubbling humor of her playing in something he had seen the year before and almost beamed on her.

And the next three were named, respectively, Mahoney, Fleming and Lawson, and were, again respectively, electrician, stage hand and stage hand. They seemed rather bored with the whole matter. Pam North seemed about to rise, but Weigand, to his own surprise, quelled her with a glance. He said a general "Thank you."

"I'm afraid I'll have to keep you here for a time longer," he said. "I shall need to talk to each of you separately. Meanwhile, make yourselves as comfortable as you can, and don't try to leave the theatre. I should prefer that, so far as it's possible, you stay on, or in the vicinity of, the stage. Right?"

Nobody said it wasn't right, although

several looked the words. Mr. Christopher sulked obviously. It was too bad about him, Weigand decided. It was going to keep on being bad. He left the circle as it began to break into groups and found the temporary flight of stairs reaching down from the stage to the orchestra aisle up which he had climbed a few minutes before. He started down them, thought of something, and called, "Mr. Kirk."

Kirk turned from Ellen Grady and said, "Yes?"

"I want your help, Mr. Kirk," Weigand said. Mr. Kirk followed.

III
TUESDAY

3:45 P.M. TO 4 P.M.

At the foot of the steps down from the stage, Weigand turned to Kirk.

"What I want," he said, "is to have you —"

He was interrupted by a heavy, official voice from up the aisle, which said: "Lieutenant?" Weigand said, "Yes?"

"The doc's here," the voice told him. "Wants to see you."

Weigand said "Right" and went up the aisle toward the knot of men about the huddled body. Kirk, after hesitating a moment, followed him. As they were halfway up, flashlights suddenly glowed, focusing on the body of Dr. Bolton. And a well-known voice said:

"Damn it! How do you expect a man —"

Weigand, followed by Kirk, appeared and Dr. Jerome Francis, assistant medical examiner, stood up.

"This," Dr. Francis said, "is the devil of a

61

place for a cadaver. You'd have to be an acrobat."

"Well," Weigand said. "I didn't put him there, Doctor. And where would you have been all these hours? Out seeing a man about a guinea pig?"

It wasn't, Francis said with some exasperation, "all these hours." It was exactly . . . he looked at his watch . . . one hour and sixteen minutes since word came through about Weigand's corpse.

"And," Dr. Francis said, "there were two ahead of you." He looked at Weigand. "Every corpse in its turn, Lieutenant," he said. "We can't make exceptions."

Weigand half smiled at him.

"Right," he said. "And now you're here?"

"Now I'm here," Francis said, "I'd have to be an acrobat. But it's a corpse."

Weigand said he thought it was. How long had it been?

"And don't put on your song and dance about exactitude," the detective advised. "We've been over that. Just a close guess, seeing as it's a nice fresh one."

Dr. Francis wanted to know if it would be all right to take it out. Weigand nodded. They took Dr. Bolton out, with some difficulty, and laid him in the aisle. Kirk made a small, distressed sound and Dr. Francis

62

looked up at him.

"You'll get used to them," Dr. Francis assured him.

"My God!" Kirk said. "I hope not."

Dr. Francis was busy. He took temperatures and examined eyes. He bent fingers and swore mildly when ink from the fingerprint pads came off on his hands. He grumbled that "they ought to wipe them off." After a while he stood up.

"Under three hours," he said. "Over an hour. I'd suggest you split the difference."

Weigand looked at his watch.

"Three hours ago it was a quarter to one," he said. "And everybody was out to lunch. An hour ago it was a quarter to three, and everybody was here and Bolton was dead. I was here myself, Doctor. And you could have been."

Francis said he wouldn't want to guess any closer. But about two hours ago, more or less, ought to place it. Say between a little after one and a little after two; say —

"During the run-through," Kirk said suddenly. "We started it at 1:15 and ran until —" He broke off. He yelled, "Jimmy!" Jimmy, from the stage, said, "Yeh, Humpty."

"Give me the times on the second-act run-through," Kirk directed.

"Today?" Jimmy called. Then, when Kirk

answered with a yell, Jimmy said, "Sure." He crossed to a table near the footlights and stared down at it and turned papers.

"One-twelve to 1:58," Jimmy called. "With four script pages to go. And it's running long, Humpty."

"It won't," Humpty said. "Wait till we get it set. Forty minutes flat." He turned to Weigand and resumed his natural voice.

"I remember, now," he said. "We didn't quite finish — had about four minutes to go, at a page a minute. I stopped them and came back to talk to Bolton; and found him dead."

Weigand said, "So."

"What about?" he said.

Kirk said there was a laugh where Bolton said there wasn't a laugh — just there, before the act wound up. Kirk had tried a new timing on it and wanted to see what Bolton thought now.

"Now," Kirk said, thoughtfully, "I guess I'll just keep it in."

They turned from murder easily, these people, Weigand thought. He had a feeling that Bolton's death was secondary to Kirk; that the long director, with the collapsing forelock, honestly felt murder irrelevant when compared to the timing of a laugh — that all the others, up there on the stage,

64

thought "Two in the Bush" more important, at the moment, and their parts in it more important, than any number of men dead in aisle seats. He regarded Kirk a moment interestedly, and then recalled them both.

"Do *you* happen to know when Dr. Bolton came back from lunch?" Weigand said. Kirk pushed back the lock of red hair. It fell down again.

"Yes," he said. "I saw him." He paused. "At least," he said, "I saw him start in through the stage door. I was up the street a little ways, and I saw his back. That was — oh, about one o'clock. I'd had a sandwich and come back —" He broke off and a surprised look came over his face. He stared at Weigand, and there seemed to be reproach in his stare.

"That's one for the book," Kirk said. "I had an appointment and damned if I didn't forget it altogether. I was thinking about the last act and got an idea and came back to find Smitty and talk it over with him. I just put down my sandwich in the middle and came back, all full of it. And then I saw Bolton going in."

"And did you see him inside?" Weigand wanted to know. Kirk thought and shook his head. He said that that didn't, however, prove anything. Bolton could have been almost any place in the theatre, and Kirk, who was looking for Smitty, wouldn't have seen him.

"And did you see Mr. Smith?" Weigand wanted to know. Kirk hadn't; Mr. Smith wasn't there. He came in after the run-through had started and Kirk by then was deep in the second act and didn't stop. And Bolton? Kirk shook his head. He supposed Bolton was in the theatre, but as for being sure —

"Look, Lieutenant," Dr. Francis broke in. "Don't let me interrupt you. But I'm going. This one's dead and you can have it taken away. We'll do an autopsy tonight, just for the hell of it, but I can tell you now he was stabbed." Weigand said he could have told Dr. Francis that. Francis nodded.

"Between the occiput and the atlas, or first vertebra," Francis said. "Just below the foramen magnum, in other words. Very neatly, with a very sharp ice-pick — by a person who knew the place to stab. And then he just twitched a couple of times. And . . ."

But Weigand wasn't looking at him. Weigand was staring down at the body. Clinging to the rough wool of Bolton's trousers, visible now that the body was straightened and laid flat, was a length of orange silk. It fell away from the body and lay bright against the neutral carpet of the aisle. It was —

"Look," Pam North said, unexpectedly behind the Lieutenant, "it's a swatch. He was going to match something."

"A what, Pam?" Weigand asked. Kirk was looking at Mrs. North with some surprise, and Dr. Francis with interest. But Weigand did not seem surprised.

"A sample," Mrs. North said. "From some material for —" she bent, not looking at Bolton more than she had to, and examined the strip of orange silk — "for a dress, I think," she said. "Something he was going to match for a woman, probably."

Weigand knelt beside Bolton's body and smoothed the silk between his fingers. Then he drew it from the loosened hand and stood up. He held it out to Kirk.

"Was one of the costumes to be made of this material?" he asked. "One of the dresses for the play, I mean? You'd know, wouldn't you?"

He waited, then, because Kirk waited to answer. Kirk made a great business of looking at the silk and a great business of thinking about it. At just the moment when thought might reasonably be concluded, he shook his head, slowly.

"No," he said. "I wouldn't know, necessarily. Not unless it had been decided upon . . . this might just have been something Mary was showing one of the girls as a possibility. So I wouldn't . . ."

He trailed off and looked at Weigand. It was an inquiring look, and Weigand recognized it with interest. It was the look of a man who wondered whether he was putting something over. Weigand nodded at him, cheerfully.

"Naturally," Weigand said. "I see how you might not recognize it."

Anything, within reason, to satisfy a suspect, Weigand believed, at this stage of the game. But Kirk knew something about the orange silk; knew something he didn't want Weigand to know. Weigand felt like shaking hands with him. Kirk had produced a ripple in waters previously too calm.

"A good detective is always more or less suspicious and very inquisitive." That was the classic definition from the "Rules and Regulations and Manual of Procedure for the Police Department of the City of New York." Weigand agreed with it entirely. He welcomed, as cases started, small discrepancies which nurtured suspicion and encouraged inquisitiveness; or, more exactly, small things which localized suspicion. Five minutes before, Weigand had been suspi-

68

cious of fourteen — no, with Jimmy Sand, fifteen — people. Now Kirk, who knew something he didn't want to tell, had taken one step forward from the even line of suspects. And every little bit helped.

Weigand changed the subject. He told Kirk he wanted to try something. Would it be possible to run through the second act again, for his benefit? Run through it, as nearly as possible, precisely as they had run through it earlier.

"Because," Weigand said, "I want to get things clear in my mind. It's all very confused now, naturally — where people were, and all that; because we can take it, I think, that Bolton was killed during the run-through. Would that be possible, Mr. Kirk?"

Kirk pushed back the hair, waited for it to fall, and said, "Sure."

"As a matter of fact," he said, "swell! We kill two birds with one stone — you get the picture, we get more rehearsal, which heaven knows we can do with." Kirk ran his hand again through the forelock and pulled it anxiously. "Every time I think of Monday I quake," he said. "The next time I let anybody talk me into opening a show cold, I'll . . ." He broke off. "Sure," he said, "I'll go line them up."

He turned and went off down the aisle,

69

calling, "Jimmy! Hey, Jimmy!" Weigand heard Jimmy say "Yeh, Humpty." Weigand looked after him and turned to Pam North, who was looking after him, too.

"He knows about the material," Mrs. North said, suddenly. "The orange silk, I mean. It belonged to the pretty girl."

"Miss Grady?" Weigand said. Mrs. North was impatient with him.

"She is *beautiful*," Mrs. North explained. "It's a great strain on her. And Mr. Kirk doesn't care. The other girl — the James girl. *She's* pretty. And Mr. Kirk does care. Therefore — the silk belonged to her."

Weigand said, "Um-m." He was about to go on when one of the detectives who, now that the body was gone from its cramped place in the seat, had been examining the seat and carpet beneath it with devoted care, interrupted him. Did the Lieutenant want to have a look before they cleared things up and took them away?

"What things?" Weigand said. Detective Stein pointed with a shaft of light from his electric torch. Weigand said "Um-m-m" again and bent closer.

There were several things to see; following the guiding finger from the flashlight, Weigand checked them off:

Wedged in between backs of two seats immediately in front of the seat in which Dr. Bolton had sat: a paper cup, crumpled at the bottom where it had been forced into the small gap. In the bottom, Weigand's finger told him, a quarter of an inch of water. For a moment Weigand was puzzled; then it was obvious. The cup was intended as an ashtray — the water in the bottom to extinguish cigarettes. There were no cigarettes in it.

On the floor, a little to the left of Bolton's chair, a cigarette, broken in two in the middle as if the fingers which held it had suddenly twisted convulsively; as, Weigand thought, they very well may have. The cigarette had been lighted, but it had fallen before more than two or three drags had been taken, and then it had, lying on the carpet, gone out. Weigand took the light from Stein and bent lower, examining the cigarette carefully without touching it. It was marked at one end with a manufacturer's insignia which Weigand recognized.

"Virginia," Weigand said. "Straight; so it went out."

"Right," Stein said. It was not parody; it was emulation.

On the carpet near the cigarette, two paper matches, both burned.

Weigand said "Um-m-m" and withdrew.

Stein pointed to the carpet behind the seat Bolton had occupied. Obediently, Weigand illuminated the carpet with the torch.

There was another burned paper match there. It was, however, a special paper match, being shaped like a bottle. Weigand picked it up and regarded it with interest.

"I think," he told Stein, "that I'll keep this one. It might come in handy."

IV
TUESDAY
4 P.M. TO 4:58 P.M.

Humphrey Kirk called Weigand from the stage.

"Ready when you are, Lieutenant," he called and Weigand, saying "Right" on the way, went up the stairs over the orchestra pit. Everybody looked at him.

"To fix times and things like that, I'm going to have you run through the second act just as you did earlier this afternoon," Weigand told them. "I don't expect an exact duplication, of course, but you ought to be able to come pretty close — with the lines to help you and everything. I want those who were not on the stage, but were somewhere else in the theatre, to go where they were earlier. I'll have one of my men go with each of you who was somewhere else. Is that clear?"

Several people nodded. Kirk said he thought they all understood.

"Right," Weigand said. "Now is there

73

anybody who wasn't in the theatre when the run-through started?"

Mary Fowler waited a moment, evidently for someone else to speak, and then spoke herself. She said she wasn't in the theatre when the run-through started.

"I'd had to go to my place for some samples," she said. "I was late getting back — not that that was unusual, I'll admit. They'd already started when I got in. And first I tried to come in the front, and that delayed me more."

"Through the front of the theatre?" Weigand asked. Mary Fowler, her protruding eyes looking at him intensely, nodded. "How was that?" Weigand said.

She had thought the front doors might be open, she told him. Sometimes they were, and since she didn't need to go back-stage at once, it would have been easier to come through the front of the theatre. But the doors were locked and, although she saw Evans inside, he pretended not to hear her and —

"Wait a minute," Weigand told her. "Who's Evans?"

Kirk snapped his fingers.

"I forgot about Evans," he said. "He's the custodian of the theatre — sort of a watchman who looks after things when it's shut

74

up. He's always around somewhere; I forgot all about him. He's not one of our crowd, really; he belongs to the bank."

"To the bank?" Weigand repeated.

The Consolidated Bank, Kirk told him — the bank that owned the Forty-fifth Street Theatre and employed Evans as watchman. Weigand nodded.

"Find this man Evans," he called to Stein. Stein said "Right" from somewhere in the rear. Weigand turned back to Mary Fowler.

"I'll send a man with you," he said. "About what time did you get here?"

It was, Mary Fowler told him, about twenty minutes after one. Weigand looked at his watch and nodded. She was to do again for the detective who would be with her, what she had done before, pretending to herself that it was three hours earlier in the afternoon. And —

"I got here late too," Christopher broke in, sulkily. "Do you want me to go out and come back?"

Weigand nodded.

"One detective can go out with you and — is it *Miss* Fowler?"

"Miss," Mary Fowler told him.

"One man can go with both of you," Weigand said. "After Miss Fowler comes in, he can wait with you. Or did you come in before she did?"

"After," Christopher said shortly. "She was sitting out front when I came in and I stopped and spoke to her."

Weigand looked at Miss Fowler, who nodded. Weigand said, "Right."

"You were the only two who weren't in the theatre when the run-through started?" he asked. Nobody said anything.

"Right," Weigand said. "You can start it then, Kirk." The detective looked at his watch again. "Start it in three minutes. That will make it 4:12 instead of 1:12, and keep our times even."

Kirk nodded. Weigand went down the temporary steps to the orchestra and stopped. He said: "Hold it."

"Were the lights on out here?" he asked. "I assumed they weren't."

"No," Kirk said. "They weren't. Want them out?"

Weigand did. Kirk yelled "Fleming!" and when Fleming came waved at the auditorium. Fleming nodded, and went off stage. The house lights suddenly went out.

It was more like a theatre now, Weigand thought, worming his way across the house to join the Norths, Dorian and Mullins on the other side. The light was where it should be; the stage was a box of light and the

76

orchestra was a cavern of shadows. Back through gathering darkness, rows of empty seats curved starkly; at intervals along the sides dim red lights marked the locations of exits. It was more like a theatre and yet for the first time forbidding. As Weigand sat in the aisle seat the Norths and Dorian had left for him when they saw him coming, he felt an odd uneasiness. His back felt unprotected from the darkness beyond.

"It breathes down the back of your neck," Mrs. North whispered to him, suddenly. "The emptiness."

Weigand nodded to her. They were sitting well down, half a dozen rows from the stage, the stage light on their faces. The darkness seemed to begin immediately behind them.

Across the aisle, in the section of seats to their right and two rows nearer the stage, Penfield Smith was sitting. He had wedged a paper cup between two seats in front of him and was smoking. Kirk came down the stairs on the other side of the house and dropped into a seat in the center section. The stage emptied; then Jimmy Sand came onto it through the door at the left, carrying a straight chair and a script bound in blue paper. He sat down and twisted in his chair.

"O.K., Humpty," he said. "Want them on?"

"Let it go," Kirk said.

Sand turned back and called, "All right, people."

Ellen Grady and Percy Driscoll came on together. Miss Grady went to a small sofa which stood a little distance from the footlights, and facing them, a little to Weigand's left of the center of the stage. She sat on it, and continued a conversation with Driscoll, who walked across the stage to stand easily near the fireplace.

"— and so they're closing it out of town," Miss Grady said. "And anyone could have told them that Florence couldn't ever play it. A good many people did tell them."

"I know, darling," Driscoll said. "Florence is a lovely person, but —"

Paul Oliver came in hurriedly through the door near Driscoll, crossed the stage to a position near the window in the rear wall and said: "Sorry. Didn't mean to hold you up."

"Of course not, darling," Ellen Grady said, with a terrible sweetness. "You never mean —"

"Curtain!" said Jimmy Sand, tersely. Miss Grady relaxed suddenly upon the sofa and became another person. Her voice lifted and took on inflections and she said:

"*Let's try to look at it simply, Francis. Let's*

try to look at it as if it were a simple thing and we were people who could. Now do you see what I mean, Humpty?"

Miss Ellen Grady had suddenly, more or less in the middle of things, quit being Joyce Barber and become again Miss Grady, Weigand decided. She stared at Humphrey Kirk, shielding her eyes with her hand.

"Where the hell are you, Humpty?" Miss Grady demanded. "Can you see what he's doing?"

"Now, darling —" Kirk said.

"Up there catching flies, that's what he's doing," Miss Grady said indignantly. "Every time I start a line he does a double take."

Oliver spoke with dark bitterness from the windows, out of which he had been, Weigand now realized, staring with rather aggressive interest.

"I thought," Oliver said, "that this was supposed to be comedy. I thought we decided there was a laugh there, when I break in on all this simplicity, and there isn't any laugh if I don't build for it." Mr. Oliver was very resigned and weary about it all. "Heaven knows," he said, "we need a laugh somewhere."

"Why don't you stand on your head?" Miss Grady demanded, turning and glaring at him over the back of the sofa. "That'll get a laugh. That'll wow them."

Oliver looked at her with great tolerance.

"This isn't that kind of a play, darling," he told her. "No cartwheels in this one."

Miss Grady turned toward Kirk and demanded indignantly whether she was supposed to take that.

"From this over-grown juvenile," she said, angrily. "From this mug-man, this — this fly-catcher?"

"Children," said Kirk, getting up and walking down to the rail of the orchestra pit. "Children!"

Paul Oliver walked down-stage. Miss Grady leaned forward on the sofa and stared at Kirk.

"I'm sorry," Oliver said. He sounded sincere, Weigand thought, wondering what to do about it all.

"Did they do this before?" Weigand whispered to Pam. She nodded.

"Almost exactly," she said. "It's as good as a play." She paused and considered this. "Better than some," she added, critically.

"I'm merely trying to do what you said you wanted, Humpty," Oliver said. "I'll be glad to come down a little, except that it will make an awfully long cross when I go out. But perhaps Mr. Smith can put another beat in the line to get me off."

"Listen," Mr. Smith said, standing up suddenly and knocking his paper cup of cigarette butts into the aisle. "That line stands! Absolutely and finally! Another beat and where's the nuance? That's what I want to know."

Mr. Smith sat down indignantly. Then he stood up again.

"That's final," he said, and sat down.

"Of course, Smitty," Kirk promised him. "But it does give Paul a long cross."

Mr. Smith growled.

"All right," said Kirk, agreeably, "we'll work it out some other way." Kirk climbed to the stage and led Oliver back to the windows. Then, grasping him by the shoulders, he led him two paces down toward the footlights. "Try it from there. All right, darling, take it up."

"— *feel things simply,*" Ellen Grady said, instantly again Joyce Barber.

She stopped and nobody said anything.

"*Darling please remember* — yours, Perce," Jimmy Sand said.

"Sorry," said Percy Driscoll, suddenly, as it seemed, awakening from an inner coma. "*Darling — please remember that simple people wouldn't be in this situation — that it's a situation —*"

"Play it, please," Kirk said. "You're just

saying it. How can we get the feeling of the thing if we don't act it?"

"Sorry," said Driscoll. "I was just thinking —"

"Listen, children," Kirk said. "Don't think. Just act. Just run through it."

"Sorry," said Driscoll. He repeated the lines, assuming the character of Francis Carter. Ellen Grady answered him as Joyce Barber, and then Paul Oliver, now evidently somebody called Douglas Raimondi, broke in. Kirk returned to his seat.

It was a play, now, Weigand realized. It was as if one mood had been turned off at the faucet and another turned on; it was confusing, but it was a play.

"She's going to marry Martin Bingham," Pam North whispered. "But she's been living with the other man — Carter — all this time and he doesn't like it. And that other man, he's the family jester. He just stands around and says things. Like Alexander Woollcott on the sofa."

"What?" said Weigand, in spite of himself.

"Behrman," Pam said, still in a whisper but a little impatiently. "Woollcott on a sofa. Of course you remember."

"Oh," said Weigand. "That."

"Hush, Pam," Jerry North said, from beyond her.

82

"But Doug," Ellen Grady said on the stage, *"he couldn't have been* under *the bed!"*

She had twisted on the sofa to look up-stage toward Oliver, and, without moving, she raised her voice and called: "Humpty!" Kirk said, "Yes, darling."

"They can't see my face," Ellen Grady said. "And I'm damn near breaking my neck. It throws the line away."

"I know, darling," Kirk said. "But it's a back-hair line."

"All my lines are back-hair lines," Miss Grady said, bitterly. "They always will be as long as you let him *lurk* upstage every minute he's on." She paused. "Doing double *and* triple takes," she added, with a voice of cold anger.

"All right, darling," Kirk said. "We'll work on it tomorrow. I'll think of something. Pick it up, Paul."

"It *was the only place he wasn't afraid,"* Paul Oliver said, walking across the stage toward the door at his left. "See what I mean about the beat, Humpty? Am I supposed to run?"

A growl started from the vicinity of Penfield Smith. Kirk intervened hastily.

"I'll work something out, Paul," Kirk promised. "Maybe I can move you in and shorten the cross."

"Why not have him stand in front of me?" Ellen Grady inquired, sweetly. "*Smack* in front of me? Wouldn't *that* be funny?"

"Children!" said Kirk, gently. "Children! Pick it up from there."

"Bell," said Jimmy Sand. "Brrrrrrr."

"Jimmy!" said Ellen Grady. "What a *lovely* bell."

John Hubbard came on. He met Paul Oliver going off and there were sounds of greeting and parting.

"That's it, children," Kirk said. "Ad lib it there."

Mullins slipped into the seat behind Weigand and leaned toward him.

"That guy Evans —" Mullins said. Weigand shook his head, stopping it. "Never mind now," he said. "Time them — when they come on and go off I mean. It will give us a framework, maybe."

"O.K., Loot," Mullins said.

They were getting on with it on the stage. Alberta James had come on. Ellen Grady moved upstage and turned to offer her left profile to the audience. She appeared to be staring absently through the windows. Kirk got up and moved a few seats toward the rear of the house, and then crossed through the row and came down to Weigand. He half knelt in the aisle beside the detective.

"Do you always have as much trouble?" Weigand asked. "Did you earlier today?"

"Trouble?" Kirk repeated, in apparently honest astonishment. "We're not having any trouble. As smooth a run-through as I've ever seen."

Weigand said, "Oh."

"Then the time's running about the way it did earlier?" he said.

"I think so," Kirk said. "Just about. It's a little hard to gauge, but it won't vary much. It never varies much. Yes, John?"

Weigand looked up. John Hubbard had dropped out of his part and come down to the footlights.

"I just remembered something," Hubbard said. "There was a cigarette, Lieutenant."

"Yes?" said Weigand. "What do you mean?"

"I was trying to think if things were the way they were earlier," Hubbard explained. "After I came on, I mean — I thought it might help."

"Right," Weigand said. "And they weren't? Something about a cigarette?"

"Somebody was smoking a cigarette back there on the aisle," Hubbard said. "The right aisle. I caught the glow as I came on and then — well, it was a little point of light, see?"

Weigand got up and moved to the pit rail. He said, "Right."

"Just after I came on, I think," Hubbard said, "it went out. That is, it didn't exactly go out — it moved down, as if somebody had lowered a cigarette from his lips. Only, thinking about it, it went down faster than that. As if somebody had dropped it, only dropped it so that the lighted end always pointed this way." Hubbard stopped and looked at Weigand earnestly. "Am I making it clear?" he said.

"Yes," Weigand said. "I get the picture. And this was just after you came on-stage?" Hubbard nodded.

He started back to his seat and turned. "You're sure it was the *right* aisle?" he said. Hubbard nodded. "Which one?" Weigand insisted. Hubbard pointed. Weigand said, "Oh, of course. *Your* right," and went back to his seat. "Right" and "Left" might be confusing in the theatre, he realized. Stage right was to the audience's left; Hubbard's "right aisle" was the aisle on the left as you entered the theatre. The aisle on which Dr. Carney Bolton had been sitting.

Hubbard waited a moment longer and Kirk said:

"All right, children. Take it from there."

They picked it up. John Hubbard and

Alberta James were, it appeared, Wade and Sally Bingham; it was their father Ellen Grady, as Joyce Barber, was planning to marry. They were, it became evident, opposed to this — it was a duel between them and Joyce Barber; a duel very deft and biting.

"This is where it starts rolling," Kirk said, still crouched in the aisle. Weigand looked across at Penfield Smith. He could see little of Smith's face, but what he could see had an expression of almost exalted approval. Kirk followed Weigand's glance.

"He likes it," Kirk said. "He knows when he's good."

The scene between Joyce Barber, Francis Carter and the Bingham children lasted about five minutes. Then Alberta James went offstage, Hubbard crossing to the door with her, an arm around her shoulders. A little later, F. Lawrence Tilford came on, rather pompously as it seemed to Weigand, in the character of Martin Bingham. Still later, Carter and then Wade Bingham exited, leaving only Bingham and Joyce Barber on the stage. Weigand listened to the smooth, flickering dialogue with half a mind and kept the rest on other things. Mullins, using a tiny flashlight, was taking notes — there was always a slight vibration when Mullins took notes, and heavy, anxious breathing. Weigand watched for others who ought to be coming in.

A dark figure sidled slowly through a row of seats from the extreme left — "*my* left" Weigand thought — aisle and took a seat a little off the left-center aisle. That would be — yes, that was Mary Fowler.

"Time her," Weigand whispered over his shoulder to Mullins. "That's Miss Fowler."

"O.K., Loot," Mullins said.

A much slimmer figure came through the same aisle and sat beside Miss Fowler and their heads went together. Faintly, Weigand caught the swing of hair — that would be Alberta James. The two got up and went back through the row to the aisle. They disappeared behind the boxes.

"Can they get through to the stage that way?" Weigand whispered to Kirk. Kirk nodded.

"There's a door there," he said. "Behind the boxes at the end of the aisle. One on this side too, which isn't usual."

Weigand said, "Right."

"Where's Ahlberg?" he whispered. Kirk jerked his head toward the rear.

"About row ten, in the middle," he said. "He came in a while ago."

A moment later, a man's figure appeared

in the aisle from which Mary Fowler and Alberta James had vanished. There was no mistaking Arthur Christopher even in the dim light.

"Must have met them back-stage, about at the door," Kirk said. Weigand nodded.

"By the way," he said, "you weren't here during the other run-through, were you, Kirk?"

Kirk shrugged.

"I was all around," he said. "It might as well have been here. I wander — get new angles. I was probably here part of the time." He broke off, started again.

"You won't get an alibi for me, Lieutenant," he said. "I can't pretend to one. I could have been anywhere."

"Right," Weigand said. "Too bad, but we can't have everything."

"How true," Kirk said. He straightened up and moved to a seat behind Penfield Smith. Smith turned his head and Kirk leaned forward. They talked and Kirk pointed at the stage. Then Smith pointed. Then they both got up, walked back up the aisle for about half its length and stood talking. Then Smith came down again and Kirk crossed through a row in the center section and walked down the left-center aisle to Christopher. He pointed and Christopher nodded. Christopher drew something which looked at that distance like an envelope from his pocket and wrote on it.

Kirk left him, walked back up the aisle and sidled through another row of darkened seats. He reached a little glow in the darkness and sat down beside it. The glow became two glows, one larger than the other. That would almost have to be Ahlberg, unless there was an added starter; Ahlberg with a cigar, Kirk with a cigarette.

Ellen Grady and Tilford were alone on the stage now, talking slowly, as if searching for words. The tempo of the dialogue was off; it no longer glinted. Tilford, as Martin Bingham, was slower, heavier, more matter of fact. He was, Weigand decided, intended to be — probably he had been cast to be. Then Ruthmary Jones, the colored maid, came on and began to clear away coffee cups. Only there were no coffee cups. She cleared away imaginary coffee cups, having answered an imaginary bell.

"Props," Pam told him in a whisper. "Isn't it funny? There aren't any yet. Because then they would have to put on a property man. So they just pretend. Like Thornton Wilder."

"What?" said Weigand. "Oh — that. Yes."

"Ask Mr. Wade and Miss Sally to come here

a minute, please Gladys," Tilford said.

"I'll ask them, Mr. Bingham," Gladys said.

She went off. After a moment, Alberta James and Hubbard came on. The tempo picked up again; the stage filled with undercurrents. It was a long scene and Weigand grew interested in it. Kirk was back beside him and he had not seen or heard Kirk coming.

"Good enough to eat," Kirk said. "Lovely scene."

"Yes," Weigand said.

The scene built up, quickening. Then it was broken, just before what might have been a climax. Driscoll and Ellen Grady came back through the door at Weigand's right. They were talking. Hubbard caught up a line from Ellen, smoothly, and twisted it. A new tempo began, slow, then quickening. The scene built again, grew sharper and more intense than the one before. There was edged laughter in it, and under the laughter a twang of stretched nerves. Weigand was, he realized, in danger of forgetting the murder.

Then the scene began to break again. Wade and Sally left the stage and, a few minutes after them, Carter. Bingham and the woman he wanted to marry — the woman who was tying his middle-aged life in knots, revealing motives in it which had long been hidden, linking it to the lives of thousands of other middle-aged men caught between new and old things — were alone on the stage. Now the tempo was slow again, and now it was quickening, building to a climax. Weigand was, in spite of himself, carried out of the world of murder into the world Penfield Smith was so artfully building in the lighted box. Bingham crossed to the window, looked out casually for a moment. Then the acting of Lawrence Tilford stiffened Bingham's body. You could see Bingham's attention caught and held by something outside; feel Joyce Barber's words glancing unheard from some new isolation. Tilford turned suddenly and Weigand could see words forming on his lips.

Then, from the rear of the theatre, there was a hoarse, galvanizing shout — wordless, then shaping into words.

"Carney!" the voice shouted. It rose high, cracked a little. *"Carney!"* And then, lower but desperate in the silence. *"My God, he's dead!"*

In spite of himself, although now he knew what this must be, Weigand started to his feet; turned to run toward the sound. Besides him Pamela North said "Oh!" Shudderingly, and beyond her, and beyond

Jerry, Weigand heard the gasp of a snatched breath from Dorian.

Kirk spoke from the rear of the theatre. He spoke quietly, now.

"And that, children," said Humphrey Kirk, "was where I found the body."

V
TUESDAY

Humphrey Kirk had pointed out a door opening off the mezzanine and marked "Private" and then, at Weigand's direction, gone back to wait with the others on the stage. Uniformed men stood stolidly at the exits and in the aisles to see that they stayed there; squad men presented leathery red faces to the suspects and gathered by twos in conference. The people on the stage watched them and wondered uneasily, uncertainly suspecting that things affecting them went forward. Now and then one of the detectives looked hard at one of the people on the stage and then turned back to his companion and spoke seriously.

"Watch Notre Dame," one said after such a stare. "That's all I'm telling you, Flaherty. Watch Notre Dame."

It would have consoled F. Lawrence Tilford, who had withstood the full, cold weight of Detective King's regard, to know

94

the burden of Detective King's communication to Detective Flaherty; to know that Detective Flaherty's portentous nod meant only that Detective Flaherty also thought Notre Dame was hot this year. Mr. Tilford unhappily construed the conversation otherwise: he put it instinctively into dialogue:

Detective King: There's our man, Flaherty.

Detective Flaherty: (Nods in agreement) Yeh.

Mr. Tilford, who had been standing easily near the fireplace, found a chair and sat down and took out a handkerchief which matched his greenish socks and wiped a brow which also, he suspected, now matched the socks.

Weigand had opened the door marked "Private" and led Sergeant Mullins into the office of the West Forty-fifth Street Theatre — an office which, in the old days, had been David Dortman's own, part of David Dortman's own theatre, part of David Dortman's own tradition. Weigand, remembering, looked for the casting couch which had once enjoyed equal fame. It was gone; the office was now comfortable and impersonal, as if it belonged to a bank which did not know quite what to do with it.

"Now, Mullins —" Weigand began, and

somebody knocked at the door. Weigand made a remark and opened the door and glared at Detective Stein, on guard and messenger duty outside.

"I thought I said —" Weigand began coldly, and then said, "Oh!" He looked at Pam North, who led the delegation, with Dorian just behind her and Mr. North, looking worried, bringing up the rear.

"I told them we'd better —" Mr. North began. Pam said, "Sh-h-h."

"We're going, Bill," she said. "Tell them to let us. We're taking Dorian down to our place to tell Martha five and see about the gin. And then you come down."

"Well —" Weigand said.

"When you can," Pam told him. "After all, you're going to have to eat some time. You're going to have to let all these people eat. And — listen!" She waited for them to listen. *"We've got Noilly Prat!"*

"No!" Weigand said.

"Genuine," Pam told him. "Jerry found it at a little place on Eighth Street. Wasn't that clever of him?"

"Very," said Weigand, meaning it. He paused. It wasn't often anybody could offer martinis with real Noilly Prat these days. And he would have to eat. And it often paid to talk things over with the Norths.

"All right," he said. "I'll try — around seven-thirty, though." He hesitated and looked at Mullins. "You want this?" he asked.

"Listen, Loot," Mullins said. His voice held appeal. Mrs. North looked shocked.

"Aloysius Clarence?" Mrs. North said, in evident surprise. "Of course!"

Mullins winced.

"Listen, Mrs. North," he said. "I know it's funny. But it's just a name, see?"

"Of course it is, Al," Mrs. North said. "Or would Clare be better?"

"Yeh," Mullins said. "Al." He looked at Mrs. North darkly.

"What's this Noilly stuff?" he inquired. "Do you drink it? Like rye?"

Mrs. North smiled at him, please. She promised there would be rye. Mullins looked relieved. He watched the Norths and Dorian disappear, with Stein going along to pass them out. A reflective pleasure remained upon his face. Then he saw Weigand looking at him and his face descended. He read the look.

"Jeez, Loot," he said. "All them times?"

Weigand nodded unrelentingly. Mullins sighed deeply and got out his notebook. He looked at what he had written there, sighed even more deeply, and said, "Jeez" again.

Then he squared his shoulders and said: "O.K., Loot."

Mullins had timed everything. He started to read and Weigand stopped him.

"It was twelve minutes after four when they started?" he said, repeating the time Mullins had just given him. Mullins nodded. Weigand said, "Right."

"To make it simpler," he said, "we'll take these times as duplicating the times earlier in the day. We'll make 4:12 equal 1:12. Right?"

Mullins looked at him doubtfully and then even more doubtfully at his notebook. Then he brightened and said, "Yeh!" He looked admiringly at a man who could thus bring order out of chaos. He continued.

At 1:12, revised time, Sand said, "Curtain," and Ellen Grady, who was already on stage, began to speak. With her on the stage at that time were Percy Driscoll and Paul Oliver. Sand was sitting at a small table down-stage right; Kirk was in a seat in the third row. Mullins interrupted himself.

"I didn't try to get Kirk every time he moved," he said. "He was all over the place. In sight, mostly. And Sand stayed where he was, looking at these papers."

"He was following the script," Weigand said. "I noticed that. Go ahead."

"Well," said Mullins, "they cussed each other out for a while — say, that Grady dame is something, ain't she, Loot." Mullins' face lighted with reminiscent fervor. "I could go for that one, Loot."

"Don't," Weigand told him. "You'll burn your fingers. Go ahead."

"Yeh," Mullins said. "I guess maybe I would. O.K. They cussed each other out for a while, and said a few lines from the play, and Kirk jumped up and down and then this guy Oliver went off the stage. The Grady dame went over and sat on the windowseat and kept looking out like she expected to see somebody coming. That was at four — no, one-fifteen. Then, couple of minutes later — 1:17 — this Hubbard guy comes on. They talk a little and then Hubbard comes down and says he saw a cigarette about where the dead guy was sitting. He musta seen it about 1:18." Mullins broke off.

"You figure that's it, Loot?" he said. "Was that when somebody bumped him?"

The fingers of Weigand's left hand patted gently against the desk before which he was sitting. They patted in due order, beginning with the little finger and ending with the thumb. After the thumb patted the shining wood, Weigand said it could be.

"Or," he said, "maybe we're supposed to think that." He looked reflectively at Mullins. He said there were alternative theories. Mullins looked doubtful and said, "Yeh," without conviction.

"Such as this," Weigand said, helping him. "Say, for some reason, the murderer wanted us to think that was the time. He could sit back there and move the cigarette as Hubbard saw it moved, hoping it would be seen."

Mullins' face brightened and then clouded.

"Yeh, Loot," Mullins said. "But where'd it get him? He'd have to be there, and if he was there anyway, where'd it get him? I mean —."

"How would it help an alibi?" Weigand clarified. "I don't know, Mullins. But there are a lot of things we don't know. Go ahead."

Mullins went ahead. Alberta James came on stage at 1:20 but stayed only a minute. As she left, F. Lawrence Tilford came on. Tilford, Grady, Hubbard and Driscoll were on together until 1:28, when Driscoll went off. At 1:32, Hubbard went off, leaving Tilford and Miss Grady alone on the stage. At 1:40, Ruthmary Jones came on; at 1:41, she went off and at 1:42, Hubbard and Miss

James came back on. Tilford, Miss Grady, Hubbard and Miss James were on then until 1:48 when Miss Grady went off. She came back three minutes later with Driscoll. Hubbard and Miss James left almost at once. Driscoll went off at 1:55, and Tilford and Miss Grady were alone on the stage until 1:58, when Kirk shouted.

Weigand drummed the desk.

"The others?" he asked.

Ahlberg came in and down the right aisle to a seat at 1:21. Miss Fowler came in at 1:22, and Miss James joined her at 1:24. They went back-stage almost at once, apparently passing Christopher, who came in at 1:25. Miss Fowler returned to her seat twenty minutes later and stayed in it until the body was discovered. Smith came to his seat, from the back-stage, at 1:27, and stayed in it thereafter.

Weigand's fingers continued to drum. Then he spoke abruptly.

"Well, Sergeant," he said, "who killed Carney Bolton?"

Mullins stared at him.

"Listen, Loot," he said. "You mean to say you know? You got it from these times and things?"

Weigand looked at him, and grinned as suddenly as he had spoken.

"I'll tell you about that, Mullins," he said. "I don't know a damn thing more than I knew before. How about you?"

Mullins looked disappointed, and said, "Oh."

"I thought maybe —" he said. "Only I guess it couldn't be."

"But," Weigand said, "these times may mean something when you boil them down. Put a fire under them, Aloysius."

"Now listen, Loot," Mullins said. "Ain't it enough that Mrs. North —"

"Right," Weigand said. "Take it away, Mullins. Find out just when everybody could have slipped around to the back, come down and stabbed Bolton. Figure he was there the whole time, dead, or alive, from, say, about 1:10 to 1:58, when Kirk found him dead. Or —" He suddenly stopped.

"Or suppose," he said, "that Bolton wasn't dead *until* Kirk found him. Suppose he was alive until 1:58 and that Kirk stuck an ice-pick in his neck and then *yelled so that nobody could hear any sound Bolton made!*"

Mullins looked at Weigand and blinked.

"What about the cigarette, if it was that way?" he wanted to know.

Weigand shook his head. Perhaps, he pointed out, the cigarette had nothing to do with it. Perhaps Bolton had merely been sitting there smoking quietly and lowering the cigarette from his lips at intervals to knock the ash off in the cup, suppose — Weigand stopped.

"Yeh," Mullins said. "Where was the ashes? Where was the butt he was smoking, because the only one was the broken one on the floor. Or if that was the cigarette, what made him break it?"

Weigand's fingers drummed again.

"Suppose," he said, "that the cigarette had nothing to do with it in the first place; that it was just Dr. Bolton smoking. But suppose the murderer wanted to fix 1:18, when Hubbard saw the cigarette glow, as the time of the murder, because at that time he had an alibi — was on stage, perhaps. Suppose Hubbard had already, not realizing it, spoken about the cigarette to the murderer. What's to prevent our man from taking the ash-cup Bolton had been using, and which may have been full of cigarette ends, and throwing it away — *and replacing it with an unused cup?* Then he could take a couple of drags off a cigarette anywhere, drop it on the floor near Bolton, and leave us to work out the 1:18 time."

Mullins looked thoughtful. After a time he said, "Yeh."

"In that event," Weigand said, "Bolton was killed after 1:18. But —" He broke off.

"Listen, Loot," Mullins said. "Don't ball it up any more. It's screwy enough now."

Weigand shook his head, and drummed the desk.

"Or," he said, "it could be this way — the murderer did go and smoke a cigarette in a seat near Bolton's and did intend to establish 1:18 as the time of the murder. He did that because, at 1:18, *he wasn't in the theatre.* I mean, of course, he wasn't suppose to be in the theatre."

Mullins scratched his head and then looked in his notebook.

"Penfield Smith, Mary Fowler, this Christopher baby — they weren't supposed to be in the theatre."

"And," Weigand said, "add Mr. Ahlberg. He came in, when we were re-playing it for times, at 1:21. Three minutes after Bolton, in a manner of speaking, left it. But perhaps all our times are a little off. The second run-through lasted almost precisely as long as the first, but that doesn't mean that every exit and every entrance coincided with the same exit and entrances in the first. Maybe, for example, they didn't have any argument at all during the first few minutes of the original run-through, but had one of about the same length toward the end. Get it?"

"Jeez, Loot," Mullins said. "Let's forget the whole business, huh? Let's just figure that somebody bumped Bolton off any old time, huh? This sort of thing will get us nuts."

Weigand shook his head. He said they couldn't just forget any part of the business. So Mullins would work out a chart showing the times it might be possible for each suspect to commit the murder; the times, that was, when each person was apparently for a long or short period off the stage, if one of the actors, or out of sight if not one of the actors. Mullins sighed. Weigand relented a little.

"You can do it later," he said. "Tonight, after we're done here. Because just now, I think we'll see some people about a murder."

He stepped to the door and spoke to Stein. He closed the door and came back to the desk.

"We're going to start with Mr. Kirk," he said. "I think Mr. Kirk ought to have some things to tell us."

VI
TUESDAY
5:37 P.M. TO 6:15 P.M.

Humphrey Kirk sat and extended himself
in the chair Weigand indicated and pushed
back the lock of red hair. It fell down again.
Weigand let the fingers of his left hand play
for a moment on the polished surface of the
desk. Then he told Kirk he wouldn't keep
him long.

"Now," he added, thoughtfully. He let the
qualifying word hang in the air for a moment and went on. "I have a way of going
about these things," he said. "Sometimes it
works. Just as, I suppose, you have a way of
going about directing a play. Perhaps, as a
matter of fact, there's a certain similarity in
the methods."

Kirk, Weigand thought, would be interested in shop talk. Kirk looked as if he were.
He looked interested and inquiring.

"I've found," Weigand told him, "that
there's no use in trying to learn everything
at once, to get all the answers the first time

over. As a matter of fact, I usually don't know all the questions the first time over. New points keep creeping in. I suppose a play develops in pretty much the same way?"

"Well," Kirk said, "it's the other way around, of course. Analysis as against synthesis. But I see what you mean."

Weigand nodded.

"Obviously," he said. "And in my job it works out this way — I don't expect a witness to give me all he has the first time I talk to him. If he did, I probably wouldn't know what to do with what he told me — I wouldn't have an outline to fit it into. Just as you don't expect an actor to give you all he has the first time he reads the line. You have to get a picture in your own mind before you know what you require of your actor. Right?"

Kirk nodded.

"Only of course," he said, "I have the script to start with. And you haven't."

Weigand felt Mullins looking at him wonderingly, and pretended he didn't.

"No," he said. "We have to write the script as we go along. We see what happens first, and fit it into a story. It's like coming into the middle of a movie — or, for that matter, like coming in on 'Two in the Bush' during a run-through of the second act. The first thing we wonder about is the relations of the people — who's fond of whom, where the hates and irritations lie. That sort of thing. Right?"

Kirk nodded. He said Weigand's job, looked at in that way, seemed like an interesting one. Weigand nodded and drummed gently on the table. "Now, Mr. Kirk," he said, "I have a strong feeling that you didn't like Dr. Carney Bolton. I don't say it was any more than that. If you want to tell me anything, I'll listen."

Kirk pushed back the red lock and held his hand to his forehead. He stared at Weigand. Weigand could see him hesitating.

"All right," Kirk said. "I didn't."

Weigand nodded.

"Tell me about him," he directed.

"Obviously," Kirk said, "he was a very able man. From all I hear he was a good doctor; anyway he had some celebrated patients. He spent a lot of time on Broadway. He went to most of the openings, always with a different girl — or almost always. He had fingers in lots of pies, and money in lots of shows. He went to the Stork and places like that. He knew a lot of people."

"And," Weigand said, "you didn't like him. Why?"

"I don't like people like that, particularly," Kirk said. "That was all."

"Now, Mr. Kirk," Weigand said. "Don't make things hard for us."

"No," Kirk said, "that really was all, at bottom. He'd been a nuisance during rehearsals; he decided to give this one his personal attention and he was full of notions. He got in everybody's hair. But as far as that's concerned, almost everybody got in almost everybody's hair. He irritated me more than — well, say Smitty for example, but chiefly because I don't like people like Bolton and do like people like Smitty. Also, of course, Smitty made more sense. But there wasn't anything else."

Weigand said he saw.

"Why was Bolton particularly interested in this show, do you suppose?" he asked.

"Because —" Kirk started, leaning forward. Then he changed his mind and settled back, adjusting the meandering lock. "I wouldn't know," he said. "Presumably the play just interested him more than usual."

"Or," Weigand said, "perhaps somebody in the cast interested him more than usual."

Kirk said he wouldn't know. He said it with a careful lack of interest.

"Wouldn't Miss James be rather Bolton's

type?" Weigand asked, suddenly. Kirk sat up.

"My God, *no!*" he said. "She's anything but his type. She wouldn't —" He broke off. Weigand waited a moment.

"Wouldn't she, Mr. Kirk?" he said. "Dr. Bolton was — helpful to a good many young actresses, wasn't he?"

"Look," Kirk said, "I tell you she wasn't the type. She never looked at Bolton."

"She had lunch with him today," Weigand said, without expression. Kirk looked amused.

"Got you there, Lieutenant," he said. "She had lunch with me."

"In that case," Weigand told him, "she's a liar. And for no reason. She says she had lunch — coffee, anyway — with Bolton at an Automat. Maybe you were along?"

"Skip it," Kirk said. "You're on the wrong track."

It was, Weigand admitted, quite possible. He said there was one other question on the same track.

"You're pretty fond of Miss James yourself, aren't you, Kirk?" he said.

Kirk wanted to know whether that was any of Weigand's damn business.

"Frankly," Weigand told him, "I don't know. If Bolton were playing around with

110

Miss James and you were pretty fond of her — well, finish it yourself, Kirk. I don't know that I'd want any girl I was fond of playing around with Bolton."

Kirk was still uninterested, but his voice was hard. He said that Weigand could skip that, too. Weigand was cheerful about it. It was, he said, something Kirk could keep in mind — until next time. Meanwhile, they'd try another track. Kirk knew this theatre — how to get in and out of it, that sort of thing. He would save Weigand's nosing about, at the moment, by telling him about that. Kirk nodded and told.

You could, he said, get into the theatre through the front doors, as the audience did. Normally when the theatre was dark, even when rehearsals were going on, those doors were locked, however. You could get in through the stage door.

"And the fire exit doors?" Weigand asked. "I suppose you can't?"

You couldn't, Kirk told him. They all, in accordance with the law, opened outward. And on the outer surfaces there were neither knobs nor handles. And when fully closed, they locked automatically, as far as entrance was concerned. Weigand nodded. So there were two possible entrances, but the front entrance was almost certainly locked. Right?

That was right.

"Now," Weigand said, "to get from the stage to the auditorium, how do you go about it?"

There were doors at the ends of the right and left aisles, behind the boxes, Kirk told him. There were the temporary steps he had seen over the footlights. And you could go through the basement. Weigand looked interested.

At the right — stage right — of the stage were the dressing rooms, Kirk told him. They opened off a corridor, into which the passage from the stage door led. From this door, there was also an entrance to the basement area under the orchestra seats — a wide, mostly empty expanse of concrete, broken by concrete pillars. Off this area there were entrances to the boiler room, where the cooling apparatus for use during the summer also was. Or you could, if you wanted to, find a door which would lead you under the stage. You could, if you knew which way to go, also find a door which led you into the downstairs lounge and from there you could, of course, go up carpeted stairs to the main floor of the theatre.

Weigand nodded and said, "Thanks."

"Did you touch Bolton's body when you found it?" he asked.

"I don't —" Kirk said — "yes, I remember. I touched his — the shoulder. It was when he sort of toppled away, across the arm of the seat, that I realized he was dead. Then I yelled!"

Weigand supposed Kirk had merely touched clothing, not skin. So he wouldn't know anything about body temperature. Kirk said, with a slight shudder, that he wouldn't. Weigand said, "Right!"

"By the way," he said, "did the rehearsal we just saw go pretty much as the earlier one did, up to the time you found the body?"

Kirk shrugged.

"Pretty much," he said. "New points kept coming up — little things, such as we take up in conferences before each session; some came up on the second run-through that didn't on the first. But we covered much the same ground."

"I suppose," Weigand said, "you always have little disagreements — among the actors, I mean?"

Kirk said Oh God yes.

"But," he said, "this show is tame to some I've directed. These people are little ladies and gents."

"Is it a good play?" Weigand said. Kirk stared at him.

"Sure," he said. "It's a great play. The last act needs a little fixing, maybe, and I'm not sure about the first scene and I want to speed up the second-act curtain, but it's a swell play. First-rate Smitty."

"Speaking of Mr. Penfield Smith," Weigand said, "how did he get along with Bolton?"

Kirk grinned at him, suddenly.

"He told you, didn't he?" he said. "Smitty couldn't bear him. His butting in was driving Smitty nuts. And when Smitty goes nuts —" Kirk looked at the ceiling and smiled reminiscently and shook his head. "Boy!" he said. "When Smitty goes nuts!"

"Was that all there was to it?" Weigand asked. His tone was carefully without expression. He was, he decided suddenly, "throwing the line away." Kirk continued to regard the ceiling.

"No," he said. "They didn't get along from way back. There was something —" He stopped suddenly and looked at Weigand. "Very nice going, Lieutenant," he said. "You caught me napping. But what the hell — a hundred people can tell you about it. Or you can read about it in Variety, if you want to go through the files. It was this way —"

The way it was was that Bolton had done

Smith a dirty trick some ten years earlier, before Smith had got going; when he was still trying to get going. So far as Kirk could remember it was on the occasion of Bolton's only appearance as an independent producer. Normally he was an "angel," backing recognized producers. But this time he appeared in his own right as the prospective producer of an early play by Penfield Smith. He went so far as to buy the play. And then — well, did Weigand know how the Dramatists' Guild contract worked? Weigand shook his head.

"It requires advance payments," Kirk told him. "You can buy a play by paying a hundred dollars down, and a hundred a month for a few months. Then you have to pay a hundred and fifty a month. And as long as you make the option payments the play is yours. Up to a year."

"So?" Weigand said.

So Bolton went into it, presumably, on the up and up, really meaning to produce the play. But he wanted changes made that Smith wouldn't agree to and they quarreled. And then —

"Well," Kirk said, "Bolton just hung on to the play. He told Smith he was going to. He sent his option checks on the last possible days of grace each month and laughed at

Smith and wanted to know what Smith was going to do about it. Smith couldn't get his play back, you see. There was another producer interested, and he tried to buy Bolton off and Bolton just laughed. He held on to the play for the full year, which ran well into the spring. And by that time the other producer was tied up with another play and there was Smitty — stuck. He got around fifteen hundred for his play, and that was all he ever got, because it had some topical value and was no good the next year. And Smitty needed money bad in those days — needed it damned bad. He'd just got married and all that sort of thing; married, in fact, on the strength of "selling" the play to Bolton. And then they started a baby and there were complications — not Bolton's fault, of course, although he just laughed when he heard about it. And somebody else might have put the play on and had a flop and Smitty wouldn't have got even his fifteen hundred. However —"

"Mr. Smith didn't like it," Weigand finished for him. Kirk agreed that Mr. Smith hadn't.

"He was sore as a pup when he found out that Bolton had money in this one," Kirk said. "He thought Maxie was on his own when he signed the contract. He tried to withdraw the play, but he couldn't."

Weigand nodded.

"By the way," he said, "did Mrs. Smith get all right?"

Kirk shook his head.

"No," he said, "Mrs. Smith never did get all right. Mrs. Smith up and died." He pushed back the lock of hair and regarded Weigand.

"So I don't think Carney Bolton was so much of a guy, do you, Lieutenant?" he said.

Weigand said he didn't seem to have been so much of a guy.

"There are a lot more nice stories about him," Kirk said. "You'll run across them, probably. So you see why I wasn't keen about —" He stopped, abruptly.

"About what, Kirk?" Weigand asked him.

Kirk shook his head.

"No soap, Lieutenant," he said. "Just make it read: 'About Carney Bolton.' "

"All right," Weigand said. "I'll make it read that way. For now. By the way, do you happen to remember where you were when Hubbard saw the cigarette — you remember where that comes in the act, don't you?"

Kirk nodded and then shook his head, spreading out his hands, helplessly.

"Sitting somewhere out front, probably," he said. "But I honestly don't know, Lieu-

117

tenant. I was all over the place. That's the way I work."

Weigand nodded and thought that was all, for the moment. He could go back and join the others. And would he, in passing, ask Mr. Smith to come back. Kirk, standing, looked down at Weigand.

"He'll love me for telling you this, Lieutenant," he said. "I just drifted into it. Or did you push me in?"

Weigand shook his head and smiled faintly and did not answer. He watched Kirk go, looking after him speculatively.

"Listen, Loot," Mullins said. "That guy's that way about this James girl."

"Yes, Mr. Winchell," Weigand said, staring at the door as it closed behind Kirk.

"And listen, Loot, this guy Bolton was making a play for her and Kirk didn't like it. Don't you figure it that way?"

"Yes, Sergeant," Weigand said. "That is just the way I figure it." Then he said, "Come in," to the person who was knocking on the door. Penfield Smith came in. He removed his glasses from his nose and a handkerchief from his pocket. He peered at Weigand and polished his glasses. He peered at Mullins and put his glasses on and looked at Mullins. He sat down where Weigand indicated and took off his glasses and

118

continued to polish them. He was still polishing them when he spoke.

"I suppose by now, Lieutenant," he said, "you know why I didn't like Dr. Bolton — why I heartily approved his demise?"

Weigand nodded at him.

"Yes," he said. He let Smith take it on from there.

"Shall I repeat that I did not kill him, in spite of that?" Smith inquired. He put his glasses on and looked at Weigand. He left them on for half a minute and took them off and put them in his pocket. Otherwise he seemed entirely calm.

"If you like," Weigand said. "It's a statement I've learned to expect."

"Naturally," Smith agreed. "Yours must be an interesting occupation, Lieutenant Weigand." He looked at Weigand closely. "I think you find it interesting, don't you?"

"Yes," Weigand said. "Quite interesting. Did you sit in the same seat throughout the first rehearsal this afternoon as you did in the second, Mr. Smith?"

Smith took his glasses out and began to polish them.

"Approximately," he said. "That is — the same seat, or back a row or down a row. I didn't notice exactly."

"And you stayed in it?"

119

"Except for getting up once or twice to talk to Humpty, yes," Smith said. "I may have walked down to the stage and back a couple of times. I stayed on that side of the house, however — I remember that."

"Why?" Weigand said. "I mean — why do you remember that, particularly?"

"Bolton was on the other side," Smith said. "I preferred not to have to talk to him. It disturbed me. I preferred to concentrate on the play."

Weigand nodded.

"By the way," he said, "it seems to be a very amusing play, if you don't mind an outsider's opinion."

Smith smiled at him.

"I'm delighted to have an outsider's opinion, Lieutenant," he said. "After all, people who pay for seats are outsiders."

"And a very good cast," Weigand said. "Or am I just a bad judge of acting?"

Smith looked judicial. He put the glasses away. Finally he said that, considering everything, he thought the cast was shaping up very nicely.

"Especially this Miss — what's her name?" He made a business of looking at notes. "James," he said. "The girl who plays the daughter."

Smith nodded.

"Very nice little actress," he said. "Very nice. Works well with Humpty too, of course."

"Of course?" Weigand repeated. He smiled slightly.

Smith smiled back, and nodded.

"Of course," he repeated.

Weigand devoted a moment to looking like a man who has encountered a new idea. He arranged to look a little puzzled. He arranged suddenly and frankly to share his puzzlement with Smith.

"Somehow," he said, "I got the idea that Bolton was making a play for Miss James — I don't know where I got it. Out of the air apparently."

Smith shook his head and said that that was very shrewd of the Lieutenant. As a matter of fact —

"Well," he said, "it won't be the first time in history that two men have made a play for the same girl, Lieutenant. Or that she has — hesitated between them."

Weigand nodded.

"Only," he said, "I shouldn't have thought that Bolton was the sort of man who lets girls — hesitate."

Smith agreed that he didn't, often. Possibly he was having difficulty with Miss James. Smith made it clear that he didn't

121

know and hadn't investigated. Weigand cast again.

"I should have thought that Miss Grady would be more his type," he suggested. "More — polished."

Smith looked at him a moment. Weigand doubted whether he was extracting anything that Smith didn't want to give, or that his finesse was escaping notice. Smith spoke, after a moment, and spoke drily.

"Miss Grady has the same thought, I suspect," he said. "Or had, up to 1:18 this afternoon."

Weigand looked at him with interest.

"One eighteen, Mr. Smith?" he said. "Why 1:18?"

Mr. Smith looked very bland and said, "Really, Lieutenant."

"When young Hubbard saw the cigarette fall," he said. "As of course you know."

"Do I?" said Weigand.

"Certainly you do," said Smith. "Your sergeant here timed it very carefully. So, as a matter of interest, did I. I made it 1:18, didn't you, Sergeant?"

Mullins looked at Mr. Smith darkly. Mr. Smith returned a sunny gaze.

"Listen, Loot," Mullins said, growlingly.

"All right, Sergeant," Weigand said. "Skip it. Mr. Smith is merely observant." He looked at Smith. "Merely observant, isn't it, Mr. Smith?"

Smith put his glasses back on and nodded brightly.

"Of course, Lieutenant," he said. "What else would it be?"

Weigand said he couldn't imagine, and that Mr. Smith could join the others. "For now," he added. "No doubt I'll want to talk to you again later. I may want to take advantage of — your habit of observation."

Penfield Smith went. Weigand stood in the door and spoke to Stein. Where the hell, he wanted to know, was this guy Evans, the custodian? Stein shrugged and spread his hands. A couple of the boys were looking for him. Apparently he had gone out somewhere.

"I want him," Weigand said. "Gone out or not, I want him."

VII
TUESDAY
6:15 P.M. TO 7:25 P.M.

Mullins was looking inquiringly at Weigand when the lieutenant closed the door.

"Evans?" Mullins repeated. "Who — oh, yeh, the janitor. Why him, particularly?"

"Custodian," Weigand said. "I gather he doesn't personally janit." He paused and considered that Pam North apparently was creeping into his speech. "And because I want anybody whose habits suddenly change when somebody's done a murder. Evans normally is always around, everybody says. Today he isn't around. And today a man's been killed."

"Yes," said Mullins. "Who next? Meanwhile?"

Weigand stopped to consider and regard his watch. There were too many waiting to include in continuous questioning without a break — a break for dinner, chiefly. And also, Weigand decided, a break for him. It was fine to get suspects tired and nervous.

But detectives also could get tired, and when they were tired miss things. He told Mullins to ask Mr. Kirk to come in a moment. Mr. Kirk, after a moment, came, brushing back his forelock.

"Are you done here for the day?" Weigand asked him.

Kirk said he had been going to come back and talk about that. Normally, yes. But he had planned an evening rehearsal, before all this happened.

"We're dragging a little," he explained. "Nothing serious, but I want to get back on schedule."

"And now?" Weigand said.

Now, Kirk told him, more than ever. He seemed worried.

"The children are going to pieces, Lieutenant," he said. "They're all out there beginning to jitter and get their minds off the play. I'd like to pull them up short; get them back to work before they go up like balloons. They're funny children, Lieutenant."

Weigand thought it over. Then he said, "Right."

"Not that we can let the murder wait for the play," he said. "We'll have to keep at them, here or somewhere else. But they may as well work between whiles. What do you want to do?"

"Let them go now," Kirk said, promptly. "Give them a call for — say eight o'clock. All right?"

"All right," Weigand said. "Let the cast go. Ask Mr. Ahlberg, Mr. Christopher and Miss Fowler to stay around for a few minutes. Or, ask Mr. Ahlberg to come in here and Mr. Christopher and Miss Fowler to stick around. After we've finished with them, we'll get something to eat and take the rest of them later."

"Right," Kirk said. "Mr. Christopher's in a pet."

"Is he now?" said Weigand. "Think of that."

Kirk pushed back the red forelock, grinned at Weigand and went out, with the faintest parody of a flounce. Mullins laughed and Weigand smiled.

"Nice guy," Mullins said. Weigand said he seemed to be. Mr. Ahlberg came in, round and anxious. Weigand said there were a few questions. Ahlberg looked increasingly anxious.

"Troubles," Mr. Ahlberg said, desperately. "Always troubles. If it ain't money it's murder or some critic can't digest his dinner. Always troubles."

"As the sparks fly upward," Weigand said.

"What did you and Dr. Bolton confer about after lunch today, Mr. Ahlberg?"

"Confer?" Ahlberg repeated. "Me and Bolton?"

"Confer," Weigand said. "He hurried back from lunch to see you. Why?"

"Oh," Ahlberg said. "That. I didn't wait. I went to the Astor and had lunch and forgot Dr. Bolton, except I got nervous indigestion from thinking about him. He was trying to ruin me."

"Really?" Weigand said. Mr. Ahlberg didn't need encouragement.

"He should write a play," Mr. Ahlberg said. "He should write his own plays. Always beefing — always wanting to fire somebody. Kirk. Grady. The colored lady."

"Really?" Weigand said. "Why?"

"He should direct," Mr. Ahlberg said. "He should act all the parts. He should produce too, maybe. Always what other people do is wrong with Dr. Bolton. Like this morning, he flares up and says he's pulling out."

"Withdrawing his backing, you mean?" Weigand asked. Mr. Ahlberg was proving very interesting.

"Absolutely," said Maxie Ahlberg. "Take out the money. And the set not paid for and opening in a week. Always troubles. So I went to the Astor."

Weigand was a little puzzled. Mr. Ahlberg had gone to the Astor for a long lunch instead of meeting his partner for an important conference?

"Sure," said Mr. Ahlberg. "I know Bolton." He paused. "I knew Bolton for years," he corrected. "Always he flared up, usually he calmed down. When he was upset I didn't confer with him."

It was, Mr. Ahlberg insisted through several more questions, as simple as that. Several things during the morning rehearsal had upset Carney Bolton to the point where he threatened to withdraw his money. He had instructed Ahlberg to meet him immediately after lunch to talk it over. Ahlberg had decided to ignore the instructions, hoping that later Bolton might have calmed down, might even have forgotten his whole intention. Mr. Ahlberg had had a long lunch, meeting several friends, and had then returned to the theatre and let himself in through the front door and come down to a seat.

"Like I did later," Ahlberg said. "When you re-enacted it, like it says in the papers."

Ahlberg, questioned carefully, was less talkative about the relations of others in the company to Bolton. He had heard of Penfield Smith's difficulties with the physician;

128

he thought it had been a dirty shame. Maybe Bolton was making a play for Miss James; who could tell? Mr. Ahlberg's shoulders disclaimed knowledge. Miss James was a nice little actress; a very sweet kid. Better she should pay more attention to Humpty Kirk, who was a nice boy. Mr. Ahlberg forgot to be worried and beamed paternally when he considered Mr. Kirk and Miss James.

"By the way," Weigand said. "Were the front doors locked when you came in? I assume you have a key?"

They were. Mr. Ahlberg did have a key. So far as he knew nobody else did, except probably Bolton.

As to the time of his entrance through the lobby, Mr. Ahlberg was pleasingly certain. He had looked at his watch as he opened the outer doors and his watch had showed 1:20, maybe 1:19. And now, at any rate, his watch was right with Weigand's, which was, because Weigand had set it half an hour before for just such purposes, almost certainly right with God. Weigand audibly approved of Mr. Ahlberg, who knew not only where he was going, but when.

"As a matter of routine," Weigand said, "did anybody see you? At the doors? In the lobby?"

Ahlberg saddened and shook his head. When he was opening the doors, anybody might have seen him. "Half the people on Broadway." But he didn't know. He had seen nobody he knew then or until he joined the rehearsal group. Weigand told him not to worry about it, and let him go.

Mr. Ahlberg went. Mullins, looking after him, said he was a nice little guy.

"It seems to me, Mullins, that you are getting very fond of people here lately," Weigand said. "You want to watch that. How are you going to give guys a going over if you love them all?"

"Now listen, Loot," Mullins said.

"However," Weigand added, "Maxie does seem like a nice little guy. Of course, that doesn't say he didn't kill Bolton."

Mullins thought it over, and nodded.

"Keys to the front door," he said. "He could've come in any time and nobody seen him. But look — if he bumps Bolton where's his money coming from for the show?"

"Well," Weigand said, "didn't you ever hear of insurance, Sergeant? Of partners mutually insuring themselves in each other's favor? I suspect we'll find that that happened here. And in that event, Bolton dead would be worth more to Ahlberg than Bolton alive and *planning to withdraw his backing.*"

Mullins thought it over. Mullins said "Yeh!" They summoned Mary Fowler.

Miss Fowler seemed sunk in calm; at peace on the bottom of a troubled sea. She stood in the doorway solidly, looking with quiet interest at Weigand out of protuberant eyes. When he invited her to sit she sat, and thereafter did not move. She seemed free from those nervous compulsions which keep most men and women uneasily in motion even when invited to repose. She thanked the lieutenant for the chair and waited. Her unhurried dignity gave Weigand no obvious approach.

He was, he told her, sorry to have had to keep her waiting. He regretted the inconvenience which was, however, inseparable from murder investigations. She said "Yes, Lieutenant," in an unhurried and huskily musical voice. It was a voice, Weigand thought, which should belong to a beautiful woman. He asked her about the afternoon.

She had, she told him, gone out to lunch when the morning rehearsal broke. She had hoped to talk with Mr. Kirk about the costumes during the morning, and confer with Miss Grady and Miss James. There turned out to be no opportunity. She had

131

gone home for samples, then up to Forty-eighth Street and had lunch at the Tavern. She had not hurried getting back; Mr. Kirk had had an appointment for lunch which would, she supposed, keep him so late that he would want to start rehearsing as soon as he got back to the theatre. It was a few minutes after one before she herself got back. This wasn't unusual; she usually took her time over lunch, having no reason for promptness. She had gone first to the front doors, and, when she found them locked, had gone down the passage at the side of the theatre to the stage door.

"As I did later during the re-enactment," she said.

Weigand nodded.

"Why did you think the front doors would be unlocked?" he asked. "Weren't they usually locked?"

"No," she said. "Not 'usually.' Sometimes they were locked, sometimes they weren't. And sometimes when they were, Mr. Evans would be in the lobby and would open them." She smiled slightly. "After a good deal of grumbling," she added.

"But today he wasn't?" Weigand supposed.

"Yes," she said. "He was; but he wouldn't hear me — I'm sure he did hear me, because I tapped on the glass with a coin and he looked around. Then he pretended he didn't hear me, or see me either, and walked off."

" 'Because he knows it teases,' " Weigand said. "Did anyone else see you, Miss Fowler? We have to check up on these things."

"Of course," Miss Fowler said. "And as it happens somebody did. A mounted policeman; and his horse. He seemed a little suspicious — the policeman — and said something about the doors being locked and to try the stage entrance. I stopped and said something to him, I think, and petted the horse. Then I went through the stage entrance and out front until Mr. Kirk and the others should be free."

"And Miss James joined you," Weigand said, "as she did when we ran through it?"

Miss Fowler nodded. Miss James had found a material she wanted to have used for her first-act dress and wanted Miss Fowler to pass on it. Miss Fowler had gone back and they had taken it to the stage door and looked at it in daylight. She had stayed with "Berta" for a quarter of an hour or so and had then gone back and watched the rehearsal through to its unexpected climax.

Weigand suddenly drew the piece of orange silk from his pocket and held it up.

"Was this it?" he said.

Mary Fowler looked at it with quiet interest.

"Oh, no," she said. "It was a blue material — a blue crepe. Not at all like this."

Weigand said, "Right," and let the silk fall on the table. It lay there brightly, but Miss Fowler, after her first appraisal, did not seem to notice it. Weigand took up another line.

"Did you know Dr. Bolton well?" he inquired. Rather to his surprise, she nodded.

"Quite well, some years ago," she said. "He was my physician at one time, when I was on the stage myself. And we were quite good friends for a time."

Weigand nodded, waiting for her to go on. She looked at him inquiringly.

"But that was several years ago," she said. "I hadn't seen much of him lately — since I quit acting."

Weigand nodded.

"By the way," he said, "would you care to tell me whether he was interested in anybody in the cast — specially interested, I mean? I suspect you would have noticed."

She smiled.

"I see you know his reputation, Lieutenant," she said. "There was usually some woman in whom he was — specially inter-

134

ested. I suppose this time it was Miss Grady. But I haven't had much opportunity to notice — I've only dropped in and out, of course. Still, I should think it would be Miss Grady. She's a very beautiful young woman."

"Not Miss James?" Weigand asked.

Miss Fowler shook her head, rather emphatically.

"Oh, no," she said. "She isn't at all the type for Dr. Bolton. I'm sure he wasn't interested."

Weigand nodded. He fingered the orange silk.

"By the way," he said, "are you sure you haven't seen this before? It seems to come in your department."

He held it out to her.

"Look at it," he urged. She looked at it, as one who does an unnecessary duty. She did not touch it. She shook her head.

"I'm not using anything remotely that color," she said. "Or even anything it would go with. Why, Lieutenant?"

"Because," Weigand said, "this silk was in Bolton's hand when he was killed. So naturally we're interested."

Miss Fowler said she saw; but she shook her head again.

"It isn't a color we could possibly have

used, Lieutenant," she said.

Weigand nodded.

"It would have been all wrong for everything — in color, I mean," she insisted.

"Right," Weigand said. He pushed the piece of silk back in his pocket. He made a business of consulting notes. He said he thought that that was all, for now.

"As other points come up," he told her, "I may have to ask you a few more questions."

She said she understood. If she could, at any time, be of any help — She stood up and Weigand stood with her. She went out, moving with uncommon grace for so substantial-seeming a woman. Weigand stared after her for a moment, and then called to Stein to send in Mr. Christopher.

Mr. Christopher came, scowling. He sat and fidgeted. He had come to the theatre after the rehearsal started, sat in one place, done nothing and seen nothing. He knew Dr. Bolton only slightly and had no views about him; he had heard that Bolton was making a play for Miss Grady, and assumed it to be true. He hadn't paid much attention.

"Once and for all, officer," he said, "I don't know anything about this. Keeping me here is merely — an imposition."

Weigand said he was sorry if Mr. Christopher had been inconvenienced. No doubt he had wasted Mr. Christopher's time and his own.

"However," Weigand explained, "we can never know that until after we *have* wasted it, of course. We have to ask the questions before we can know the answers. A great deal of everybody's time is necessarily wasted in this business."

Christopher did not look particularly mollified, but he nodded.

"And now you're through with me, I gather?" he said.

Weigand nodded.

"I should think so," he said. "For the time being at any rate. Oh — one more thing."

He took out the piece of orange silk and held it up before Christopher. Christopher stared at it, and at Weigand. No, he had never seen it before. It was interesting that it had been found in Dr. Bolton's hand but, Christopher's tone commented, not very interesting.

Would it, Weigand wanted to know, be a color which would clash with the colors of the set — one that Miss Fowler would, therefore, not think of using? Christopher appeared more interested. After looking at the silk he shook his head slowly.

"Not necessarily," he said. "The set is

fairly neutral — we plan to fill it with color. Something like this might fit in." He stared at Weigand with an expression which seemed accusing. "People all the time talk about clashing colors," he said. "An artist can put almost any colors together. You'd think most people are blind."

"So," Weigand said, "this might conceivably have been used?"

"Yes," Christopher said. "Although I haven't seen it before, and of course I would have to be consulted. But we might have used it, if one of the girls had been sold on it."

"Right," Weigand said. He looked at the silk with new attention.

"By the way," he said, "this could be used with blue, couldn't it? As trimming or — something?"

"As an accent," Christopher enlightened him. "With some blues, certainly. Rather obvious, of course — but so many people prefer the obvious, don't you think, Lieutenant? I —"

Weigand was saved from answering, and Christopher from finishing the sentence, by the appearance of Stein in the doorway, heralded by a quick knock.

"Sorry, Lieutenant," Stein said. "But we've found Evans — the custodian. He's out, cold."

"What?" said Weigand. He stood up and moved toward Stein. Mullins followed him and waved Christopher into limbo in passing. Christopher looked indignant.

"Where?" Weigand demanded. "How bad's he hurt?"

In the basement, Stein told him, leading the way. Evans was out, apparently concussion.

"It looks," Stein said, "as if he'd fallen down stairs and landed on his head. That's what the boys say. They just found him. Only he wasn't near any stairs."

"No?" Weigand said. "Where was he?"

He was in a sort of supply closet in the basement. It was a closet with a snap lock. And Evans was locked in when they found him.

"Locked in and knocked out," Stein repeated. "Nice for Mr. Evans."

They went down carpeted stairs from the mezzanine to the orchestra floor and then down more stairs to the downstairs smoking lounge — a long, rectangular room with chairs and sofas which looked more comfortable, Weigand suspected, than they would turn out to be, and a fireplace in which no fire had ever burned. They met Detective Brown of the precinct there, and he led them to an unmarked door at one end of the room. It opened on a steep, short flight of stairs, pitching down to a concrete floor. And then they were in a shadowy, shapeless area, broken by steel and concrete columns.

"This takes us under the main part of the theatre, Lieutenant," Brown explained. "The orchestra seats are above us. If you go straight ahead, you can get under the stage. Over there to the left is a stairway leading up to the dressing-room corridor backstage. It's pretty dark, ain't it?"

It was not so much dark as gray and full of shadows. Their feet scuffled on a gritty cement floor. Then, thinly, they heard the plaintive warning of a siren above.

"Ambulance," Brown said. "We sent for it as soon as we found him."

A cluster of flashlights off to one side identified the whereabouts of Evans and his finders. Evans was lying on the floor, with a rolled coat under his head, and was breathing heavily. Two detectives and a uniformed patrolman stared down at him. They drew back to make room for Weigand and Mullins. They stared down at him. Weigand knelt beside him. There was an ugly, lacerated bump on the right temple. Weigand touched it gently and the bones near it. It

140

didn't feel like a fracture.

He stood back and looked at Evans. Evans was a little, gnarled man who might be in his sixties, with scraggling gray hair and a tooth missing near the front of his mouth. He wore a cheap blue suit, which was now covered with dust. There was a triangular rent in the knee of the right trouser leg.

"Well," Weigand said, "he does look like a man who has fallen downstairs. But it would be quite a fall that would land him where he ended up. And behind a locked door."

A door banged open somewhere and a light appeared at one distant end of what was, Weigand decided, more a grotto than a room. Somebody yelled, "Hey, where is it?" Somebody else said, "Over there, Doc."

The white-clad interne followed the circle of a bobbing flashlight across to them. The interne said that they were certainly keeping the ambulances rolling. He knelt beside Evans, examined his eyes, felt his pulse, ran fingers lightly in the vicinity of the bruise.

"Concussion," he said. "Pretty bad at the moment. But it doesn't feel like a fracture." Another man in uniform joined him. His cap bore the word: "Bellevue," and he carried a stretcher. He joined the interne in staring down at Evans.

"Musta fell downstairs or something," the

141

newcomer suggested. He looked at the faces around him. "Yeh," he said, with renewed confidence. "He musta fell downstairs."

They took Mr. Evans out to the ambulance, then, a patrolman assisting the driver with the stretcher. The interne started after them.

"How long before he can talk, Doctor?" Weigand asked.

The interne shrugged.

"Quite a while, at a guess," he said. "Hours, maybe. Perhaps a couple of days. We'll let you know."

"You do that," Weigand said. He turned to Detective Brown.

"All right," he said. "Where was he?"

Brown pulled open a door a few feet away. It opened on a closet full of cleaning brushes, cloths, cans of polish, cartons of paper drinking cups, cardboard boxes of disinfectant tablets. Brown waved at it. Weigand looked in.

"Sorta doubled up on the floor," Brown explained. "Like he'd been dragged in and dropped, and the door pushed shut and the catch snapped."

Weigand nodded.

"He didn't fall in there, certainly," he said. "Maybe he didn't fall anywhere. Or maybe he was pushed."

He called Stein.

"Get the boys busy here," he said. "And get some pictures. I think somebody was after Mr. Evans."

Weigand swung the beam of a flashlight slowly about the shadowy cavern. It caught dimly, and remained, on the short stairs down which they had come from the lounge. Weigand said, "Um-m-m" and walked over to them. He focussed his light on the floor at the foot of the steps and called, "Mullins!" Mullins went over and looked down.

"Blood, ain't it?" he said. He looked up the stairs and then down again to the faint mark on the cement floor.

"Looks like he tripped and pitched down," Mullins said. "Landing on his head. Don't it, Loot?"

Weigand nodded and said it did.

"Or," he said, "was chucked down. Or pushed down."

"Yeh," Mullins said.

"And," Weigand said, "perhaps taken for dead and stowed away in the closet just to confuse things. He must have looked pretty bad — particularly to the person who pushed him."

"Yeh," Mullins said. "You might take him for dead, if you was in a hurry. Particularly before he started to breathe heavy."

Mullins looked at Weigand, and there was reproach in his stare.

"Listen, Loot," he said. "We got another screwy one. A sure enough screwy one, Loot."

Weigand nodded slowly. It looked, he had to admit, as if they had.

VIII
TUESDAY
7:35 P.M. TO 8:45 P.M.

Jerry North was beating a canvas bag of ice on the hearth and Dorian was sitting on the sofa watching him. Mrs. North's head appeared around the kitchen door and said, "Hello, you're late," to Bill Weigand and Mullins. Weigand said there had been complications.

"Complications and concussions," Mullins said, unexpectedly. Everybody looked at him and he looked surprised. Then he smiled, pleased.

"Canapes," Mrs. North said. Her face saddened. "Remember how Pete loved them?" she said. She looked very sad. Jerry North looked sad with her. Jerry said that, after all, Pete had been getting old. Pam said they all did, that was the trouble, and the next time a Siamese.

"Only," she said, "it will get old too, unless we do first. I sometimes wonder. Who got concussed?"

145

"A man named Evans," Weigand said, and Pam North said, "Oh." Then she said, "Oh, not *Evans*?" Weigand nodded. "Not the man who made us put out cigarettes?"

"Well," Weigand said, "I suppose so. The custodian."

"Oh, no!" Pam said. "But he was nice." She paused and considered. "In a way," she added. "Crunchy."

"Crotchety," said Mr. North. "Is he badly hurt? And who did it?"

Weigand said they thought he'd come around. And that they didn't know.

"Presumably, in case somebody did do it, the person who killed Bolton," Weigand said. "Only it is possible that Evans just fell downstairs. And, conceivably, partially recovered consciousness a minute or two later and got to the closet under his own power, because he had some purpose we don't know about. And then fell again and pulled the door closed in falling, so that the lock snapped."

"Stumbled over a coincidence, probably," Pam said, still in the kitchen door. "And then it dragged him into the closet. Really, Bill! Jerry, come here. I want you."

Jerry North looked a little surprised and then said "Oh." He went into the kitchen, following Pam. Then he stuck his head out.

146

"Oh, Mullins," he said. "Come here a minute, will you?"

Dorian looked after Mullins and smiled at Bill, who took her hands, held out to be taken, and pulled her to her feet. With his lips against her hair he said that it was a dirty shame. Dorian clung to him a moment, and didn't say anything. Then she said, "What does it matter, really, as long as we know?"

"It matters," Weigand told her, "a hell of a lot. Don't be so pure, baby."

"Well," Dorian said, "if you prefer *dead* bodies." She drew back enough to look up at Bill Weigand. "I don't know why it is, Bill," she said, "that you make me say things like that."

"Don't you, Dor?" he said, and grinned at her. She put her head back where it had been. She murmured something into his coat and Bill said, "What?" Dorian emerged, looked at him through eyes which had, for the moment, no greenish cast whatever, and said: "How long will it take?" Bill shook his head.

"I don't get it." Mullins' voice came from the kitchen. Dorian shook gently with laughter in Weigand's arms.

"I don't know," Bill said. "But we'll hurry it!"

"And then, as soon as you catch a man and start him for the electric chair we can — oh, *Bill!*" Dorian drew back in real earnest this time, and stared up at him. The green was back in her eyes. Bill shook her, gently.

"Now who's stumbling over a coincidence, Dor?" he said. "Suppose I'm a mail carrier. Suppose it's just when I get back from carrying the mail. Public service."

"I know," Dorian said. "It *sounds* all right. Only you're not carrying the mail." She continued to look up at him. Her hands tightened on his arms, then relaxed. "Well," she said, "this is the way it is. And I can't do anything about it, can I?"

"No, Dor," Bill said. "Not easily."

"Then it has to be all right," she said. "I mean — I can just take it as all right, can't I?" Her hands were behind his shoulders, pressing him to her. "Really," she said, so softly that he could hardly hear her, "really it's lovely, Bill. Only catch him quick."

"All right, children," Pam North said from the kitchen door. "If we're all tactful in that kitchen much longer Martha will never get dinner ready. And we had to explain it all to Mullins." She looked back at Mullins, who appeared following her. "Birds and bees," she said. "Love, Mr. Mullins." Mr. Mullins,

148

as one who hears a forbidden word in polite company, flushed. He said, "Aw!" Pam looked at him, turning.

"I think he's *sweet,*" she said. "And so big, too!"

Jerry appeared with a tray of shaker, glasses and little dishes.

"Let him up, darling," Jerry said. "He's had enough!" He grinned at Mullins, who grinned back.

"Hell," Mullins said, "I can take it, fella."

Jerry put the tray down on a coffee table and began to pour. He twisted lemon peel over glasses and passed them around. Pam sipped and said, "Um-m-m!" She said you could tell it was really Noilly Prat, and wasn't it a pity that they invaded Neuilly. Everybody looked at her and Jerry said, anxiously, "What, Pam?"

"N-e-u-i-l-l-y," Mrs. North spelled. "Where Neuilly Prat comes from. Came from. A little town in the south of France."

They all looked at her. Then, without speaking, Jerry North got up and went to the kitchen. He returned with a bottle and pointed out the label. Pam looked at it and said, in a very disappointed voice, "Oh." Jerry sat down and resumed his cocktail.

"But Jerry," Pam said, "you told me this was *real* Neuilly Prat. Imported. And it's just pretending."

"Listen, Pam," Jerry said. "It's Noilly. It's always been Noilly. Since the world began."

"Why Jerry," Pam said. "How can you? Just to make us feel better!" She tasted her drink. "It's a very *good* imitation," she said. "Only not from Neuilly. You can tell that."

"Darling," Jerry said. "It was always Noilly. Not Neuilly. What do you think 'Prat' means."

"Well," Pam said, "after all, Jerry."

"Look, children," Dorian said. "Why not just skip it? And Bill will tell us about Evans, and who killed Dr. Bolton. And then some time, when there's a lot of time, we'll go into Noilly Prat. Thoroughly. We'll put Sergeant Mullins on its trail."

"Not me," Mullins said. "I hold with rye." He held with rye during a long swallow. "Mount Vernon, this is," he said. "Named after a guy."

"All *right,*" Weigand said. "Do you people want to know about Evans?"

Three cases earlier, Weigand had abandoned as untenable the correct position that a police officer should not talk about cases to civilians. He had succumbed, as nearly as he could remember, to the Norths' tacit assumption that they were, when murder arose, associate detectives; and when Dorian

150

appeared, for Weigand so brightly, she had been absorbed into the body of unofficial advisers. So Weigand told them about Evans. Without much pressing, while the cocktail shaker emptied, while broad Martha set the table and beamed at Mullins, of whom she was particularly fond, he told them also about the inquiry to that moment.

His report continued to the table. They listened to it over crabmeat cocktails and through clear soup and into roast ducks. Then Mrs. North held a fork of duck suspended and said it would be better if there weren't so many.

"I think it's very good as it is," Mr. North said, tasting it. "So many what, Pam?"

"People," Pam said. "The case, not the duck, silly. I think Martha's very good with duck, myself."

It would, Weigand agreed, be better if there were fewer people. Murder cases would always be better if there were fewer people.

"If," Dorian said, "we have to have them at all, I'd settle for two people. One to do and one to be done to. Then Bill could just arrest the survivor and there we'd be." She paused. "He could take the rest of the time off," she added.

"Speaking of times," said Jerry North, "what do they show? Can't you figure something out from that?"

That, Weigand told him, was what Mullins ought to be doing now.

"Instead of eating more duck," he added, as Mullins, after a hopeful look at Mr. North, passed his plate. Mullins said, "Listen, Loot!" Weigand added that, as a matter of fact, the times, so far as he had checked them, gave pretty much everybody an opportunity.

"Unless, of course," he said, "we take it as certain that Bolton was killed when Hubbard saw the cigarette go out." He looked at the others. Mrs. North tapped her head.

"Hubbard is the young actor who plays the brother," Weigand reminded them. "The brother of the girl Alberta James plays. Alberta James is the girl with the long reddish hair — very pretty. Hubbard says he saw a cigarette fall when —"

"All right," Pam North said. "I remember now." She thought a moment. "Of course," she said, "maybe he did it himself and then just said he saw a cigarette fall then at —" she wriggled insistent fingers at Mullins who, sighing, laid down his fork and took up his notes. "About 1:18," Mullins said, after consulting them. Pam resumed:

152

"One-eighteen," she said. "Because then he was on the stage himself along with — along with who . . . ?"

Mullins sighed more deeply and put down his fork again. It now had a piece of duck on it. He consulted his notes.

"Ellen Grady," he said. "This Driscoll guy — Percy. Paul Oliver. No, take that back. He'd just gone off. Grady, Driscoll, Hubbard. Three."

He put the notes down quickly, seized his fork and conveyed the duck to his mouth.

"Got it that time," he said, pleased. Pam said she was sorry.

"But," she said, "we've got to help Bill solve it, because he's got other things to do." She paused again in thought.

"If it wasn't Hubbard," she said, "and he was right about the cigarette, it couldn't have been Ellen Grady or Mr. Driscoll. Because they were on stage when it happened. But if it *was* Hubbard then the cigarette doesn't mean anything and it could have been either of the others."

She paused to look bewildered and the others joined her, except for Mullins who ate rapidly.

"I don't know," Pam said, frankly, "that that gets us anywhere, precisely. It sounds a little confused to me."

153

"Yes," said Mr. North, gently. "It does sound a little confused, somehow." He looked at Pam and nodded encouragingly. "Although," he added, "how you ever came to notice it, darling, is —"

"Jerry!" Pam said, decidedly. "Leave me out of it. We've got enough without me. How about Tilford? How about the producer? How about Mr. Kirk?" She paused. "How about everybody?" she said. "We ought to be able to work something out. Only now we'll let Mr. Mullins eat."

"Thanks, Mrs. North," Mullins said. He ate. The others ate. Then Mrs. North broke in again.

"Motives?" she said.

Weigand shrugged. He said it was early days yet. However —

"Kirk may have been jealous of Bolton, because of Alberta James," he said. "Assuming I'm right in thinking he's fallen for her."

"You are," Mrs. North said, with assurance.

"Also," Weigand added, "he's not telling something he knows — maybe a lot he knows. That's to be gone into."

"Ahlberg," he went on, "possibly because of some financial hookup, which hinges on the fact that Bolton was threatening to pull out. Penfield Smith — that's the author,

154

Pam — because of the dirty trick Bolton did him." Weigand paused. "I hope it isn't," he said, "because I'm afraid I'd sympathize. Miss Grady — no motive that I see."

"Well," Mrs. North said, "maybe Bolton was going to put her out of the show and give her part to Alberta, if Bolton was chasing Alberta. Or maybe Bolton had scorned Miss Grady. Or maybe — maybe it's something we haven't found out yet."

That of course, applied to any of the others for whom no motive was evident. Like Tilford. Like Hubbard. Like Mary Fowler, the costume designer. Even like Christopher, the scenery man.

Mrs. North shook her head over Christopher and said she wouldn't pick him.

"Too —" she said, and let it hang. Nobody required enlightenment.

"How about Driscoll?" Dorian said. "Any reason for him?"

Weigand shrugged, and said none they had come upon. Nor had they found any for Paul Oliver and Ruthmary Jones, colored, the other members of the cast.

"It doesn't seem to me," Pam North said, accusingly, "as if you'd got very far. Probably you should have urged us to stay and help."

"Listen, Pam," Jerry said, but Weigand

155

grinned at him, and then he found that Pam, also, was smiling her pleased recognition of a rise to bait. Jerry said, "Oh, all right," and why didn't they have coffee in the drawing room. They withdrew to the end of the living room, which became the drawing room for purposes of coffee, and had coffee and then turned on Mullins.

"Times, please," Pam said. "Wait, I'll get us all some paper. Then we'll figure out who would have had time to."

It took a while, with a good many erasures, but they came up with a list. It was not altogether satisfactory. Pam said she was a little disappointed in it, at first glance.

"For one thing," she said, "anybody could have killed him if he got back before the rehearsal started, as apparently he did. And, of course, if they got back, too. I mean if he got back, too. Or she. Whoever murdered. So up to twelve minutes after one, anybody who was in the theatre could have killed Bolton." She shook her head over the fact. "It isn't as neat as I'd hoped," she said.

With the exception of the time before the rehearsal began, when no one was accounted for, the list agreed upon went like this:

Opportunity:

Ellen Grady — From 1:48 to 1:51, when

156

she was off the stage.

(Pam: "Not much time." Weigand: "Perhaps just enough.")

Percy Driscoll — From 1:28 to 1:51; 1:55 to discovery of the body at 1:58.

Paul Oliver — any time after 1:15, when he left the stage.

(Mullins: "Looks like he's got an easy job, Loot." Weigand: "Maybe he works harder in the other acts.")

Alberta James from 1:12 to 1:20; 1:22 to 1:42, although conferring with Mary Fowler for part of this time; 1:52 to 1:58.

John Hubbard — 1:12 to 1:17; 1:32 to 1:42; 1:52 to 1:58.

Tilford — 1:12 to 1:21; on stage from 1:21 to discovery of the body.

Ruthmary Jones — any time except for the minute between 1:40 and 1:41.

Mary Fowler — out of theatre until 1:22; 1:24 to about 1:45, conferring with Alberta James; 1:45 to 1:58 if she could slip unnoticed from her seat in the orchestra.

Penfield Smith — prior to 1:25 (about) and thereafter if he left his seat unnoticed.

Christopher — out of theatre until 1:25 (about); any time t.i.h.l.h.s.u. (Pam: "I'm not going to write it out every time, for anybody.")

Ahlberg — out of theatre until 1:21

(about): any time thereafter if unobserved.

Kirk — almost any time, except during first few minutes of the run-through. (Mullins: "Although every time I looked for him, I saw him. Of course that don't mean I could of earlier." Weigand [automatically]: "Could *have,* Mullins.")

"And, of course, Evans could've any time," Mrs. North pointed out. "Except when he was concussed, and we don't know when that started. Maybe he just bumped his head against a wall to make an alibi." She paused. "Only," she said, "I don't really think that."

Weigand took the tabulation from Mrs. North and looked at it thoughtfully.

"It doesn't," he admitted, "tell us much. Not even as much as I'd hoped." He drained his coffee cup and shook his head. "We'd better get back on it, Mullins," he said. "Back to digging, Sergeant."

Mullins sighed and rose.

"Wait," Pam said, "is it still at the theatre?"

Weigand nodded.

"Then," Pam said, "I don't see why we don't all go. When there is so much room."

Mr. North was doubtful for a moment. But in the end they all went.

IX
TUESDAY

Weigand explained carefully that the privacy of the Norths' home was one thing and a formal police investigation something else; he explained that, although he couldn't keep the Norths and Dorian out of the theatre, he would prefer to talk to his own men in reasonable and official privacy. So the Norths and Dorian could go away and play or, if they would keep out of trouble, go away and detect. He was no longer Bill Weigand; he was now Detective Lieutenant William Weigand.

"And," he said, still very grave and official, "I can't have Pam confusing my men. Except Mullins." He paused and looked at Mullins. "And it's changing him," Weigand said, with the mockery of gloom. "He's softening."

Pam said that she thought Mr. Mullins was getting sweeter. "If anything," she added. Mullins said, "Listen, Mrs. North,"

159

and everybody smiled at him with affection. Then the Norths and Dorian wandered off into the darkened auditorium and down toward the stage, on the edge of which Humphrey Kirk stood and pulled at his forelock and said: "No! *No!*" Mr. Kirk advanced with a long stride and took Alberta James' shoulders and moved her to the left. "There," he said. "Now say it and turn!"

"It isn't that we do want you to be —" Alberta said obediently, in the voice of Sally Bingham. She turned downstage. "Is that what you mean, Humpty?" she said.

"Beautiful, darling," Humpty said. "And now you cross to the door and then you say: *'But Joyce, and so on and so on and so on.'* "

Alberta crossed to the door.

"But Joyce," she said, *"and so on and so on."*

"All right," Humphrey Kirk said, "now we'll take it over from where she says: *'You can't call it wheelchair snatching.'* "

"Isn't it wonderful?" Mrs. North said to Jerry in a whisper. "You'd never think there'd been one."

Mr. North agreed that you wouldn't.

Weigand and Mullins sat in the theatre office off the mezzanine and absorbed routine.

160

Edward Evans was still unconscious at the hospital. There was no fracture and the concussion was not severe. But it probably would be hours before he could be questioned. Precinct men were dutifully, but without much hope, canvassing hardware stores, and cut-rate "bargain" stores and five-and-ten-cent stores in the hope that somebody might remember somebody who had bought an ordinary ice-pick that day or the day before or at any time within the last few days.

"For 'ice-pick' read 'needle,' " Weigand commented. "But it's the way we earn our money. We are very thorough, Sergeant."

Mullins said, "Yeh."

"It 'ud be nice if somebody went in and said, 'I want an ice-pick to kill a heel named Bolton,' only nobody would of," he said. "People ain't considerate."

They weren't, Weigand agreed. And so the precinct men were probably wasting time — probably, but not certainly. "Always remember the Fogerty trunk, Mullins," he said. "It should be an example."

Mullins remembered the Fogerty trunk which had, when it showed up on the platform of a receiving station of the Railway Express Agency, contained Mr. Fogerty. Mr. Fogerty was newly dead; discovery came because Mr. Fogerty had seeped. Somebody vaguely remembered that a taxi had driven up an hour or so before and that two men, one of them the driver, had lifted the trunk to the platform. Then, presumably, the taxi had driven away. It was a puzzling case, because Mr. Fogerty, while all of a piece, was entirely naked. And the police broke the case within a little more than an hour, because Mr. Fogerty's room-mate, when he purchased a trunk from a luggage dealer on Sixth Avenue, had neglected to notice a half-erased chalk mark on the bottom.

That chalk mark, described to half a dozen detectives and by them to fifty-odd luggage dealers, had led to Mr. Fogerty's roommate, who was about to leave for the West and had been surprised and disappointed. The case, Mullins agreed, showed what routine would do.

"Only," he said, "was there a chalk mark on the ice-pick?"

Weigand admitted that there was not, and that that was the rub. However — routine was good practice; it turned up that hundredth chance. They continued it.

Ahlberg had been, as he said, at the Astor, where many had seen him. He was not with Bolton. It was impossible to trace the visit of Alberta James and Dr. Bolton to the

Automat. But Kirk had had, as he said, a sandwich at a nearby counter. And Mary Fowler had lunched at the Tavern in Forty-eighth Street.

"And," said Detective Stein, reporting on such matters, "she did try to get in in front; tapped on the door, like she said. A man from Traffic saw her. He's outside, with his horse."

He came inside, without his horse — Mounted Patrolman Callahan of Traffic A. Early in the afternoon he had broken up a traffic jam in West Forty-fifth Street and admonished the driver of the impeding truck. He had been sitting on his horse, looking around, when he saw a woman trying to get into the West Forty-fifth Street Theatre, which he knew was closed. He described her, and with her Mary Fowler.

It was none of his business, of course, but after watching her for a moment he called across and told her the theatre was closed, adding that the stage entrance might be open. She had knocked once or twice again and turned away, shaking her head and frowning. But she hadn't seemed very mad, Patrolman Callahan reported.

"Sort of peeved and smiling at the same time," he said. "And when she came up to me, she patted Henry's nose and sort of

163

smiled. She said, 'He's in there, but he pretends he can't hear me.' She rubbed Henry's nose and said, half under her breath. 'The old fool!' Then she went down the passageway leading to the stage entrance."

Yes, Patrolman Callahan knew about what time it was; he made a point of knowing about what time everything was. "I gotta sense of time, Lieutenant," he said. Weigand said that was fine. And what time, about, was it that the woman had tried to get into the theatre?

"I'd make it about 1:20, a minute or so either way," Patrolman Callahan reported. "It couldn't have been much earlier, because it was 1:15 when I rode down from Broadway and it took me a few minutes to break up the jam. Some guy thought it would be bright to double park."

Weigand said "right" and waved the patrolman on his way. But when Callahan reached the door there was another question for him.

"By the way," he said, "could you see into the lobby? Did you see anybody?"

Callahan shook his head. Not from where he was sitting, he couldn't. But he supposed the woman had seen old man Evans in there puttering around, and that it was Evans who

164

had refused to let her in.

"He's a funny old guy," Callahan said. "He'd think it was fun to let her knock. By the way, I hear he got hurt?"

Weigand told him, briefly, about Evans. Callahan nodded.

"Somebody pushed him, all right," Callahan said, with conviction. "He's got a lot of people around here sore on him. I know half a dozen kids who'd be glad to give him a shove, only they'd rather do it off the Empire State." Callahan paused. "Not that he ain't all right when you get to know him," he said. "He just don't like kids."

"Right," Weigand said. "Thanks, Callahan."

Weigand and Mullins continued with the routine. They looked for discrepancies in stories, for people seen at wrong times.

And there was a point at which Weigand's drumming fingers were quiet for a moment on the desk, and then picked up their beat at a slightly faster tempo. Weigand stared at the wall for a moment and then said:

"Well, that's interesting."

Mullins involuntarily looked at the wall and then, hurriedly, back at Weigand, who hadn't noticed. Mullins waited, hoping for clarification, but Weigand merely stared a moment longer at the wall.

"Something, Loot?" Mullins said. Weigand abandoned the wall and looked at Mullins instead. After a moment he apparently saw Mullins and after a moment longer he nodded slowly.

"Something that doesn't match," he said. "You heard it, Sergeant. Only —" He stopped and stared at Mullins again.

"You know, Mullins," he said. "Things aren't neat. Why didn't Evans have a watch to break and stop when he fell downstairs? Everybody who is going to fall downstairs and knock himself out ought to have a watch. For the police force to go by."

Mullins thought this over and grinned at Weigand.

"Maybe he had to hock it, Loot," Mullins said. "You can't be too hard on a guy." Then Mullins, remembering with a pang that there was thought to be engaged in, sobered. "Is there something screwy in the stories, Loot?" he asked, hopefully. "Something that don't fit?"

Mullins waited hopefully. But after a moment the Lieutenant shook his head, as Mullins had been afraid he would.

"We've got to keep you in training, Sergeant," Weigand told him. "Think it over, Mullins."

Mullins obediently, but without much

hope, wrinkled his forehead and made a start.

Weigand watched him a moment, smiling slightly. Then he interrupted.

"And," he said, "here's something else for you, Sergeant.

Weigand opened an envelope and spilled its contents on the desk. Its contents was burned paper matches. Mullins stared at them and then at Weigand.

"Stein," Weigand said. "I've had him collecting them. Borrowing here, borrowing there. Giving himself nicotine poisoning, probably. And remembering where each match came from, and not throwing the match away after he used it." Weigand spread the matches out on the desk top.

"Looking," he said, "for this baby."

The baby was wider than the other matches; wide enough to carry printing down its face. "The Pipe and Bottle," the printing said. Looking at it, Mullins began to nod.

"The bottle-shaped one," he said. "Like you found on the floor behind the stiff."

"Right," Weigand said. "Stein got it on his fourth cigarette. The one he lighted with a match he borrowed from Mr. Humphrey Kirk."

"Well," Mullins said. "Think of that."

■ ■ ■ ■

They finished the second scene of the first act for the third time and Humpty Kirk uncoiled himself from a seat near the center of the fourth row.

"All right," Kirk said. "Where the hell is she? Who the hell does she think she is? Helen Hayes? Katharine Cornell? Somebody we should stand around all night waiting for?"

Nobody seemed to have an answer to this series of questions. Then Jimmy Sand appeared, carrying the blue-bound script. It adhered to him, Pam North decided, watching.

"O.K., Humpty," Sand said. "I guess she's on her way. Nobody answers."

"On her way!" Kirk repeated. He spoke bitterly. "On her way where? She was 'on her way' when you called half an hour ago. She's been on her way all night. Who the hell does she think she is?"

Kirk stopped and glared at everybody.

"All right," he said. "All *right*. Take it from Martin's entrance — no, take it from the start of the scene. We'll twiddle our thumbs for her. Take it from the start."

"Oh," Pam said to herself. "Not *again*!"

I know it word for word, Pam thought. I could play all the parts. I could say it in my sleep. I've never been so bored.

It was strange, Pam thought, to be bored in the middle of a murder *and* in the middle of a play. It wasn't being the way she thought it would be. I thought temperament, Pam thought, and everybody tense and excited, because it's a rehearsal *and* a murder both together. She looked at Jerry, who was staring at the stage without expression and obviously thinking about several other things. Business, Pam thought, and he just sits there. I wonder where Bill is? She looked around for Dorian and remembered that, ten or fifteen minutes before, Dorian had stood up and wandered off, dreamily, and Pam hadn't asked where because she thought she knew. But Dorian hadn't come back.

"And I'll bet," Pam said to herself, "she's found Bill and is right in the middle of things, and here I am and nothing happening!"

She started to stand up and Jerry looked at her abstractedly.

"Drink of water," Pam said. "I'll be right back."

Perhaps, she thought, Jerry will come with me, and we'll find out what's happening.

169

But Jerry merely nodded and went back to thinking, with the look of a man who is thinking about business. Pam sighed and looked at the stage. They were going through the second scene of the first act for the fourth time, and forgetting lines and Jimmy Sand was prompting in a tired voice. Humpty Kirk seemed to have subsided somewhere.

"Probably in a coma," Pam said to herself. "I should think he would."

Pam walked up the aisle, thinking she would find something going on, but there was nothing. There was a drone from the stage and empty seats and no sign of anybody chasing murderers. Pam crossed back of partitions between the orchestra seats and the lobby doors and started down the aisle at the extreme right with the desultory movements of a person who may decide to sit down at any moment. But before she was halfway down her steps quickened. Pam North had an idea.

"I'll see what it looks like back there," she said. "And where they really go when they go out the doors." She said it to herself, but with almost audible determination. If they didn't want her to go back-stage, they could always say so, if they didn't see her, and nobody had said she mustn't. She passed back of the curtains which cut off the stage boxes and stumbled on a short flight of steps. She said "ouch" under her breath and "this must be it" under her mind. There was a door at the top of the short flight of steps and it opened toward her. Pam North stepped through, cautiously.

Caution was required. At her right was something infinitely complicated, and having to do with electricity. There were switches and buttons and, just as Pam feared, wires. She shrank to the other side, brushing against tall wooden frames over which canvas was stretched tightly. On the back of one of the frames was stenciled: "Teddy Must Run." Pam could just make it out in light, which, starting bravely from unshaded bulbs, lost itself amid looming obstacles.

" 'Teddy Must Run,' " Pam repeated to herself. "Oh — I remember that. But it was years ago. This must be part of its scenery, just left around."

Something brushed against her face and she jumped. In a moment she would have screamed, but in a moment she discovered that she had brushed the dangling end of a piece of rope. She looked up, and the rope disappeared in darkness. She could look a long way up, and there was a steel framework, with ropes dangling from it.

"The grid," Pam said to herself, proud to have remembered. She edged forward and the space widened. It was bounded now, on her right, by a rough brick wall and, on her left, by a canvas structure which she recognized, almost at once, as the other side of Martin Bingham's apartment in the East Sixties. It was stenciled, too — "Two in the Bush." Through it she could hear voices. A voice said: *"— to keep this one small place free from —"*

"All the noisy bitterness of the world." Pam finished to herself. It was still the second scene of the first act. Pam hoped it wasn't really as dull as it had now begun, to her, to sound.

She went on, and then, beyond another pile of canvas frames, stacked against the brick wall, a man was sitting in a kitchen chair, leaning back against the bricks. He was smoking a cigarette and looking at Mrs. North without interest. Pam smiled at him and he nodded absently. Then Pam remembered who he was, or almost who he was. He was one of the stage hands, or perhaps the electrician, who had sat in the semicircle when Bill was identifying people. He didn't seem to mind her being back-stage and she went on until the brick wall was in front of her, as well as at the right. She turned to her left, and realized that now she was directly behind the set — yes, here were the other sides of the two doors, which led out of Mr. Bingham's apartment. On this side of the doors there was a little platform, built up and reached by stairs — Pam wondered a moment, and then remembered that the doors, from the other, visible, side of the wall opened off a platform of similar height. Of course — the actors couldn't be caught climbing as they came in the doors. They had to have something on the other side to start from. It was interesting, Pam decided, to find out about these things. And now along the back there should be windows — the other side of windows. She came to the windows curtained and, after the first two, angling away, so as to cut off a corner of the room. It was funny, Pam was thinking, how small the set really was, seen thus unprotected in its essential wood and canvas, and how much more of the stage they could have used if they had wanted to — all this wasted space between the walls of the set and the real, brick wall of the theatre — and it was funny — Then Pam interrupted herself, because she heard voices. She had wondered where everybody was, and where all the actors went when they went off the stage, and now here were at least two of them, just around the corner of the set — around the blunted corner made by the windows. Pam hesitated, wondering if they would mind her being there, and then started to go on to meet them, because she was really not doing any harm. Then she stopped, because Humphrey Kirk, who ought to have been out front, was back here instead, and talking earnestly.

"They haven't yet, but they will," Humphrey Kirk said. "You can trust them for that, Berta. It would be too easy if they didn't. Oh, darling — *why!*"

It didn't sound as Humphrey Kirk usually sounded. The "darling" was not its usual casual substitute for "hey, you!" And Kirk's voice was different; it had an odd, urgent note; it was — Then Pam identified the note, or thought she did, because she had heard something like it in another voice, often. It was the voice of a man who was worried through a deep fondness; who was brought up against, and baffled by, some alarming vagary in one deeply loved. Only this was not a little vagary — not one of those half-assumed, although still essentially real, variations from the understandable which both the man and the woman, without ostensible admission of the fact, en-

174

joyed. This was about something which was, to Kirk, extremely real. Nor was there any doubt how he felt about Alberta James.

Now, she realized, Pam ought to cough, or fall noisily over something, or, more simply, walk on around the corner and interrupt. If people were to lurk, the people should be paid policemen and — But Pam did not go on around the corner, because now Alberta was speaking.

"But Humpty," she said. "I had to. Just that once. You know I did. I couldn't just let it drop — not with everything unsettled. And —"

"You didn't want to let it drop. You didn't plan to, not really." There was bitterness, and unhappiness, in Kirk's voice now. There was a little pause and then the girl spoke slowly.

"I can't make you believe me, Humpty," she said. "That's the way it was — there was never anything, really, and what there was was over. Oh yes — that's clearer now than it was a while ago. Even than it was yesterday. I — he confused me, Humpty. For a while I didn't — It was all — complicated. But you know it was complicated. I couldn't just — *stop.* It was all — tangled up."

"That's the trouble." Kirk's voice was

175

quick, this time, as the voice of a man who sees his point and drives toward it. "*You* were tangled up. That's why the rest of it was tangled — *you* weren't clear, sure in your own mind." He paused. "Or in your own feelings," he added. "God knows I've tried not to think that."

"You didn't have to, Humpty." Alberta's voice was low. "Oh, Humpty — dear — you didn't have to. Not ever. . . . What do you think I am?"

"You know what I think you are, darling," Humpty said. "Oh — forget what I said about your feelings. It wasn't that you felt confused. You *thought* confused. You wouldn't take the simple way. You had to go on with it — 'working things out,' as you said." He stopped, suddenly and then went on. "Well," he said, and now his words had an inflection of almost hopeless finality. "We've worked it out, all right. Among us."

The girl didn't say anything for a moment. Then she said, "Oh, Humpty!" Her voice seemed to be coming through tears.

This is awful, Pam thought to herself. I oughtn't to be doing this. There were other sounds — a slight movement, a low murmur. Pam could almost see them, holding each other desperately against danger. I hate myself for this, Pam thought. I'll always hate

176

myself for this. And I'll never tell; if they are both murderers, I'll never tell.

Humphrey Kirk's voice was quieter when he spoke again. He said he was a fool.

"But I always knew, really," he said. "I was — well, jealous. Stupidly jealous. But I always knew. You know that?"

The answer was very low, its burden more evident in tone than in words. She had known.

"Now," Kirk said, in still another voice. He was, Pam thought, pushing back that unstable forelock of his. "Now — we've got to get things clear. You say you just dropped it."

"I must have," she said. "That's the only way. And somebody — must have found it. Or perhaps he found it after I went out. That would explain it."

Damn, Pam thought. Found what? It was annoying to have the guilt of eavesdropping, and such illusive gain. Found what?

"But Humpty," the girl said. "We can't just *explain* it — think up something it could have been. We have to *know*! We're not safe unless we *know*! We're tangled up in it."

Humphrey Kirk sighed.

"If you'd only dropped it long ago, darling," he said. "You could have gone to some other man. There are plenty of other men just as good as Bolton — as Bolton was. Or if, instead of that, you had quit seeing him the other way. As your aunt said."

"Her aunt?" thought Pam North, who was no longer even pretending to herself not to listen avidly. "What's her aunt got to do with this? And what *is* it?"

Pam listened and tried to think it out at the same time. Alberta had lost something and somebody had found it. She had made Humphrey Kirk jealous, but probably needlessly jealous with, presumably, Dr. Bolton, and she "could have gone to another man," which was an odd thing for Humphrey Kirk to tell her. Unless by "man" he meant "doctor," Pam nodded to herself. Alberta could have gone to another doctor; therefore, she was seeing Bolton professionally. But Kirk would not have been jealous if she had been seeing Bolton *only* professionally. And Alberta's aunt, like Kirk himself, had been opposed to her dual relationship with Bolton.

"There wasn't any 'other way,' " the girl said, "not for a long time."

Again there was a moment during which neither spoke. When Kirk did speak, then, there was a note in his voice which made Pam feel that something had been settled

178

between them.

"There's always F. Lawrence," Kirk said. His tone was speculative. Alberta said, "Why?" and Kirk made dim, hesitant noises. Finally he said it wasn't clear.

"Except for the obvious hookup," he said. "And I'll admit that's remote. But it would give the police a trail — something else to bay on. And that would give us time."

"What good's time?" Alberta asked. There was, it seemed to Pam, an odd note in her voice. Apparently the note seemed odd, also, to Humphrey Kirk. He asked Alberta, in a voice suddenly sharpened, what she meant. Her answer was silence, and Pam wished she could see them; the girl was, she thought, looking at Humpty in a certain way. But what way is it? Pam thought. What is she saying with her eyes and the line of her mouth? Whatever she was saying, it was clear to Kirk.

"Darling!" Kirk said. There was urgency and a kind of command in his voice. "Don't think that! You *mustn't* think that!"

Damn! Pam thought to herself. What mustn't she think? Alberta mustn't think — Pam tried to fill out the sentence. "You mustn't think — *I did it.*" Could that be it? Or — *"I think you did it!"* Or — but it slipped through Pam's mind. Were they talking,

179

really, about somebody else entirely; somebody else of whose innocence Alberta had doubt; somebody close to her who, to Alberta dreadfully, might have killed Carney Bolton?

It was, Pam decided, entirely unsatisfactory. She added up. Humpty Kirk and the girl with reddish brown hair were in love, and it was not an easy and comfortable love; it was love shot with jealousy and doubt. She had lost something and somebody had found it and "it" was connected with the murder of Bolton. Kirk wanted time for something and Alberta felt that time was of no use to them. Alberta had been a patient of Bolton; Alberta had an aunt who had disapproved of Bolton. Alberta was thinking something she mustn't think and —

"Well," a low, musical voice said behind Pam North. "Are you waiting for something — Mrs. North?"

Mrs. North jumped and said, "Oh!" She looked, she was convinced, as guilty as she felt — as guilty as she was. Mary Fowler looked at her quietly and seemed a little amused. But the amusement was not friendly.

"Oh," Mrs. North said again. "I was just exploring."

I wish, she thought, that that sounded

more convincing. If she's been there for any time at all she knows I'm not exploring; I'm just standing still. And now I'll have to walk on with her and pretend to be looking at things, and we'll simply fall over those two and everybody will know I was listening. Oh, damn!

Mary Fowler's words, when she spoke, then, seemed to take Pam North's statement as full and satisfying information. Miss Fowler said, "Of course." But Pam would have preferred, she decided, another tone.

"It must be interesting to you," Miss Fowler said. "Back-stage and everything. It always interests people who aren't professionals. It's — I'll never forget how exciting it was for me, a long time ago, when I was only a girl and stage-struck."

She smiled at Mrs. North.

"Only," she said, "one almost needs a guide the first time, don't you think? If you had asked me — or anyone — we'd have been glad —"

It was hard to tell what Mary Fowler was thinking; whether the note in her voice was irony. Or more than irony. But she must, Pam decided, pretend that she was believed.

"I know," Pam said. "It was foolish of me. Only everybody was busy."

She spoke without lowering her voice, so

181

that nobody who might now, in turn, be overhearing would think she had anything to hide. She felt Mary Fowler's unexpectedly strong fingers on her arm.

"We'll go on around, my dear," Miss Fowler said. "Be careful you don't stumble over something."

Pam tried not to look at Miss Fowler suspiciously. Stumble over something? Was that irony?

They went on around the corner blunted by the windows and — *and there was nobody there!* Or, more exactly, there were several people there, Alberta James among them. And Humphrey Kirk was not among them. There was a short bench just under the farthest window and it was about right as to distance and direction, Pam thought, to have been the refuge of the girl and Humpty Kirk when they were talking. But now nobody was in it. Alberta was standing farther on, with John Hubbard and another man whom Mrs. North had not seen before, and they were talking.

"Oh," Miss Fowler said from beside Mrs. North. "I thought Humpty was here. Have any of you seen him?"

"He was here," Alberta James said. "Five minutes or so ago. I don't know where he is now."

She spoke casually, as if it didn't matter at all to her where Humpty Kirk had got to. She didn't look guilty of anything, Pam North decided. But, of course, she was an actress. And Mary Fowler didn't look as if she had any secret knowledge which concerned Alberta and Humpty and, unfavorably, Pamela North. But Miss Fowler had, Pam remembered, once been an actress herself. Pam looked at Miss Fowler's rather heavy face, marred by the startling eyes, and wondered about that. She must, Pam thought, have played very special parts.

Pam decided to be somewhere else. She smiled vaguely and said something about the deep anxiety which might, by now, be presumed to be consuming Mr. North; she asked directions and was given them. Hubbard gallantly guided her through apertures to another door and told her to watch the stairs. Through the door and down the stairs she was back in the auditorium.

They were still on the same scene. Just as Mrs. North found a seat, Alberta James came on stage and spoke the lines of Sally Bingham. Humphrey Kirk was coiled in a seat in the third row with the air of one who has never left it. Jerry North was slumped in the same seat he had previously occupied and still, Pam decided, looking at him across half the auditorium and in a very bad light, thinking of business. Then Weigand and Mullins came down the right-center aisle from somewhere in the darkness to the rear and Weigand spoke.

"What's this, Kirk, about Miss Grady being missing?" he said. "Have you heard anything from her?"

Weigand's voice was sharp and demanding, Mrs. North noticed. And there was, she thought, a note of anxiety in it. He was, she decided, worried about Ellen Grady's absence.

And that's fine, Mrs. North told herself. Now he wouldn't want to hear about Alberta and Kirk, even if I were going to tell. Which I wasn't. But now I don't have to feel guilty about not telling.

"Although," Pam added to herself, "I'm going to feel guilty whatever I do."

X
TUESDAY

Kirk stood up and walked back to meet Weigand. He shook his head as he walked back.

"Not a word, Lieutenant," he said. "La Grady seems to think she doesn't have to come to evening rehearsals. D'you want her?"

"Damn it all," Weigand said. "I want everybody. I can't have people wandering off and not coming back." He walked on down, Kirk falling in a step behind him, and addressed the cast.

"I want all of you to understand that," he said. "Just because we let you go on here as if nothing had happened doesn't mean that nothing has — or that any of you can wander off without talking to us first. Do you all understand that?"

He was, Pam thought, being very stern for Bill Weigand. He watched several in the cast nod; heard F. Lawrence Tilford say, with due attention to each syllable: "I am sure we all understand perfectly, Lieutenant."

"After all," John Hubbard added suddenly, "*we're* all here, Lieutenant. Ellen's the only one who wandered off."

"Right," Weigand said. "But I want you to understand, all of you. We want you here for questions, when we get ready to ask them. And if you go, we want to know where, so we can — look after you." He looked at them slowly. "I suppose," he said, "that one of you is a murderer. We'll look after that one, in time. The rest of you are, I suppose, innocent. But several of you haven't, I think, told everything you should tell. Some have had a chance and haven't come clean; some haven't had a chance. And remember this — any one of you may, perhaps without realizing it, know some fact which is dangerous to the murderer — *something the murderer would kill to keep us from knowing!*" He paused, rather dramatically. Pam looked at him in some astonishment and then looked quickly at Jerry. Jerry looked amused, and nodded his head as if in approval. Now why was Bill —

Oh, of course, Pam thought suddenly. Because they're all theatrical. He's — he's making it dramatic for them. Then she nodded, too, and caught Jerry's eye across the space which separated them and smiled with him.

"Is the situation perfectly clear?" Weigand went on, still to the cast and to the others of the company. "Nobody is to leave the theatre without permission. We are to know, as nearly as possible, where everybody is at a given moment and what everybody is doing." He paused, looking from one to another. This time there were no comments, only here and there a nod of acceptance. "And," Weigand said, "if I were you I would stay in groups of at least three. That's all."

He turned, and as he turned spoke Mullins' name. Mullins came down the aisle saying, "O.K., Loot." They met near Pam North who had dropped into a seat.

"I want you to find Miss Grady, Sergeant," Weigand said. "Find her and bring her here. They say she isn't at her apartment, but start there anyway. Perhaps her telephone is out of order; perhaps she's just decided not to answer it. If she's there, bring her here. If she isn't, find her."

"O.K., Loot," Mullins said. "You think maybe —"

"I think I don't want them wandering," Weigand said. "Also I want to talk to Miss Grady. Right?"

"O.K., Loot," Mullins repeated. He started back up the aisle, and Pam North spoke suddenly.

"Mr. Mullins," she said. "I want to go with you."

Mullins stopped and looked at her, and Weigand turned and looked at her. Both looks were inquiring.

"Because," Pam said, "there ought to be a woman along. In case — in case she isn't dressed or something."

It sounded very lame, Mrs. North realized. It sounded very lame to her, and it evidently sounded very lame to both Bill Weigand and Mullins. But it was the best the spurred moment provided, and she nodded at both of them earnestly.

"Of course there ought to be a woman," she said. "And anyway, Bill — I won't get in Mullins' way."

Bill Weigand smiled at her.

"Just for the ride, Pam?" he said. "It's all right with me. And doubtless very fine with Mullins. Only won't Jerry be jealous?"

"Bill!" Pam said. "You're ridiculous. Come on, Aloysius."

"Listen, Mrs. North —" Mullins said. But he said it to Mrs. North's back, which was preceding him up the aisle. It was a back which moved jauntily, because Pam was pleased with herself. If I had stayed, she thought, I would have forgotten and told

Bill about Alberta and Mr. Kirk, and I promised myself I wouldn't. And if I go now why — well, maybe something will come up so that it won't be worth telling. And then I won't have to worry.

"And anyway," Pam added to herself as she and Mullins, with the red lights blinking officially on the car's prow and the siren demanding clearance up ahead, "anyway, it's a nice ride." The siren screamed at a loitering truck; the police car lurched, caught itself and went around. Pam clutched the door handle. "Whee!" Pam said. "Ride 'em, Al!"

Mullins beamed at her with the near side of his face.

"Mostly the Loot won't —" he said. The siren drowned the rest of it.

Their course was across town, almost to the East River; then up for a dozen blocks. In ended when the car swerved into the curb in front of a small, sedate apartment house, from which the doorman hurried.

"You can't —" the doorman began, and saw the police shield on the car's nose. "What — ?" the doorman said.

Mullins told him. Miss Ellen Grady's apartment, and no need to telephone Miss Grady. Because apparently she wasn't in. The doorman looked puzzled.

"I'm almost sure she is," he said. "I'd have seen her go out. Is there something — ?"

"That's what we're here to find out," Mullins said. The doorman was looking wonderingly at Mrs. North's trim, non-authoritative figure. Mullins' manner became more official than ever and rolled over the doorman's implicit inquiry. At a repeated command the doorman, his expression slightly baffled, led them into the sedate lobby and took them up on the very modern, very subdued, elevator. He took them to the fourth floor and along a corridor and to a door marked "4-F." The doorman pushed a button and a refined buzz answered him from within. But nothing else answered. He pressed the button again. Mullins brushed him aside and knocked harshly. The sound of his fist on the door panel was noisy and intrusive in the corridor. It filled Pam North, waiting behind the men, with an odd feeling of discomfort and alarm. Mullins tried the knob. Nothing happened, except that the doorman made a small, disturbed sound.

"She isn't in, sir," he said. "She must have gone out without my noticing. If you would like to leave —"

"I'd like a passkey," Mullins said. The weight of his official assurance bore down

190

protest. The doorman looked unhappy, but reached for a ring of keys hooked to his belt.

"I don't know what —" he said. Mullins gestured impatiently. Pam felt sorry for the doorman, who could never finish a sentence, but not very sorry. She was feeling, obscurely, more afraid than sorry. Mullins took the keys and used the one the doorman had sifted from the rest. The door opened on a quiet apartment.

It was a small apartment, decorated by a decorator. "Furnished," Pam decided. "The very best furnished." The door opened onto a small living room, with a wooden mantel on one wall pretending to frame a fireplace. The pretense was only formal and not expected to deceive. Beyond, through a door, was another room. Pam followed Mullins into it. The doorman stood just inside the living room, trying to look as if he were still outside. Mullins stopped in the doorway to the next room and said, "Well!" Pam peered around him.

It was a bedroom, not so "furnished." The bed was wide and low and spread with yellow silk and there was just room, near it, for a deep chair, also in yellow silk. There was a glass dressing table, too, with intricately shaped bottles almost filling it, and in front of it powder had spilled on a raspberry carpet. By the bed was a soft, thick white rug.

And over all these things there was a scattering of other objects. One slim, extravagantly heeled shoe lay on its side on the white rug; its mate stood impertinently on the dressing-table bench. Stockings festooned the deep chair and in the middle of the floor there was a satin girdle, tiny and unexpectedly forlorn. A brassière hung dejectedly over the edge of the bed. And halfway to one of the doors in the right wall of the room, a trail of silk and lace lay on the floor. Pam looked at the negligee, estimated its presumptive cost quickly and shook her head mentally. A couple of hundred dollars, she thought, lay trailing thus casually on the carpet, which could hardly be that clean. Mullins, staring in, said he would be damned.

"Somebody's searched the joint," he said. "Jeez."

Pam's laugh was tiny and subdued.

"Mr. Mullins!" she said. "She's just dressed to go out. And left what she didn't want."

"Huh?" said Mullins. "Left the place like this?" His tone was disapproving, but Pam was not listening. There was, she thought, something wrong over that explanation.

192

There was — her eyes went over the room. The shoe, that was it! The shoe on the dressing-table bench. Because if Ellen Grady had been going out, she would have sat on the bench the very last thing and if the shoe had been there then she would have brushed it off. But if she had been changing shoes *after* she had finished making up, then she would almost certainly have sat on the bench to change them and couldn't have put the shoe there because *she* was there.

"Wait," Pam said, because now she knew what the room looked like. She started toward the doors in the right wall and then stopped suddenly. She turned to Mullins.

"You go," she said. "Because it looks as if — as if she's gone to take a bath. And hadn't come out again!"

Mullins was across the room before she finished and had one of the doors open. And then he stood in this doorway and Pam could tell from his back that he had found something. He said "Jeez" again, but this time the tone was different. And, wishing she had never come — wishing that now she could make herself turn and run from the apartment — Pam followed him.

Ellen Grady had been a very beautiful woman. Lying small and naked in her bath, with hair floating around her face, she was still very beautiful. Mullins, looking down at her, swore slowly and with a strange sadness, because no man looking down thus on Ellen Grady, dead and defenseless and still singularly beautiful, could have been other than saddened at the waste. And even Pam, who had no reason to feel as a man would have felt, had another feeling beside her horror — a feeling that the bodies of the dead should not be so beautiful; should not, above anything else, look, in their slender whiteness, so dreadfully alive.

There was no mark on the body and the face was just above the water.

"No blood," Mullins said. He tested the water with a finger and shook his head. "Just warm," he said. "Anyway, she couldn't have been scalded."

He turned, conscious of Pam North's presence.

"Jeez," he said. "We'd better — I guess we'd better get the Loot."

He looked back again at Ellen Grady's body, and said "Jeez" once more, and followed Pam North into the living room. Pam sat down very sudenly on the bed and watched and then put her head down to force back the circle of dark which seemed to be narrowing about her. She heard

194

Mullins talking into the telephone.

"Well," Detective Stein said, speaking into the wall telephone in the passage off the stage entrance of the West Forty-fifth Street Theatre, "he isn't here, Sergeant. He's at the hospital. Evans came out of it." Stein listened. "I'll get him on the phone. And I'll send the gang." He listened. "Jeez," he said. "In the bathtub, huh? What? Well, I'll be damned."

He hung up the receiver and turned to Detective King.

"Well," Stein said, "they found the Grady dame, all right. In her bathtub. Dead as a beefsteak. The Sarge thinks maybe she was drowned."

Lieutenant Weigand sat beside the hospital bed and listened to a small, wizened, angry man. Edward Evans had come out of it and, what was more, remembered a good deal about it. What he remembered made him very angry. At the moment his anger seemed rather more intense than a man could endure while remaining flat on his back. Weigand told him to take it easy.

"I gather," Weigand said, "that you don't think you fell. You think somebody pushed you. Right. And before?"

"What the hell?" Evans said. "Me fall on those steps? After I've gone up and down them a thousand times, maybe? You're a fool, officer!"

Weigand's voice was gentle.

"No," he said. "I think you were pushed. I just want to get it straight. Will you tell it once more, Mr. Evans?"

"Yah!" said Mr. Evans indignantly. "What's the matter? Can't you hear, or something?"

Weigand smiled at the angry little man and waited. After a moment, Evans almost smiled himself.

"I guess I'm sort of sore," he said. "Here it is again —"

He couldn't, he said, be sure of times. He had been around when the members of the company started to come back after lunch. He remembered Kirk coming back; he remembered that, a minute or so before, Dr. Bolton had come in through the stage door and looked around as if he expected to see somebody and then gone back into the orchestra section. A few others had come in; Evans hadn't noticed particularly. He had left the back-stage and gone through the auditorium to the lobby. Not, it seemed, for any particular reason.

"I've got to keep an eye on things," he

explained. "I'm responsible. Nobody'll keep an eye on things if I don't."

So he had gone to keep an eye on the lobby. He had picked up a cigarette butt or two from the sand-filled urns there and "had a look around." Weigand could see him looking around — irascible and inquiring and very responsible. Evans had stayed in the lobby "a few minutes." He thought he might have left it about 1:15. It might, however, be five minutes either way.

"Now," Weigand said, "did you see anybody while you were there?"

"See anybody?" Evans repeated. "Why would I see anybody?"

Weigand hadn't, he said, any idea. He merely wondered. Was there anybody in the lobby? Or at the doors leading to the street?

"No," Evans said. "I didn't see anybody."

"Suppose," Weigand said, "somebody had been trying to get into the lobby . . . from the street, I mean . . . and, finding the doors locked, had knocked. Would you have seen them? Or heard them?"

"Well," Evans said, "that depends. If I was down near the doors, sure. If they knocked loud enough for me to hear, I'd have heard. But nobody did."

"But," Weigand said, "it's possible that you may have been some distance from the

197

doors, with your back to them, and not have seen somebody who was trying to get in. Perhaps not even have heard them if they knocked? How is your hearing, by the way?"

That was, Weigand realized, a futile question. Evans bristled again.

"Nothing wrong with my hearing," he said. "Nothing wrong with my eyes. Nobody tried to get in while I was there."

Now he was certain, where before he had been doubtful. But the facts were not clarified. Evans' hearing might be less acute than he supposed; very probably, considering his indignation at the question, was less acute. With street noises to drown a tapping on the glass, he might have heard nothing when Mary Fowler tried to get in. Weigand was inclined to think that Evans had not seen her, whatever she thought. But she might merely have been wrong in thinking he saw her, and not wrong in saying he was there. The question stayed open.

"Right," Weigand said. "You stayed a few minutes in the lobby. Then you went downstairs to the lounge. Right?"

"Sure," Evans said. "Like I told you. I looked around there, and then went to the door leading down to the basement — only it ain't a basement, really. Not a real basement. Just a place under the orchestra and stage."

"Yes," Weigand said. "I've seen it. That's where we found you, remember. Now, tell me again what happened."

"Well," Evans said, "like I said, I opened the door. I hadn't switched on the lights, except there was a light in the men's lavatory and the doors were open, so it was sort of light. Enough to see your way around. I opened the door and started to step down and then I heard somebody. I started to turn around —"

He had just relinquished the doorknob and stood at the head of the stairs when he heard the sound; an indescribable sound of movement. He had started to turn and in a moment he would have seen who was behind him. But he never completed the turn. Something struck his shoulders heavily, hurling him off balance. He felt himself pitching foward and then —

"Well," Evans said, "next thing I was here, in this bed." He glared. "Somebody pushed me," he said. "Somebody tried to kill me so I wouldn't see them. But they didn't. I'm tougher than that."

The last was said with evident gratification, and some pride.

"Tougher than I look,' he added. "Where'd

you say you found me?"

Weigand told him again about the little closet. Evans looked puzzled.

"I don't get it," he said. "Why didn't they finish me off?"

"I don't know," Weigand said. "Maybe they — he or she, whichever it was — thought you *were* dead, and just hauled you off to the closet so we wouldn't find the body. An inexperienced person might make that mistake. Or maybe, being sure you hadn't seen enough to identify anybody, the person who pushed you didn't care whether you were dead or not. If you had had a moment more to turn around, so you had really seen — well, then it might have been different. As long as you hadn't seen, and weren't given a chance to, you were no more dangerous alive than dead."

Evans said he'd like to get his hands on the guy who did it. Weigand said they would try to do that for him.

"Meanwhile," he said, "you take it easy here. You're perfectly safe."

Weigand, remembering another man who had not been perfectly safe in a hospital, felt a slight qualm. But, after all, there were men on guard, this time. And it was, or seemed to as city-bred a man as Weigand, easier to protect people in New York than in

200

a little town like Brewster.

Not, Weigand told himself, that Evans was not in some danger. The person who pushed could not have been absolutely sure he was not recognized. Therefore, he must have thought that Evans was dead or, alternatively, must have been planning to go back later and see that he was dead. Weigand would pass the word around that Evans did not know his assailant, which might help. Or might, if murderers are, like detectives, always suspicious, fail to convince the person who had tried to end Mr. Evans.

Weigand wondered which of his suspects would be most likely to mistake an unconscious man for a dead man, and after wondering shrugged his shoulders. Almost any of them, he decided. Unless one or more had special experience of which he, at present, knew nothing.

"You'll be all right, now," he told Evans, standing up. "I'm leaving a man to see that nobody bothers you. Later, perhaps, we'll try to —"

He didn't finish. A nurse came in quickly. Weigand was wanted on the telephone, urgently, by a Detective Stein. He was to hurry.

Weigand said "Right," and hurried.

Bill Weigand stared down at Ellen Grady's body and felt, as Mullins had felt before him, that curious, impersonal sense of loss, being for a moment all men lamenting the destruction of loveliness. He said nothing and turned away and went back into the bedroom, in which men were working.

"All right," Lieutenant Weigand said to one of them. "Get your pictures. And where the hell do you suppose the M.E.'s man has got to?"

The question was rhetorical, and the police photographer acknowledged its existence by a routine shake of the head. He said, "Come on, Joe," and Joe went on, with flashlight bulbs. The bulbs began to flash in the bathroom. Weigand stood a moment watching the fingerprint men, who needed no advice from him and were covering everything diligently, and went out into the living room. Mullins was there, and a uniformed policeman stood at the door, and Pam North, looking very small and a little dazed, sat in a chair.

"Jeez, Loot," Mullins said.

"Right," Weigand told him. "A hell of a note."

"Bill!" Pam said. "It's dreadful. She was so — so lovely. And she would have been like that for a long time yet. And —"

"Right, Pam," Bill Weigand said. "Don't think about it. Try not to, anyway. We'll — hello, Doc. You're early, aren't you?"

Dr. Francis stared at him, haughtily. Then he looked at Mrs. North.

"Well," he said, doubtfully. "You again."

"Doctor!" Pam's voice was protesting. "Don't say it like that! You make it sound —"

Dr. Francis of the Medical Examiner's office said he was sorry.

"However —" he added, vaguely. He let it ride.

"And as for being early — there wasn't anybody ahead of you this time, Lieutenant." He stared at Weigand. "You certainly have 'em, don't you, Bill?"

Weigand nodded, not pleased.

"All right," Dr. Francis said, in resignation. "Where's this one? Somebody said in the bathtub?"

Weigand motioned him toward the bedroom. Dr. Francis followed the gesture. Weigand looked down at Pam.

"Did you see anything, Pam?" he asked. Pam merely looked at him. "So you did," he said. "What was it, Pam?"

Mrs. North said she didn't know whether it meant anything. But it was funny.

"The shoe?" Weigand suggested. "On the bench?"

Pam looked at him in honest surprise.

"Why, no," she said. "What's funny about that? She just dropped it as she was passing, because it was still in her hand after she had pulled it off. Or she was standing on one foot to take it off and put it down on the bench to catch her balance. Or any number of things. There's nothing funny about *that*."

Weigand merely waited. Mrs. North seemed to hesitate a moment. Then she said probably it was nothing.

"Only," she said, "I wondered where her dress was, didn't you? I mean, you could see the other things she took off and just threw around, but there wasn't any dress."

Weigand's mind re-pictured the room. He nodded.

"I remember," he said. "No, there wasn't any dress. But wouldn't she have hung it up in the closet?"

Pam looked at him, and he could see she was puzzled.

"Well," she said. "I wouldn't have thought so. She didn't hang things up — left that for the maid, probably. She just threw things. Did you see the negligee?"

"Yes," Weigand said.

"Well," Pam said, "the dress she had on this afternoon was nice — green, but a nice green and from a good shop. But it was just something she wore to rehearsals. And the negligee was ever so much nicer, and it looked new and she didn't bother with *it.* So why did she hang up the dress? I'd have thought that, at the most, she would have tossed it on the chair, or on the bed. But it's hung up."

"Is it?" Weigand said. "You looked."

Pam nodded. She said to come on and she'd show him. She led him into the bedroom and to the door which opened beside the bathroom door. It was closed.

"It was closed before," Pam said, in response to Weigand's unspoken enquiry. "I opened it."

Weigand said, "Oh." Then he said, generally to the fingerprint men, that one set of prints they would find would be Mrs. North's. He opened the door, using a handkerchief to protect the knob. Pam watched him.

"That's just what I did," she said, mildly. "So there *won't* be a set of Mrs. North's prints, Lieutenant."

One of the fingerprint men laughed and swallowed it. Weigand said he was glad to see Pam was advancing. A light came on in the closet as the door opened and Weigand and Pam looked in. Pam pointed to a green dress.

"There," she said. "That's the one she was wearing."

The dress was hanging on a hanger. Weigand looked at it. He said it was a little odd, come to think of it. Pam said she thought it was. Not just the dress, but the belt. Weigand said, "What belt?" and looked again. Pam said that apparently he hadn't seen it, after all. She pointed.

"Buckled," she said. "The dress is hung up, which is odd. And then, instead of just letting the belt dangle the way anybody would — the way even a neat person would and she wasn't — she buckles the belt together across the front. And that's very odd. Isn't it?"

Weigand looked at the dress and nodded slowly.

"You're sure it's the same dress?" he said.

Pam merely looked at him. Weigand said that, as far as that went, he was fairly sure himself.

"Of course," he said, "it may have been a dress she was particularly fond of."

Pam looked at him again and shook her head.

"Actresses don't wear dresses they're *particularly* fond of to rehearsals," she said. "Do they?"

They might, Weigand thought.

"Supposing there was some man attending the rehearsals they wanted to impress," he said.

"Your numbers are funny," Pam said. "Or is it tenses? They always are when it's about collectives, aren't they?"

"What?" said Weigand. "Oh — I see what you mean. Don't quibble, Pam."

Pam said she was sorry, and that it wasn't really quibbling.

"I keep thinking of — in there," she said, looking at the bathroom and quickly away again. "It keeps my mind off. But I think the dress is important — oh!"

"Oh what?" Weigand wanted to know.

Pam said it was oh nothing, really. She'd just thought. Bill Weigand waited, but she said nothing more.

"If you've thought of something, Pam," he

said, "you really ought —"

Then Dr. Francis came out.

"Well," he said, "it's classic. But I never actually saw it before. All the same Mr. Smith and the brides of Bath."

Weigand said he'd be damned and Mrs. North said, "What Mr. Smith?"

There had been a Mr. Smith in England, he told her, who married and insured his wives and drowned them in bathtubs. He had drowned several before the police began to notice the coincidences, and even then it was a little hard to prove that Mr. Smith had not merely run into a series of nasty accidents.

"People are fairly helpless in bathtubs," Weigand pointed out. "If you move suddenly — pull on their legs, push down on their shoulders. They drown. I gather Miss Grady drowned, Doc."

Dr. Francis nodded.

"And," he said, "there's a bump on the back of her head. Probably she bumped it against the back of the tub when she was jerked down into the water. She'd be apt to. And it may have been enough to make her a little groggy, which would make it easier. Or maybe whoever did it grabbed her hair first, and banged her head on the tub, and then jerked. Anyway, she's drowned. She floated up a little — the weight of her body in the sloping tub brought her head up, after she was dead. I don't think the autopsy will show anything else."

Dr. Francis stopped and looked at Weigand as if he were just seeing him.

"Pretty, wasn't she?" he said. "Seems a pity, somehow."

"Right," Weigand said. "It does indeed. And by the way —"

"About the other one," Dr. Francis said, preceding him. "We've just started on him, but he died of a stab wound in the back of the neck — punctured the cord. And he'd eaten about an hour or so before. Was that what you wanted?"

Weigand said it was.

"Well," Dr. Francis said, "send this one along and we'll go through it. And find it was a case of drowning in slightly soapy water. And then we'll know as much as we do now."

Dr. Francis went out into the living room.

"And try," he called back, "not to have any more tonight, huh?"

Weigand said they'd try. He and Mrs. North followed into the living room. Weigand told Mullins he wanted the doorman. The doorman was procured. He said he was John Smith.

"Huh?" said Mullins, incredulously. "What do you think you're . . ." He stopped, because Weigand was shaking his head at him.

"Somebody has to be," Weigand told Mullins. "It's the law of averages." He looked at Smith. "I suppose?" he said. Smith nodded. He said, suddenly, that it was no fun, if they wanted to know.

"Nobody believes it," he said. He seemed resigned to fate.

"Well," Weigand told him, "remember the man who was really John Doe. And the draft board wouldn't believe it and the Army wouldn't believe it. Very upsetting to Mr. Doe. Now . . ."

Now, Weigand wanted to know, what about Miss Grady's maid? Was there one, and when, and where was she?

The maid, John Smith explained, was part of the house service, if a tenant wanted a maid, and Miss Grady did. Miss Grady wanted very complete service — breakfast late in the morning, apartment cleaning, some laundry work. Maggie was the maid assigned.

"Maggie?" Weigand repeated. "Maggie what?"

Smith didn't know. It would be on the records. As far as he was concerned, merely

Maggie. She had been there that day and finished about four o'clock. Smith had been standing in front of the building and seen her come out the service entrance and had said goodnight to her and watched her go down the street.

"Right," Weigand said. "Now — who visited Miss Grady later? This evening, I mean after she came in. Did you see her come in, by the way?"

Smith had. She had come in a few minutes before seven and spoken to him. She had come by cab and gone straight to her apartment. That was, say, about 6:45.

"And — ?" Weigand said.

After that, Smith said — about half an hour after that — a man came to see Miss Grady.

"Mr. Ahlberg," Smith said.

"So," Weigand said. "Mr. Ahlberg. Do you know him?"

Smith did. And, also, Mr. Ahlberg had had himself announced. Miss Grady hadn't sounded much as if she wanted to see him, when Smith talked to her on the house telephone, but had said, finally: "Oh, all right, send him up." Ahlberg had gone up.

"And when did he come down again?" Weigand wanted to know.

Smith looked puzzled.

"Come to think of it," he said. "I don't know. I didn't see him come down at all."

"But you would have seen him?" Weigand insisted.

Smith started to nod, and then shook his head.

"I might have," he said. "But then I might not."

He explained. The elevator was automatic, operated by the passengers. And Smith had not been uninterruptedly in the lobby or on the sidewalk.

"A couple or three times," he said, "people wanted cabs and there weren't any at the stand. Then I went up to the avenue and flagged one. He could've come out one of those times."

He did not know when the times were.

"And," Weigand said, "anybody who wanted to could have come in while you were out after a cab, got in the elevator and gone up to the Grady apartment. Right?"

Smith admitted it was.

"Did you see anybody else?" Weigand went on.

"Yes," Smith said. "There was a girl came in and said she was going to see Miss Grady. Said not to bother to announce her, and I had some people coming out who wanted a taxi and — well . . ."

"You let her go," Weigand said. "Although you are supposed to announce everybody. Right?"

"All right," Smith said. "Suppose I did? Mostly people don't mind. And if they have to wait for a cab they do mind."

"And," Weigand explained further, "if you get them a cab you get a tip. Right?"

"All right," Smith said. "So what, Captain?"

"Well," Weigand said, "I wish you hadn't, this time. But you couldn't know, of course. What did the girl look like?"

She had been a pretty girl, slight and with brown hair — sorta light brown hair — hanging down almost to her shoulders, and no hat and large eyes and —

"She looked like a million," Smith said. "Maybe that's partly why I didn't stop her."

Weigand nodded slowly, thinking of the only girl he had seen in recent hours who matched the description of the attentive Mr. Smith. So Alberta James had also visited Miss Grady during the last hour or so that Miss Grady was alive. Weigand heard Pam say "Oh," in a small, hurt voice beside him. Weigand discovered, a little to his surprise, that he felt much as Mrs. North sounded. The male, encroaching on the policeman, hoped for an instant that another attractive

213

female was not going to be wasted.

Smith seemed to know nothing more. He went back to the lobby. Mullins looked after him, and then looked at Weigand.

"You know, Loot," he said, "it's pretty near got to be a dame. Maybe not this James dame, but a dame. Because she wouldn't have let no guy — well, see her — (Mullins looked embarrassedly at Mrs. North) — well, nude sort of."

"Naked," Pam said. "I wondered how soon you'd think of that, one of you."

Weigand smiled at her.

"I'd thought of it, Pam," he said. "Only — don't be too innocent, you two. It could have been —"

"Oh, of course," Pam said, sounding rather cross with herself. "Her lover, of course. Some man she wouldn't mind seeing her." She paused. "Or really'd like to have," she added, unexpectedly. Then she, in turn, looked embarrassed.

"Right," Weigand said. "Or it needn't even have been that. She wasn't — well, strict. At least, I suppose she wasn't. Her virtue aside, I mean. She wouldn't have minded, particularly if there was some man she wanted to see and knew pretty well and if she were in a hurry to dress and go out, if —" He paused, the sentence beyond him.

214

"If he'd sat here in the living room, or even in the bedroom and talked through the door," Pam finished for him. "Left open a crack so he could. Of course not."

"And then," Weigand said, "if this man went in suddenly she might be surprised for a moment and not move and then — well, it would only need a moment."

"Of course," Pam said. "So where are we? It could have been either a man or a woman. And it needn't be either Mr. Ahlberg or Alberta, because anybody could have come in. And — and —"

"Only," Mullins said, "if it was Mr. Ahlberg, she'd have been dead when the James dame came and the James dame would have — noticed it. And said something. Wouldn't she?"

Pam thought a moment.

"Unless," she pointed out, "Mr. Ahlberg went first and pretended to leave when Alberta came and then went back and drowned Miss Grady. It could have been that way."

Weigand had almost stopped listening. But he broke in to tell them it was foolish to spend time guessing.

"After all," he said, "we can always ask questions; else what are policemen for?"

Mrs. North was uncharacteristically silent

215

on the ride back to the theatre. She sat beside Weigand in the back seat while Mullins, driving almost sedately with the Lieutenant to observe, coasted them along the lighted streets. She was so silent that Bill Weigand, conscious of her under his own thoughts, broke his own injunction against speculation.

"What did she know, I wonder," he said, half to himself. "What did she know or what had she seen? And who would Evans have seen if he had turned around?"

Pam still did not speak, but only stared out of the window nearest her.

"Tired, Pam?" Bill asked.

She shook her head and after a pause said she wasn't tired.

"But I'm afraid I'm worried, Bill," she said. "Because I don't want it to be the way it is. The way I think it is."

And also, Pam thought, because I ought to tell him what I heard, back there behind the set and . . . She compromised with her conscience.

"One thing, Bill," she said. "Ask Alberta James whether she has ever worked in a dress shop. Sometimes actresses do when they're out of engagements. Because maybe . . ." She let it hang there, and turned toward Bill Weigand to find him looking at her and smiling, without much enjoyment.

"Oh, yes, Pam," he said. "I'll ask her that, all right. And also Miss Fowler." He paused, reflecting. "And of course," he added, "there's always Mr. Christopher. Mr. Christopher likes nice things."

Neither spoke again until Mullins pulled in in front of the theatre.

"Although," Weigand said then, "we may be barking up the wrong tree, Pam. Maybe she did it herself."

"The wrong clothes tree?" Pam said. "Or is it clothes horse? But why should she? It wouldn't have been in character."

Weigand's shoulders answered. They went on through the lobby.

XII
TUESDAY
11:35 P.M. TO WEDNESDAY, 12:15 A.M.

"All right," Weigand said, curtly, to Humphrey Kirk. "Get everybody on stage."

Kirk looked puzzled and worried, but Weigand's face did not encourage enquiry.

"Everybody on stage," Kirk called. "The Lieutenant wants to say something."

When he had them there, Weigand spent more than a minute staring at them; letting his gaze go over them slowly, without friendliness.

"All right," he said, finally. "One of you killed Ellen Grady. For the benefit of the others, killed her by drowning her in her bathtub some time after seven o'clock this evening. The same one of you killed Bolton and tried to kill Evans by pushing him down the stairs from the lounge to the basement. Anybody want to say anything?"

Nobody did. Weigand waited.

"Right," he said. "And once more, to all but one of you — anybody who knows

218

anything he hasn't told is in danger. Ellen Grady knew something. She's dead. Evans almost found out something. For the benefit of everybody, he didn't. He doesn't know who pushed him. . . . But he is in the hospital, and it's only luck he isn't in the morgue." He paused again. "One of you doesn't care who he kills," he added. "I'm warning the rest."

He waited, looking at them coldly. They were uneasy now, finally, there on the lighted stage with the shadows behind them; with the shadows of the now unlighted auditorium dark behind the thin crescent of light which lay across only the nearest seats. They looked at Weigand and then away from him; they looked quickly at one another and then away. Those standing or sitting nearest the shadows, nearest the doors and windows and the fireplace which opened into the set, edged forward into the light.

"I'll have men around," Weigand told them. "They'll do what they can. But maybe it won't be enough. If one of you knows something, it won't be enough for him. I can't promise it will be." He pushed again. "Stay here until I tell you you can go," he directed. "That's all."

"Shall we go on rehearsing?" Kirk asked. Weigand stared at him.

"I don't care what you do," he said. "So long as nobody leaves the theatre. But I want Miss James."

Kirk seemed about to say something. Weigand waited for him, making the wait obvious. Kirk finally shrugged and turned away.

"Miss James," Weigand said, raising his voice. "I want to talk to you now. Detective Stein will show you where."

The girl looked very small beside the detective as they went up the aisle, out of the crescent of light into the darkness. Weigand watched them go. He'd let her wait a bit, he decided. He summoned Mullins with a gesture and started toward the door upstage left. Kirk watched him.

"If you want —" Kirk began. Weigand stopped him.

"I don't want anything," Weigand said. "I want to look around."

Weigand led Mullins behind the set, along the passage made by the canvas wall of illusion and the brick wall of real estate. They rounded the corner by the windows, and came out into a relatively open area. Here was waste space, full of oddments — nondescript chairs, a bench along one wall; a wall of canvas masking a door opening off the set. Ahead of them was the beginning of a corridor, and Weigand headed for it. It was short and ran to a flight of stairs leading down to the stage door. Just beyond its opening onto the stage area, another corridor branched from it to the right and off this corridor a flight of iron stairs rose.

"Dressing rooms up there," Mullins said. He pointed up the stairs. "And back there." He waved along the branching corridor.

"Right," Weigand said. "Where's the door to the basement?" He found it before Mullins could answer, and said "Right" again, this time to himself. As they faced the stage door, the door to the basement area was on their left. It was only a few feet in from the stage door itself. Weigand opened the basement door and stared down into the shadows. There were stairs leading down from this door also, he discovered. He said, "Um-mmm." Then he turned, walked back, opened the door which led into the set, stumbled over the two-by-four which made an awkward threshold and came out on the stage. Everybody stared at him. He paid no attention. He went to the windows which cut off the corner of the room and stared out of them. Then, to Mullins, whom he had left behind, he called suddenly:

"Move around a bit, Sergeant."

There were the rather heavy sounds of

Mullins moving around a bit.

"Right," Weigand said. He paid no attention to the people who were staring at him, went back through the door in the set, and collected Mullins from the corridor.

"Could they of?" Mullins asked.

"Yes," Weigand said, "they could of."

"Have," Mullins said.

"Have is right," Weigand said. "Come on."

He led Mullins around a corner, found the door leading to the orchestra, and went along the side aisle, up the slight slope, to the rear of the auditorium. Then he paused and looked back.

"Either way would have worked," he said. "Only why take a chance?"

"Yeh," Mullins said. "Under or over. Maybe because it was quicker?"

Weigand said it could be. Only there seemed to be no reason why anybody should cut it that close.

"Of course," he added, "there may have been reasons."

He led on up the stairs to the mezzanine and opened the door into the office. The lights there were momentarily blinding, although they were bright only by contrast to the shadows elsewhere. Stein, who had been sitting beside the desk, stood up as Weigand and Mullins came in. Weigand nodded and jerked his head toward the door.

"Hang around where they can see you," he directed. "Maybe somebody will want to spill something."

He walked around the desk and sat down behind it. Mullins pulled a chair up so he could rest his notebook on a corner of the desk. Then they both looked across at Alberta James, sitting on a straight chair facing them. She looked very slight and her soft hair framed her face disarmingly. But she was pale and her hands clutched each other in her lap. Weigand's voice when he spoke was level and impersonal.

"I have a good many things to ask you, Miss James," he said. "You don't have to answer. If you had nothing to do with these murders, you'll be wise to answer. If you had something to do with them, I'd advise you not to talk. Whatever you say, Sergeant Mullins will take down, and after it is transcribed, I'll ask you to initial each page and sign the last page. Is that understood?"

"Yes," the girl said. Her voice was very low.

"As an alternative to this," Weigand said, "I can take you to the station house, and have one of the assistant district attorneys question you with me. You'll be allowed to telephone a lawyer, if you want one. We may let him in, if we have to. But we don't have to without an order, or unless we charge you with something. Is all this clear?"

"Very clear," the girl said. "I haven't done anything. I'll answer any questions you like."

"Right," Weigand said. "I'm telling you all this, Miss James, because there are several circumstances you'll have to explain. We know a good deal more now than we did earlier."

"I haven't done anything," the girl repeated. Her head was back and she was facing the detectives and her eyes were afraid.

"Right," Weigand said. "I hope you haven't. Now — you heard me say that Ellen Grady has been killed?"

She nodded.

"Very well," Weigand said. "You went there this evening; went to see Miss Grady. Why?"

"What makes you —" she began. Then she stopped. "All right," she said. "I went to see her. For a very foolish, trivial reason."

"Which was?"

"She is — she was — the lead. So she could decide, with the help of Miss Fowler, what she wanted to wear in the different acts. And she could object if I wore something which she thought clashed with her

224

clothes or — made them less effective. I wanted to wear a blue dress in the first act, accented with orange. I didn't know whether that would be all right with her. I didn't get a chance to ask her today and so — well, it was on my mind and I thought 'Why not go around now and ask her?' So I did."

She spoke with little hesitation, as if she had formed the explanation in her mind while she waited. As, Weigand decided, she unquestionably had. Which, he qualified to himself, proved nothing — whether it was true or false, she would have known the explanation would be needed, and would have formulated it in her mind.

"Right," Weigand said. "You saw Miss Grady?"

"Yes, for a moment. She said it would be all right."

"I see," Weigand said. "Now — tell me about it. Was she alone? How long did you stay?"

"She was alone," the girl said. "I only stayed a minute or so. She said she was getting ready to take a bath. She was in a negligee, as a matter of fact, and the tub was running. I only stayed a minute."

"Where?" Weigand said. "I mean, did you stay in the living room? Or go into the bedroom? Did she let you in herself?"

225

"I rang the bell," the girl said. "She opened the door a little and saw who it was and said to come on in. She said: 'You may as well come in, too. Everybody does.' "

"Did she seem angry, upset?"

"No." The girl thought. "She seemed — oh, sort of resigned and — amused. As if there had been a string of little things. But not irritated."

"Right," Weigand said. "Then you went in?"

Ellen Grady had, the girl said, opened the door and then walked on through the living room to the bedroom. Alberta had closed the door behind her and followed. Ellen had sat down in the chair and offered her a cigarette and Alberta had sat on the bed and taken up the matter of the first-act dresses. Ellen had been pleasant about it, and agreed at once to Alberta's choice. Then Alberta, seeing that Ellen wanted to go on with her bath — "she kept sort of looking toward the bathroom," Alberta explained — had crushed out her cigarette and —

"I said I hoped I hadn't bothered her, but that I'd wanted to get it settled," Alberta said. "Miss Fowler wanted to know, and so did I. She said it was all right, and she was sorry to hurry me away, but that somebody was coming and she wanted to get her bath in first. So I just went."

"Right," Weigand said. "And she?"

As Alberta went on into the living room on her way to the door, she said, Ellen had already started to take off the negligee and was walking toward the bathroom.

"She waved at me," Alberta said. "Sort of — oh, 'good-bye-be-seeing-you' and — oh, I almost forgot."

"Yes?" Weigand said.

"Just as I was going out she called after me," Alberta told him. "She said to snap the door so it wouldn't lock. It usually locked when you closed it, I suppose."

"And you did?"

She had. She had supposed, naturally, that the other person Ellen Grady was expecting had been told to come on in and that Ellen wanted the door left so that she could come on in.

"She?" Weigand repeated. "Did she say it was a woman?"

"She just said 'somebody,'" Alberta told him. "But I naturally supposed it was a woman, since she was — well, she certainly didn't act as if she were expecting a man. Unless —" She stopped.

"Unless?" Weigand repeated. The girl looked at him, and half smiled.

"Do I have to fill it in, Lieutenant?" she said.

Weigand shook his head. What, he wanted to know, had Miss James done then.

Then, she said, she had gone on across town by taxi to the Algonquin, where she was meeting Mr. Kirk for dinner. She met Mr. Kirk, they had dinner, she came to the theatre. Weigand said he saw.

"Was Mr. Kirk there when you got there?" he asked, casually.

"No," she said. "He was late as it hap— oh!"

"How late?" Weigand asked.

"Only a few minutes," she said. "Hardly any time. I waited in the bar, where we were going to meet. Then, in just a minute or two, he came along."

"Right," Weigand said. "We can always check on just how long you waited, if it seems important. Now — how did it happen that Dr. Bolton had in his hand, when he died, a piece of material which belonged to you, Miss James? A piece of orange silk you were showing Miss Fowler, as a sample of what you wanted for the accents on your blue dress?"

There was no sound from the girl for a moment, but her eyes seemed to grow wider. Weigand watched her hands; saw them twisting together in her lap. Then she said: "Oh — I —" and stopped.

"Well, Miss James?" Weigand said.

She seemed to stiffen to meet the moment. She swallowed and when she first spoke her voice was uncertain. Then it, too, steadied.

"Humpty said you'd find out," she said. "And that you'd suspect — all sorts of things. And not believe that I really lost it. It was — I was afraid to explain. But —"

"But?" Weigand repeated, when she did not go on.

"I simply don't know," she said. "I must have lost it some place. And somebody must have picked it up. Perhaps Dr. Bolton himself. I don't know why it was in his hand when you found him —"

"Simply because, Miss James, it was in his hand when he was killed," Weigand told her.

She nodded, and said she supposed so.

"And I still don't know," she said. "I had it this morning and showed it to Aun— to Miss Fowler. Then this afternoon it was gone when I wanted to try it with the blue and —" She was hurrying, now — hurrying away from a slip of the tongue. But Weigand stopped her.

"To Aun—" he repeated, echoing her syllable. "Your aunt, you were about to say, weren't you, Miss James. And then you said, 'Miss Fowler' instead. And — *is Miss Fowler your aunt, Miss James?*"

Slowly, unwillingly, she nodded.

"Everybody knows that," she said. "It isn't any secret except —"

"Except," Weigand said, "from the police. Why from the police, Miss James?"

He was surprised, a little, when the girl smiled, and seemed to relax.

"You know," she said, "I haven't the least idea. She wanted it that way — said we'd better not mention it, because it would merely be another confusion that had nothing to do with the murder. As of course it didn't. But she seemed to feel — oh, the more complicated the relationships of all of us, the more you would have to spend going down blind alleys. Like her and Mr. Tilford — everybody knows that, too."

"Except," Weigand told her, without inflection, "the police. What about your aunt, Miss Fowler, and Mr. Tilford?"

"Only," the girl said, "that they used to be married — oh, years ago."

"Well," Mullins said, "I'll be damned."

Weigand looked at him and Mullins said, "Sorry, Loot, but jeez!"

"What other 'relationships' are you people keeping from the police?" Weigand wanted

230

to know. "Keeping from us just to make it simple for us?"

The girl shook her head, the long reddish brown hair swaying. Nothing, she told him. Nothing that mattered. "Except," Weigand said, "your 'relationship' — whatever it was — with Bolton."

It was a stab. Watching her closely, he could not tell whether it had reached a mark. Perhaps her eyes widened a little again; perhaps her newly won relaxation faltered a little. But it was hard to tell.

"Relationship?" she repeated. "There wasn't any —"

And then, with no warning, the door opened violently and Humphrey Kirk stood violently in the doorway. He spoke, loudly:

"You can't —" Humphrey Kirk said, and stopped. Weigand stared at him, and was suddenly rather amused. Because it was almost ludicrously evident that the scene which confronted Mr. Humphrey Kirk was by no means the scene he had expected. The hero had leaped furiously from his horse and found the maiden having tea with the dragon. The hero was left at a disadvantage.

"Well, Mr. Kirk," Weigand said, in a voice which was incongruously low and quiet. "What can't I, Mr. Kirk? If you mean I can't ask Miss James questions, you're quite wrong. And if you mean I can't have you thrown out of this office, or if necessary out of this theatre, you're wrong again."

He stared at Kirk, who stared back. Kirk looked, Weigand decided, slightly embarrassed.

"What did you think we were doing with her, Mr. Kirk?" Weigand asked, his tone very dry. "Shining a light in her eyes? Or beating her up?"

"Well —" Kirk said.

"You read too much, Mr. Kirk," Weigand told him. "Such men get foolish ideas. Sergeant Mullins and I are merely asking Miss James some questions. She understands that she doesn't have to answer. So far she has preferred to answer. Isn't that right, Miss James?"

Alberta James spoke to Humphrey Kirk.

"It's all right, Humpty," she told him. "They're not *doing* anything. But —"

"As a matter of fact, Mr. Kirk," Weigand cut in, still in a patient, quiet voice, "you may stay if you like. Now you're here."

"Well —" said Kirk.

"Sit down," Weigand said. "There may be some questions for you, too. For example — what made you late in meeting Miss James for dinner this evening?"

"Oh, that," Kirk said. "I got tied up — with Smith. I lost track of time. I wasn't more than a quarter of an hour late, anyway."

Weigand looked at the girl, who looked down and reddened slightly.

"Well," she said. "Perhaps it was a quarter of an hour. There wasn't any clock."

Weigand said he saw.

"Did you use that fifteen minutes to kill Miss Grady, Mr. Kirk?" he asked. His tone was entirely conversational.

"What the —" said Kirk. "*No!* Why should I?"

"We assume," Weigand said, "that whoever killed her did it because she knew something about the Bolton killing. Did you kill Dr. Bolton, Mr. Kirk?"

"Listen," Kirk said. "What the hell goes on?"

A police investigation, Weigand told him. The asking of questions to get answers. Had he, to repeat, killed Dr. Bolton? Kirk said, *"Hell, no!",* violently.

"Right," Weigand said. "And don't ask me why you should. Because I could make a guess about that. It would concern Bolton and Miss James here."

Weigand's voice was still low, but much harder. Kirk pushed the dangling lock of

233

hair violently from his forehead and stood up.

"Sit down," Weigand said. Kirk hesitated. Mullins half rose from his chair, but Weigand's fingers flickered at him. "Sit down, Kirk," Weigand said. "You won't get anywhere jumping up and shouting. I'm telling you why you might have killed Ellen Grady. She might have known you killed Bolton. You might have killed Bolton because you were jealous of him. You might have been jealous of him because he was — how do you say it nicely on the stage? — taking her away from you."

"I didn't have anything to do with Bolton," the girl said quickly, her voice low but with a vibrating quality in it. "Humpty knows that."

"Of course I know that," Kirk said, almost too quickly. He glared at Weigand.

"Can't a girl go to her doctor?" he demanded.

Weigand smiled at him. He transferred the smile, which was not a warming smile, to Alberta James.

"The relationship of patient and doctor *is* a relationship, Miss James," he said. "Or had you just forgotten it?"

The girl looked up at him, her hair swinging back from her face. Her expression was one of innocence — "young girl misunderstood," Weigand said to himself. "These actors!"

"But Lieutenant," the girl said, "I thought of course you meant something different. Of course he was my doctor. I have — almost everybody has, you know — a little sinus trouble. But it's important for an actress, and Dr. Bolton was very good. And I knew people he'd treated. So naturally I went to him. But do you call that a 'relationship'?"

You could, Weigand told her. And why had she thought he meant anything more?

"You said," he reminded her, "that — read it back to her, Sergeant."

Mullins back-paged in his notebook.

" 'Relationship?' " he read, his voice a remarkable parody of the girl's. " 'There wasn't any —' Then this guy busted in."

"Right," Weigand said. "What *did* you think I meant, Miss James?"

He waited, and Kirk waited. But Miss James, looking down at her twisting finger, said nothing.

"Listen," Kirk said. "You know what she thought you meant. We all know Bolton was a chaser." He spoke contemptuously.

"Right," Weigand said. "Was that it, Miss James?"

The girl nodded.

"And why," Weigand said, abruptly, "did you jump at the conclusion I meant that, Miss James? Because other people had suggested it? And sit down, Kirk!"

Still the girl didn't speak.

"For God's sake," Kirk said. "You can hear *anything*. If a girl spoke to Bolton, Winchell heard about it."

"All right," Weigand said. "That answers it. And you still insist you weren't jealous, Kirk?" Kirk spluttered. "All right," Weigand said. "We'll make a note of it. Now — how serious was this sinus condition of yours, Miss James?"

Both Kirk and the girl looked surprised, and then relieved. The girl said that Dr. Bolton seemed to feel it was rather serious. At any rate, he had talked about the possibility of a minor operation and, recently rather urged her to have one.

Weigand said he saw.

"And were you going to?" he asked, in a tone of slight interest.

"I hadn't decided," the girl said. "But probably it will have to be done, some time. I'd have gone right ahead before now, only Aunty — Miss Fowler, you know — didn't want me to. She said that I should never 'let any doctor poke around in my sinuses.' She

236

said it was dangerous. But of course that's all nonsense."

"Well," Weigand said, "that's out of my sphere, obviously. But I like to get a full picture. Now, Miss James — did you ever work in a department store? Or in a clothes shop, or some place like that?"

Both Kirk and the girl looked completely surprised and puzzled, Weigand decided. And she answered without hesitancy.

"Why," she said, "yes, I did. Last year, and a while the year before. I modeled the first time and then I sold for several months. When I was 'resting.' " Her voice put quotation marks around the actor's euphemism. Weigand said "Right."

"I suppose," he said, "that both of you know how to get to the basement, or whatever you call that area under the orchestra? Know you can get to it from both the lounge and the stage-door passage?"

They both nodded. They weren't puzzled this time.

"Of course," Kirk amplified. "So does everybody in the theatre."

Weigand said he supposed they did.

"Now," he said, "let's see. You say you don't know what happened to the piece of orange silk between the time you showed it to Miss Fowler before lunch and the time it was found in Bolton's hand. Is that right, Miss James?"

The girl nodded.

"Right," Weigand said. "Now if I say anything which isn't as you remember it, stop me. You knew Bolton. He was your doctor, and as your doctor you naturally saw him frequently. You had lunch with him today at an Automat. Or" — (he held up his hand) — "coffee, anyway. You didn't see him after that until Kirk here found his body. You hadn't been seeing him, you say, except as a patient sees a physician, but even that may have led to talk in connection with a man like Bolton. You went to see Ellen Grady this evening and she was alive when you left and —" He checked himself.

"Something I'd forgotten," he said. "Can you describe the bedroom as it was when you left? You were in it a few minutes. I don't mean the room so much — not the permanent things. But — oh, other things. I don't want to lead you."

The girl looked puzzled and then, when Weigand waited, considering.

"Things were scattered around," she said. "Shoes and things. I remember one shoe on the dressing-table bench, standing up. And a girdle on the floor. And the dress she had just taken off over the back of the chair.

And stockings somewhere. I think on the chair, too. I remember that when she sat in the chair she struck a match and part of the head flew off and I was afraid it was going to burn the dress. But it didn't. I think that's all. Is that what you meant?"

Did she remember rather too well? Weigand wondered.

"Yes," he said slowly. "That's what I meant. I'm glad you remember so clearly, Miss James. Now, to get on — you met Kirk, who was fifteen minutes late, at the Algonquin. You came back here with him. You didn't kill Miss Grady or Dr. Bolton. Now let's see. Your aunt objected to your having Bolton operate."

"To having anyone operate," the girl corrected. Weigand said, "Right."

"You have worked in a dress shop, as model and salesgirl. You parted from Ellen Grady on good terms; at her request, you left the door to her apartment so that it could be opened from outside without bothering her if she were still in the tub, when the visitor she expected came. You know — you both know — about the area under the orchestra, and the two ways of reaching it. And —" His fingers drummed on the desk for a moment. "I guess that's all. Do you want to add anything?"

The girl shook her head.

"Right," Weigand said. "We'll have you sign this when it's ready. That's all for now."

Kirk and the girl stood up. They moved, as if instinctively, closer together. Weigand watched them.

"By the way, Kirk," he said, suddenly. "Have you got a match? I don't seem to have any."

"Sure," Kirk said. His hand went to his pocket and came out with a folder of matches, and tossed the folder to the desk. Weigand picked it up, pulled loose a bottle-shaped match and looked at it. Then he looked at Kirk, who seemed only puzzled.

"Where did you get this," Weigand said, abruptly.

"What?" said Kirk. "The match? God knows. Around somewhere. In a restaurant, or a cigar store, or borrowed it from somebody. Probably I borrowed it. People say that's where I get all my matches, and cigarettes too, for that matter. Why?"

"Well," Weigand said, "if you don't know — we found one, earlier . . . under conditions we thought were interesting. But if you just borrowed it, it doesn't matter, unless you remember who you borrowed it from?"

Kirk shook his head.

240

"I wouldn't know about that," he said. "I wouldn't have the faintest idea."

Weigand let them go, then. He stared after them, his fingers drumming on the desk.

"Whata you think, Loot?" Mullins said, after a moment.

Weigand looked at him.

"Well, Sergeant," he said. "Things begin to fit. Let's talk to Mr. Ahlberg."

XIII
WEDNESDAY
12:15 A.M. TO 12:55 A.M.

Max Ahlberg's round face sagged; his plump optimism seemed to be settling. He looked at Weigand and began shaking his head, dismally.

"I should have such luck," Mr. Ahlberg said. He was very sad. "First somebody kills my angel," Mr. Ahlberg told Weigand, and was almost accusing in his gloom. "Then somebody kills my leading lady. Next somebody should kill me, only it ain't worth it."

Weigand started to speak and Maxie Ahlberg held up a dissuading hand.

"You should ask did I kill Ellen," Maxie said. "Why should I kill Ellen?"

"I don't know," Weigand said. "Why should you, Mr. Ahlberg?"

"Don't joke," Maxie said. "All I ask it, don't joke!"

Weigand said he wasn't joking. Why should Mr. Ahlberg kill Miss Grady? Why should Mr. Ahlberg visit Miss Grady at, to

242

put the best light on it, a few minutes before she was killed?

"Yes," Maxie said. "I should have such luck. I go to see Ellen and then somebody kills her and you think that Max Ahlberg, he kills her."

Mr. Ahlberg thought this over and groaned audibly.

"Would I kill my partner?" he demanded. "Would I kill the best actress we got, a *week* before opening?"

Weigand persuaded Mr. Ahlberg to sit down. He drew out the story.

Ahlberg admitted without argument that he had gone to see Ellen Grady, and had seen Ellen Grady. He had gone to her for a very simple purpose: to raise money. It had been, he indicated, an appeal more or less of desperation. Because, it became clear, Mr. Ahlberg was up against it. The death of Dr. Bolton had put him up against it.

"Insurance?" he echoed, when Weigand made the suggestion. "Of course there was insurance. Until three days ago there was insurance. And then I figured we were in and why should I pay any more premiums on the Doc?" He sighed deeply. "How should I know he hadn't paid for the scenery?" he asked.

He had assumed the scenery paid for, as

scenery in the show business comes only for cash. But Bolton's backing was as good as cash; to give him credit, his word was as good as cash. Dr. Bolton had been about to pay for the scenery — this afternoon or tomorrow he would have written checks. But dead men write no checks. Ahlberg had taken a chance which was, in reason, no chance; he had let the insurance on Bolton's life, for which he was paying, lapse when the last day of grace came and went. It had looked like the saving of a few hundred dollars. Now it looked like bankruptcy.

Because now Mr. Ahlberg had no money. Unless he could find money, "Two in the Bush" would remain in the bush. And Mr. Ahlberg would, reluctantly, secede from the theatrical business, in which he had spent his life. Mr. Ahlberg had been for several seasons on the down swing, in that pendulum beat which affects all but a scant half-dozen Broadway producers. Now the pendulum was at nadir, and seemed about to stop.

"For five thousand I got a hit," he assured Weigand. He looked at the Lieutenant with sudden interest. "You got five thousand?" he enquired, affectionately. Weigand shook his head. Ahlberg's hope, a tiny thing, withered.

"Who's got five thousand?" he demanded. "The Government," he added. The thought evidently depressed him. Weigand pulled him back to the subject.

He had gone to see Ellen Grady, Ahlberg said, and put it up to her. He was pretty sure she had five thousand, or could get it. He put it to her that it was five thousand or no show, and he stressed the acclaim she was certain to win in the part.

"For her it was important, I told her," Ahlberg said. "Maybe after this show she would be a star. And where, I asked her, would she get another part like it for this season? Answer me that, I told her."

Miss Grady had, Ahlberg indicated, been impressed. She did not deny she had, or could raise, the money. She had confidence in the play, and liked her part. But she hesitated.

"She said she should think it over," Ahlberg explained. "But I thought she'd put it up. I thought we were going to be okay."

She had, Ahlberg said in answer to the Lieutenant's questions, talked to him in the living room of the suite. He was still arguing the numerous advantages of putting up the money when she looked at her watch and suddenly stood up.

"She said I would have to go away," Ahlberg said. "She said she would think it over, but now I should go away. She had to take a bath and dress and get dinner if she was to get back to the theatre. She said, 'Don't worry, Maxie. I think we can work it out.'"

Ahlberg stared at Weigand.

"Don't worry, she says to me," he repeated. "And so somebody kills her!"

She was wearing the negligee when he talked to her. He did not notice anything particularly in the bedroom, although from where he was sitting he could see into it. She had started toward the bedroom as he went out, and he closed the door behind him. So far as he knew, the snap lock worked. But he had not tried the door from outside. Then he had gone to Dinty Moore's and had dinner, and then to the theatre. And then he heard that somebody had killed his star who was, moreover, beginning to sprout the wings of an angel.

"I should have such luck," he said, returning to his starting point. Then he looked at Weigand.

"You're thinking: 'That Max Ahlberg, he thinks only of the money,'" he said. "You think: 'What's it to Max Ahlberg that a beautiful little girl gets killed? To Max it ain't nothing but five thousand!' " He shook his head.

"Believe me, it ain't so," he said. "I gotta heart, Lieutenant. Ellen I liked — she was an actress, but I liked her. About it I'm very sad, but about the money, just now, I'm crazy. Because what should I tell Becky, Lieutenant?" He looked at the Lieutenant and shook his head, and as the extent of his impending ruin impressed itself more deeply upon him, Max Ahlberg gained in dignity.

"Without this, I'm sunk, Lieutenant," he said. "Max Ahlberg is out of the theatre."

Saying that, Weigand thought, Max Ahlberg did not mean that he would be out of a job, with those things happening which happen to men who are out of jobs. He meant that he would be out of life. And then Weigand remembered, suddenly, recalling a phrase out of something long ago read or overheard, that this Max Ahlberg had been for a good many years Max Ahlberg, Jr. And that before him there had been a Max Ahlberg — in Berlin, was it? or Vienna? — whose name reached even those who thought little about the theatre, so that when you read it in the phrase "A Max Ahlberg Production" you thought with a kind of vicarious pride of superlative accomplishment and with a kind of personal bitterness of changes which made continuation of such achievement impossible.

The present Max Ahlberg, now standing up and looking at Weigand, and waiting for Weigand to let him go, would do almost anything to stay in the theatre. To do that, if it came to it, he might very well kill. But it seemed, so far as they had got, that murder was pushing him out of the theatre, not keeping him in. If that were true, they would have to look beyond small, round, unhappy Mr. Ahlberg for their murderer.

Ahlberg had not seen Alberta James in Ellen Grady's apartment, or in the building, or on the street outside. Ahlberg had come out, and got into a taxicab and driven to the Astor, and had been full of hope.

Weigand waved him out, and sat drumming with his fingers on the desk.

"Are we getting places, Loot?" Mullins wanted to know.

"Maybe, Sergeant," Weigand said. "Maybe. Get this guy Tilford, will you?"

Weigand watched Mullins go to the door and then stared a moment at the telephone. Suddenly he pulled it to him and dialed a number. He identified himself to Dr. Jerome Francis at the other end of the wire, and asked a question. It took Dr. Francis some time to answer, much qualification apparently being required. Weigand had thanked him and pushed back the telephone when Mullins returned with Tilford.*

No descriptions could have been less appropriate than "this guy" applied to F. Lawrence Tilford. When Mr. Tilford entered the office he filled it with his presence. Mr. Tilford was stately and when he spoke his voice rolled — perfectly pitched, perfectly modulated, almost perfectly artificial. In a world of type casting, of ingenues famous at twenty, Mr. Tilford was an actor. And if there had once been a thin, wavering line between Mr. Tilford, himself, and Mr. Tilford, actor, that line had long since been obliterated. He stood before the detectives and acted the dignified gentleman, politely curious; the good citizen, ready to be of help. If any of his earlier uneasiness remained, manner blotted it out, as Mr. Tilford saved the surface and, with it, everything.

He thanked the lieutenant and the ser-

* No clue is hidden here. Weigand, as a layman, merely sought a professional opinion on a clue already in evidence. The lay reader, with the same evidence at his disposal, may easily ask Weigand's question of some friendly physician, although he may have difficulty in getting an answer.

geant for his chair. He composed himself in his chair. He waited. Weigand, his fingers gently tapping on the desk, looked back at him and half smiled in tribute to perfection. Thus, Weigand decided, Tilford on the stage must, in heaven knew how many mystery plays, have confronted enquiring inspectors of Scotland Yard and lied like a gentleman for the lady in the case. Only, Weigand thought with faint amusement, on such occasions Mr. Tilford had not needed to worry about his lines.

"I understand," Weigand said, "that you were once married to Miss Fowler?"

Tilford looked, for an instant, startled. This was not, clearly, the conventional beginning. But when he spoke his voice revealed nothing.

"That is correct, Lieutenant," he said. "It is, in its small way, a matter of history. We of the theatre —"

"Right," Weigand said. "Why didn't you say so earlier?"

"Chiefly," Tilford said, "because you didn't ask me earlier. Although I should not, in any case, have thought it germane to your purpose."

Mullins said "Huh?" and Weigand's fingers tapped toward him. Mullins shook his head and returned to his notebook.

"We're interested in anything we can find out about anybody mixed up in this," Weigand told him. "We were interested in discovering, only a few minutes ago, that Alberta James is Miss Fowler's niece. We'd be interested in discovering, say, that Humphrey Kirk is your — son. He isn't, is he?"

Tilford smiled and shook his head.

"Berta is Mary's niece," he said. "I was Mary's husband at one time. Neither of those relationships has ever been a secret. You couldn't, indeed, have kept any secret about Mary in those days — not about Mary Evans."

"Mary who?" Weigand wanted to know.

"Evans."

Tilford's smile excused Weigand's bewilderment. Naturally, for people not of the theatre . . .

The Lieutenant might not know, Tilford thought, about Mary, although surely the name? Mary Evans? It could hardly fail to convey something, even to so young a man as the Lieutenant. Mary Evans as Hedda? As Joan? As the lovely Maria in "The Lady Forgets"? As Juliet once, and another time as Nora? Tilford scanned Weigand's face and shook his head.

"Ah," Mr. Tilford said, "the public! The public!"

He was gentle, but despairing. But Weigand was remembering — not clearly, but remembering.

"*That* Mary Evans?" he said. "But surely —" He broke off.

"It was a good many years ago, Lieutenant," Tilford said. "Before your time, almost. Twenty years ago. Mary was very lovely, then, when we were all so much younger. And a very great actress, who had a tragically short career. Half a dozen years, when she might have hoped for twenty — for thirty or more. I, myself, although never as successful as Mary, have been in the theatre more than forty years, Lieutenant. Although you would hardly think it, to look at me."

"Wouldn't I?" Weigand said to himself. But to Tilford he nodded, the nod being an invitation to go on.

"Mary now is somewhere in her late forties," Tilford said. "I could tell you of actresses that old who still — but no matter. She might still be playing but —"

"What happened?" Weigand asked. Tilford raised his eyebrows.

"But surely, Lieutenant," he said, "you've noticed. You could hardly fail to notice — her eyes. Quite tragic, in its way."

Naturally Weigand agreed, he had noticed the eyes. But he had assumed — well, he had assumed that Miss Fowler's eyes must have been — noticeable — all her life. He had never thought of eyes changing, in quite that fashion. Tilford nodded.

"It was strange," he agreed. "The doctors could make nothing of it. It happened — within a few weeks. Or so I've been told. It was after Mary and I had separated."

That, Tilford said in answer to more questions, was about fifteen years ago — fifteen years ago the June just past; fifteen years ago on the twelfth of that June. He remembered very accurately, Weigand decided. They had then been married about five years, their marriage spanning the period of Mary Evans' greatest success. The name? That was simple. Mary had been married before, briefly to a young actor named Evans. They were divorced, but by that time she had begun to be known under the name of Evans. She kept it, for stage purposes, during her marriage to Tilford.

And then it was Tilford who stopped and stared at Weigand.

"Evans," he repeated. "*Evans!* But surely, *not that Evans!* It would be — preposterous!"

"Why?" Weigand said. "Did he die, the young actor named Evans? Did you know him, at all, personally?"

"No," Tilford said. "I never ran into him. He was out of Mary's life — we hardly spoke about him. I don't know whether he's alive or dead. If he's alive he'd be — well, somewhere in his fifties, probably. And this janitor — this Evans in the hospital is — how old would you say, Lieutenant?"

He would, Weigand said, have guessed the middle sixties. But, —

"He might look older than he is," Weigand agreed. "His job wouldn't — well, keep him young. Especially if he had thought, once, of quite a different life. However, there's no use guessing. We'll find out. It would be a coincidence, of course."

But, Tilford pointed out, an entirely reasonable coincidence.

"We of the theatre," he said. "We stay in the theatre. Doormen have often been actors, you know. And wardrobe women. Evans might have found some job he could do in the theatre when it turned out he couldn't succeed as an actor. As Mary found a job, finally, in the theatre after she couldn't go on acting. And if both of them stayed in the theatre for a good many years, their paths would cross a great many times. As they may have now."

"We'll find out," Weigand said. "Guessing gets us nowhere. Get Stein on it, Mullins."

Mullins went to the door and called. When Stein appeared, he got Stein on it.

"Pending that," Weigand said, when Mullins was back at his notebook, "we'll get on. Mary Fowler, under the name of Mary Evans, was a successful and widely known actress —"

"Actor," Tilford corrected. "A great actor. We prefer that in the profession. Some of us."

"Right," Weigand said. "She had been — great — for some five years, during most of which time you and she were married. Then fifteen years ago, you separated. Right?"

Tilford inclined his head.

"Why?" Weigand said.

Tilford hesitated. Then he smiled.

"It was long ago," he said. "But vanity lingers on. Even now I hesitate . . . However, Lieutenant, to put it bluntly — she left me for another man."

"And the man was?" Weigand said. Tilford hesitated again. Then he spoke without embroidery.

"Bolton," he said. "Carney Bolton."

The name hung in the air for a moment. Then Weigand nodded, slowly.

"I wondered whether that was it," he said. "How long did it last?"

"About a year," Tilford told him. "Until

255

— she had to leave the stage. When that happened — well, shall we say she no longer interested Dr. Bolton?"

There was more than the actor's inflection now in the elderly actor's voice. The words curled with bitterness.

"He ditched her?" Weigand said. "When her eyes — went bad; when she couldn't act any longer — he ditched her?"

"Yes," Tilford said, "that was the way it was, Lieutenant."

"And she?" Weigand said. "How did she feel about that?"

Tilford shrugged.

"How would she feel?" he asked, simply. "There was a time when I — well, Lieutenant, when I would have been glad to stick a dagger in Bolton's neck. A bare bodkin, as Shakespeare says. How must she have felt?"

Weigand started to speak, and then waited as Tilford seemed about to go on.

"But, oddly enough, there was never anything to show that she did feel bitterly toward Bolton," he said. "She must have, but if she did it was hidden. She seemed — well, rather resigned than anything else. I saw her infrequently, of course. Others may have seen more. But to me she seemed only that — resigned. It was as if, with so many things happening, she merely drew into herself; allowed herself no feelings. Of course, we of the theatre —"

"Quite," Weigand said. "Some people do behave so. Not only in the theatre, Mr. Tilford. And, naturally, we can only guess how she really felt. How you felt, now —"

Tilford looked for a moment surprised, and then his voice became casual — almost convincingly casual.

"But my feelings, Lieutenant," he said, "how can *they* matter? To be sure, I once felt resentfully toward Bolton — he had taken away a woman I loved deeply, and had abandoned her in an hour of need. But that — that was a very long time ago, Lieutenant. I am — too old a man to encompass such emotions nowadays. I must leave emotions for the young, Lieutenant."

Tilford's voice became ten years older as he spoke. It quavered slightly. By it, he was eighty.

"By the way, Mr. Tilford," Weigand asked, "just how old are you?" He saw Tilford hesitate. "The Theatrical's 'Who's Who' will tell me, of course," he added. Tilford smiled, amused.

"Oh, will it, Lieutenant?" he said. There was mockery in the tone.

"Well," Weigand said.

"However," Tilford went on, "I don't

mind telling you, Lieutenant. I was sixty-four last month. When Mary and I were married I was in my forties." He paused, reflectively. "A good age, Lieutenant," he said. "A good time, the forties. Enjoy them."

Weigand said he hoped to. But to get back.

"I'm to take it, then," he said, "that whatever you may once have felt against Bolton, you have felt nothing of late years? You were — indifferent toward him?"

Tilford seemed to be reflecting.

"I seldom thought of him," he said. "I still preferred not to be in any contact with him. When I found he was backing this play I — however, it is a good part. An actor hates to turn down a good part."

"And," Weigand went on, "so far as you can tell, Mary Fowler felt no real bitterness toward him?"

"So far as I can tell," Tilford agreed.

"Why Fowler?" Weigand said.

It was, Tilford told him, her maiden name. After she divorced him, and after she was forced to leave the stage, she returned to it.

"It gave her — well, anonymity," Tilford said. "From the questions of strangers, at any rate. From pity. But it was never intended to conceal who she really was, of course."

"Right," Weigand said. "Now, as to Miss

258

James. Tell me about her."

There was, it seemed, little to tell. She was an orphan, the daughter of Mary Fowler's younger sister. Both her parents — who were not of the profession — were killed in an automobile accident when Berta was two. After that, Mary Fowler took care of her.

"She was only a little girl when Mary and I were married," Tilford added. "During the last year or two of our marriage she was away at school. She was a very sweet child." He paused. "And is," he added.

"Yes," Weigand agreed. "But about her parents — you're sure about them, Mr. Tilford? Of your own knowledge? She couldn't for example, be Mary's own daughter, and perhaps the daughter of this Evans?"

Tilford looked, Weigand decided, as if this were his first contact with that idea. The actor shook his head slowly. "I had always taken Mary's account without question," he said. "I still do. I see no reason why she should prevaricate about Berta's parentage. Certainly there could be no disgrace in having a daughter like Berta. But of my own knowledge — that is a different matter. I never knew the Jameses, certainly. And, naturally, I never asked to see Berta's birth certificate."

259

"Naturally," Weigand said. "It's something for us to check on. But I imagine Miss Fowler is really her aunt, as she says. We merely — have to clean things up as we go along."

Tilford waited for more questions. When they came they were routine. He had not been near Ellen Grady's apartment that evening. When Kirk let them go, he had taxied downtown to The Players for a drink and dinner. He had met several men he knew, both in the bar downstairs and in the dining room. From The Players he had come back to the theatre by cab, stopping nowhere and seeing no one. He was, he said, shocked by Ellen's death and could imagine no reason for it.

"She saw something," Weigand told him. "Or knew something."

Tilford said it was dreadful. Weigand agreed, abstractedly, and let him go. Weigand sat, and his fingers pattered on the desk. Then he sent Mullins for Mary Fowler.

XIV
WEDNESDAY
12:55 A.M. TO 1:15 A.M.

But Mullins, on his way to get Miss Fowler, was interrupted at the door, which opened without ceremony. Mullins said "Ouch!" as one of Pamela North's high, sharp heels came down on his foot and Pam said, in an abstracted tone, "Sorry, Mr. Mullins."

"Well," Weigand said, looking at Mr. and Mrs. North and Dorian, "I was wondering where you had been." He looked at them again. "And been up to," he added.

"As for me," Mr. North said, "I've just been sitting. As for Dor, she's been drawing pictures. As for Pam — well." He looked at his wife with mingled doubt and affection. "Pam's been into things. That's why we're here."

"Not me," Mrs. North corrected. "I'm here because you two made me, although I told you it was confidential." She looked at Dorian and Jerry, with slight rebellion. "It just proves," she said, "that when you simply have to tell sombody something you shouldn't. Because they won't."

"Won't what, Pam?" Weigand asked, feeling things slipping.

"Won't not tell," Pam explained, as if it were very obvious. "They always think it's their duty or something."

"Well," said Jerry, reasonably, "you can't hold out on Bill. It wouldn't be legal."

Bill Weigand shook his head, and inquired mutely of Dorian, who smiled at him, with a special smile.

"Aren't they?" she agreed. "The point is, Pam heard something. Back-stage somewhere, when she was exploring. And she wasn't going to tell you, because it was eavesdropping. But then she told us, because she was worried after Ellen Grady was killed. It's about Mr. Kirk and Alberta James."

"I don't think it's anything," Pam said. "And anyway I've forgotten and it's all vague. Except that they'd lost something. Or she had. They kept talking about that, and it worried them."

Pam stopped, rather unexpectedly.

"That's all, really," she insisted, after a moment.

"Go on, Pam," Mr. North said, firmly.

Pam still hesitated, but finally she went

262

on. She told Weigand how she had come across, or almost come across, Kirk and Alberta James back-stage.

"I didn't really mean to listen," she said. "Especially when they were so much in love."

"Are they?" Weigand said. "Both of them? Or only Kirk?"

"Both of them," Mrs. North told him, with finality. "She just as much as he. And they're terribly worried, because of the something she lost which has something to do with the murder. But it couldn't be the weapon, because we've already found that. In Dr. Bolton."

"Presumably," Weigand told her, "it was the piece of silk we found in Bolton's hand. It was hers — she admitted that, finally. She says she doesn't have any idea where she lost it or how it got to Bolton. Which may or may not be true. If it isn't true . . ."

He broke off.

"Yes," Mrs. North said. "That's it. If it isn't true, then it's terrible, because they're so sweet, really. And of course it was the excuse."

"I —" Mr. North began. He spread his hands. "I'm not keeping up with this," he said. He looked at Weigand accusingly. "You're not keeping us as well up with things as usual," he said. "You're getting secretive, Bill. What was the excuse, if you know what she means?"

Presumably, Weigand told him, the piece of silk. That, at any rate, was the simplest explanation of its presence in Bolton's hand. Somebody had been showing it to him; asking his opinion about it. It gave a reason for leaning over to him and made easy the use of the ice-pick.

"In the dark?" Mr. North objected.

"Matches," Weigand explained. Or perhaps the murderer had a flashlight which he — or she — either produced, or made as if to produce. But perhaps instead of a flashlight, the murderer merely produced the ice-pick and, taking advantage of Bolton's preoccupation with the silk, used it.

"Why anything?" Mr. North said. "Why not just go up to Bolton and talk about something and, while talking, stab. Why make it complicated?"

Weigand shrugged. Possibly, owing to the relationship between Bolton and the murderer, some more than usually urgent pretext had to be established before he was approached. Possibly the silk, somehow, furnished it. That wasn't important; what was important was who had showed him the silk. Mrs. North nodded to that.

264

"And the natural person," she said, "would be Alberta. And I'm afraid . . ."

She stopped and looked at Weigand.

"Had she?" she said. "What I told you to ask?"

"Yes," Weigand said. "But it could be a coincidence."

Pam looked at him, hopefully, and then shook her head. She waited for him to go on.

"All right," he said. "Here it is, to date. See what you make of it."

Rapidly he sketched what they knew. Start, he said, with the idea that it was done this way: Some time, a little after one o'clock, somebody went from back-stage to the rear of the orchestra by using the area under both. Whoever it was could slip through the door opening off the dresing-room corridor, cross in a few seconds to the door leading into the lounge, come upstairs, kill Bolton, and return the same way. With luck, nobody need ever notice that the murderer had left the back-stage area.

"Why?" Mr. North wanted to know. "Why not somebody already in the orchestra — Kirk, Ahlberg, Smith, Mary Fowler."

"Because, Jerry," Weigand explained, "the murderer pushed Evans. And he pushed Evans because he was using the basement passage. And Evans was in the way, and also about to identify him."

Pam looked for a moment as if she were thinking this over. Then she shook her head.

"Why *both* ways?" she asked. "Why *from* back-stage before the murder? Why not just to back-stage after it? That would account for Evans. And then the murderer could come from back-stage openly, as if she'd never been anywhere else."

Bill Weigand nodded. Then he stopped a nod in midnight.

" 'She' Pam?" he repeated. "Why 'she'?"

"What?" said Pam. "Oh — why — well, it's always 'he' when the sex is indefinite. And I just changed it so — well, it just seemed to be 'she's' turn and —"

She warmed to it.

"There's no reason that I can see," she told them, "why the human race should always be summed up as male. It's just as much female — more, if anything. I've just decided — after this, whenever I don't know which, I'm going to say 'she.' And I think all women ought to for — for self-defense. I think I'll start a — crusade or something. Will you call it 'she,' Dor? From now on, so —"

"All right, Pam," Bill said. He smiled at her.

266

"That was very nice going, Pam," he said. "Very nice. I wouldn't argue with you. We'll call the murderer 'she.' And you're quite right that she needn't have come from the stage area. She may quite as well have been out front and gone back after Bolton was killed. Which takes in more territory."

Pam looked at Bill and, for him alone, shook her head. She shook it, it seemed to Weigand, sadly.

"How much territory?" Jerry North said. "Have you boiled it down any? Or skimmed it off?"

Weigand nodded slowly.

"Some of them don't seem to fit in," he said. "I can't see Paul Oliver in it, for example."

"I can't see Paul Oliver at all," Mrs. North said. "Who is he?"

He was, Weigand told her, the young actor playing the role of Douglas Raimondi.

"The one Ellen Grady quarreled with," he amplified. "The one she said was catching flies."

"Oh," Pam said, "that one. Yes, I guess he's out. If I couldn't even remember him."

Jerry looked at her and shook his head sadly and wanted to know what that had to do with it.

"Particularly," he added, "since he is the

only one who had a quarrel with Miss Grady, and particularly as Miss Grady got killed."

Pam and Dorian and, after a moment, Bill Weigand all shook their heads at him. So, reflectively, did Mullins. Mullins also said, with finality, "Huh-uh." Mr. North looked faintly rebellious.

"Because," Weigand told him, "Ellen Grady was killed because she saw the murderer . . . through the windows."

Everybody stared at him.

"Do you know that, Bill?" Dorian wanted to know.

Bill Weigand said he as good as knew it. Because during the time presumably crucial — the time, that was, immediately after John Hubbard had seen what they assumed to be Dr. Bolton's cigarette as it fell from his dying hand — she was looking out of the windows — and, Weigand thought, saw the murderer come up from the basement. And, later, realized what she had seen and perhaps told the murderer, for reasons of her own.

They still looked baffled.

"I tested it," Weigand said, "with Mullins. Probably you don't remember, but before Hubbard came on stage and saw the cigarette, and for several minutes afterward —

268

up to the time that Alberta James came on stage — the business called for Miss Grady to stand at the windows and look out. She did and apparently did look out; and looking out at that angle, she could see the door leading from the basement into the passage which goes to the stage door. I know she could see it, and whoever came out of it, because I put Mullins there, and looked through the window and saw him. And so, casually looking out the windows, Ellen Grady saw the murderer, and died of it."

He paused a moment.

"And then Grady and Driscoll were on stage," he added. "Driscoll is another of the actors, Pam. And Hubbard was on when he saw the cigarette." He waved away words which seemed to be forming. "Right," he said. "Maybe he was lying; and until we know better — or worse — we're using that as our fixed point."

"How?" Pam wanted to know.

"Something to measure from," Weigand told her. "Take it more or less arbitrarily, because it doesn't violate anything we know to be true — and because, to me, Hubbard seems to have told the truth." Pam started to speak again and he said: "Wait a minute."

"Somewhere," he told her, "we have to start acting as if what we believe to be true, on our best judgment of truth, is true. In solving any problem, simple or complex. It is a basic assumption — if it turns out to be wrong, of course we have to make another and start from that. Right? Well, my best judgment is that Hubbard is telling the truth when he says he saw a cigarette fall — that he is approximately right about the time, and that the cigarette fell when Bolton was killed. So far, nothing definitely contradicts that. The fact that Ellen Grady was looking out of a window at that time, and could have seen Bolton's murderer, and later was killed, presumably by the same person, supports it. Those two facts support each other. This may be coincidence. If we get another fact supporting those two, it probably isn't coincidence. If we get half a dozen facts supporting one another, then we rule coincidence out. Right?"

"I guess so," Pam said. "It *sounds* right, I guess."

Mr. North nodded firmly. He said that it was extremely logical, and he said it with relief.

"Then," Weigand said, "we rule out Driscoll and Hubbard, who were on stage at the time and, of course, Miss Grady herself. And —"

"Everybody who wasn't in the theatre

yet," Pam said, interestedly. "That would be —"

"Ahlberg, Arthur Christopher, the designer, Mary Fowler," Weigand told her. "On the face of it, anyway. Unless there was some dodge."

"Was there?" Pam wanted to know.

"There's always the chance of a dodge," Weigand said.

"Why," Mr. North said, "don't we take them up — opportunity, motive and so on. One at a time. Or doesn't that help?" He looked at Weigand. "Or," he said, "do you by any chance already know, Bill?"

Weigand shook his head and caught Dorian's eyes on him. He looked blank, but Dorian smiled and nodded.

"I think he does," she said, "or thinks he does."

"Well," Weigand said, "I have a theory, yes. But it's vague, and it wouldn't hold in court. And —" he broke off to look at his watch — "we'll take a few minutes to check. Nobody's going to get away. So —"

"We've tentatively cleared Hubbard and Driscoll, and Grady's death clears her — anyway, we'll assume it does."

"Only," Pam said, "somebody could have killed her *because* she killed Bolton."

"Please, Pam," Bill said, running a hand

through his hair. Then he looked at Jerry North, who was doing the same thing. They both laughed.

"Leaving that out," Weigand said, "and since we can't arrest her anyway, we'll write off the three of them. No opportunity, no motive that I've discovered. Now, let's go on with the cast. Take Alberta James. Opportunity, yes. . . . No motive we've discovered."

"Oh —" said Pam, quickly. She stared at Weigand.

"You really think that, Bill?" she said.

He answered with a question: "Don't you, Pam?"

Slowly she nodded.

"I'm afraid I do," she said. "Possible motives, anyway. Based on her loving Humpty Kirk. Maybe — well, maybe Bolton was going to kick Kirk out as director. Maybe — oh, maybe Bolton had some hold over her and wouldn't let her go and she had to because she was in love with Humpty." She looked at the others, none of whom seemed impressed. "All right," she said, quickly and with a peculiar, hurried lightness. "I was just supposing. Probably you're all right."

She felt Bill Weigand watching her, and tried not to show that she felt it. There was a little pause.

"By the way, Mullins," Bill Weigand said, "make notes on this, will you? Miss James — opportunity for both murders; motive unknown. Now, take — (he pulled the program proof from his pocket and looked at it) — Ruthmary Jones."

Everybody looked blank.

"Ruthmary Jones, colored," he said. "Opportunity, yes. Motive, none known."

Nobody contradicted.

"F. Lawrence Tilford," Weigand said. "Opportunity, yes for the first murder, probably for the second. It's too late to check much at The Players," he added, as an aside. "We can tomorrow, if we need to. His alibi may be all right; it may not. Probably it will be hard to prove either way. Motive — I think so."

He told the others of Tilford's previous marriage to Mary Fowler, of the exactitude with which he seemed to remember dates concerning it, which argued, perhaps, that emotions still etched memory deeply; of the end of the marriage when Mary, then beautiful and successful and known as Mary Evans, went to Bolton and of what happened to her afterward.

"And out of that," he asked, "do we get a motive for Tilford? After all these years?"

They thought about it.

273

"It might be," Dorian said. "Things go deep, sometimes. And something — something we don't know about, some little thing — may have released the bitterness in Tilford, and turned it into hate."

Weigand nodded.

"We leave him in," he said. "And that's the cast. Driscoll, Hubbard, Oliver, Ruthmary Jones — probably out; Grady, certainly out. Alberta James and Mr. Tilford still in. Now outside the cast. Mr. Kirk to start with. Opportunity: probably, although there seems to have been no reason for him to use the basement passage. Motive: jealousy of Alberta, who had been playing around with Bolton."

"Had she?" said Mrs. North. "Do you know?" She spoke anxiously.

Weigand said he didn't know. He thought she had, perhaps innocently; perhaps only flirting with an attractive and influential man who happened to be her doctor, which made it easy.

"Or perhaps," Weigand said, "Kirk only thought she had. The motive would be the same. He did think she had, didn't he, Pam?" This last came quickly; before she could catch herself, Pamela North nodded. Weigand smiled faintly.

"So we add him to the list," he said. "Now

the author, Penfield Smith. Motive — I'd think so. I'd enjoy killing any man who did to me what Bolton did to Smith. Opportunity: so far as we know. Leave him in. Ahlberg? Since he came in after the time we think Bolton was killed, no opportunity. If he's telling the truth — on which we'll check tomorrow — on the insurance policy and what not — no motive. But we'll leave him in until we check. Christopher? In too late; no evident motive."

"Maybe," Dorian said, "Bolton criticized his set. And Mr. Christopher got in a pet and stuck him."

Weigand shook his head at her.

"Christopher out," he said. "Mary Fowler. In too late. Motive: obvious — if Bolton had died fourteen years ago. But he died today. And fourteen years is a long time to nurture hate, as we felt in regard to Tilford. Evans . . ." Weigand broke off.

"Which reminds me," he said. "See what Stein found out, Mullins . . . about Evans and Mary Fowler."

"Evans," Mrs. North pointed out, while Mullins went out the door, "was unconscious, or at least in a hospital bed, when Miss Grady was killed."

Weigand was nodding when Mullins came back. Mullins came back hurriedly.

"He was just coming to tell us," he said. "At the hospital, they won't let him talk to Evans. And the Fowler dame — she ain't here! She's just — gone! Ain't that the helluva note?"

XV
WEDNESDAY
1:15 A.M. TO 1:35 A.M.

It seemed to Pamela North, watching them, that the others were disturbed unreasonably by the news that Mullins had brought them. It was natural, of course, that Bill should be disturbed and annoyed that a suspect, because Pam could see that Bill might regard Mary Fowler as a suspect, should have sifted out of a place from which nobody was supposed to sift. It reflected on the efficiency of his men, and hence on his own efficiency. But he could not, Pam thought, really feel as perturbed about it as his voice sounded; as angry with the men of his detail as his words — rather unexpected words from Bill Weigand — sounded. Mrs. North shook her head, wonderingly.

Dorian might be expected, as things were, to feel what Bill felt. But that hardly explained why she should rise quickly when Mullins indignantly spluttered his message and look at Weigand from widened eyes and

277

say, "No, Bill! Don't let it be that way — !" with quite that odd note in her voice. Dorian didn't, Pam realized, understand it even yet, because it was evident that she thought Mary Fowler was in danger — or, at any rate, that somebody was in danger.

"But now nobody is," Pam told herself, watching Mullins and Weigand, with Dorian after them, leave the lighted little office and disappear in the shadows of the mezzanine lounge, where chairs and sofas were dim, deeper darknesses in the gray dark. "Because there's nobody left who could be."

Jerry had started after the others, but now he stopped and Pam realized that she had been speaking aloud.

"Could be what, Pam?" Mr. North said, hurriedly. But he gave her no time to answer. "Come on, Pam," he said. "Something's happening."

"All right, Jerry," Pam said. "I'll come. Only it's happened, really — all of it. Except the very last of it."

Jerry, who should have known better, took promise for performance. He went out and was in the darkness when he called back, still hurriedly. "Come *on,* Pam!"

Pam said, "Yes, dear," and now she did follow him. But she did not hurry, because she did not think that anything important was going to happen.

"It's only that she knows," Pam said. "And doesn't want —" Pam realized that she was talking aloud to herself again, and broke off, because she believed, without much conviction, that she should not talk aloud to herself. At least, she thought, following this new tack because it somehow made her feel that what must inevitably happen, and what she did not want to have happen, was being delayed if she did not think about it — at least, people don't like other people to talk to themselves, and it worries Jerry. Although he ought to know I'm not crazy.

"Or at least," Pam said to herself, "no more than most people. Anyway, I don't think so. And just *because* you talk to yourself doesn't prove anything, although what you *said* to yourself might."

This sounded perfectly clear in Pam North's mind, although, with a little smile to herself, she realized that it mightn't to some people. Except Jerry, of course. To Jerry it would be almost as clear as it was to her, only he would want, probably, to "clean it up." That was what actors wanted to do to lines which were not flatly coherent, Pam had discovered. "Clean them up" and "put another beat in" or take a beat out. Such suggestions from the actors had been enraging Mr. Smith all day and he kept saying: "But that's the way she" (or "he" if it were a he) — *"would* say it! That's *character!"*

Pamela, slowly following Jerry and the others, who now apparently had gone down the stairs from the mezzanine to the main floor, where she could hear raised voices, willfully let her mind wander.

It's all right to talk to yourself if what you say is interesting, Pam thought. And often, although probably I shouldn't think it, I'd rather talk to myself than to other people. Because other people go all around Robin Hood's barn, and cross every "i."

"Dot," Pam said to herself correctingly. "And cross every 't.' And the trouble with that is it's so slow."

She was out in the shadows of the mezzanine, now, walking toward the stairs, and moving slowly because she hoped it would be over when she got there — because surely, now, Bill must know! — and because it was too dark to hurry. It seemed darker, indeed, than it had a moment before and, without putting her mind on it, Pam wondered indifferently why it should become darker.

"Because it's night already," Pam thought. "It must be terribly late, really."

It was too late, Pam thought, the word

leading to the thought, and her mind going back remorselessly, to what she wanted to keep it away from. It is too late for the murderer, she thought.

"And, to be perfectly honest," Pam said to herself, "I'm on her side, although it was a dreadful thing to do. Because it wasn't to make things easier for herself, or not only that. And anyway, if it had to be somebody, it had better have been Dr. Bolton than almost anybody else."

Mrs. North was almost at the head of the mezzanine staircase, now. She could see the shadowy shapes of the balustrades going down, and the light below.

"It was Ellen, really," Pam said to herself. "That was dreadful, and that was the mistake. Because if it hadn't been for that I wouldn't have known. That made it —"

"Don't go any further, Mrs. North," the voice behind her said. "This is as far as you're going."

And at the same moment, Pamela North felt something small and hard against her back — something like —

"Why, it's a gun!" Pam said. She said it with incredulity in her voice, and only then, hearing her voice, realized that she had been hearing it for several moments. She could hear her voice saying, in that strangely fixed instant, "if it hadn't been for that I wouldn't have known."

I'm beginning to do it without realizing it, Pam thought to herself. I must really stop doing that.

And then, with thoughts jumbling through the incredulity which filled her, Pam realized two things. It looked desperately as if she might stop doing a great many things, besides talking to herself. "Like breathing," Pam thought, her mind aghast. "And beating." But what she said was about none of these things.

"So that's why it got darker," she said. "You turned the light out in the office?"

"Of course," the husky voice said. "When I realized."

And now, finally, Pamela North, turning slowly from the staircase which led to safety at the command of a prodding gun which pressed just under her left shoulder-blade, realized fully what was so incredible in this moment, so that even as she turned she could hardly believe in what was happening. *The voice in the shadows behind her was the wrong voice!*

"Don't scream, Mrs. North!" the voice behind commanded, as the speaker sensed — perhaps because some convulsive movement was conveyed through the weapon which pressed hard into Pam North's back — a new tension in the slight figure which obediently turned back into the shadows. "I don't want to do it — here. They'd come too soon."

The voice was reasonable and measured, explaining quite logically. Explaining, Pam thought, why I'm not to be killed here and now, and have it done with. It is strange that everything is so clear. But that's because it is happening to somebody else, really. It can't be happening to me.

"I shan't scream," she said. "I — I almost laughed. Because, you see, you were quite wrong — until a minute ago you were quite wrong. That's because *I* was wrong, you see."

Pam felt that she, in turn, must be completely logical and clear.

"I never suspected you at all," she said. "I wasn't any danger to you. I thought . . ."

Pam let it trail off. What was the good of it? She waited to hear the voice again, but for a moment, as she walked, the gun commanding, through the shadows of the mezzanine, moving across the theatre from the stairs, there was only silence. When she heard the voice again there was a note in it, hard to understand. It was as if the speaker were fighting down doubts.

283

"You knew, Mrs. North," the voice said. "What will it get you to lie? Because, anyway, *you know now, don't you?*"

Mrs. North, in the darkness, slowly nodded her head.

"So," the voice said, "it really doesn't make any difference, does it? You see that, don't you? Even if I was wrong before, *you know now!*" There was a pause.

"Ellen Grady knew," the voice said, "when she saw me. So I had to — I was sorry about that. I'm sorry about this, Mrs. North."

"I told you no one," Lieutenant Weigand said. His voice was angry. "Somebody's going to pound pavements for this!"

Detective Niccoli wilted perceptibly.

"Well?" Weigand said. "Where did you see her last? Where was she going?"

Detective Niccoli, in a small voice for so large a detective, told Weigand.

"And what could I do?" he asked, heartened by the sound of his own voice.

He could, Weigand told him, have gone to the door with her. He could have parked there and waited. If he didn't know there were two stairways leading up from the downstairs lounge, he should have asked somebody who did. Instead of waiting trustingly at the head of one flight while Mary

284

Fowler went up the other.

"If we don't find her, you go back to uniform," Weigand told the diminished detective. "If there's another killing, you go out of the department if it's the last thing I do." He glared at the detective. "Don't stand there gaping," he ordered. "I want her — alive."

Detective Niccoli moved off, uncertainly.

"Kirk!" Weigand shouted. He was walking down an aisle toward the stage, having left Niccoli behind him. *"Kirk!"*

Kirk's voice came from the shadows of the auditorium.

"Yes?" he said. "What's happened?"

Weigand told him, curtly. Miss Fowler, disregarding his order that nobody was to wander off, his warning that safety lay only in numbers, had outwitted her guardian and disappeared. Kirk came up behind Weigand, brushing back the forelock.

"For God's sake," he said. "Is there going to be another? Do you think — ?"

"I want to find Mary Fowler," Weigand told him. "That's all, for now. I want the theatre lighted up. She may still be in it — or —"

"Or her body may," Kirk finished for him. "Is that what you think, Lieutenant? Because I —"

285

"Think later," Weigand said. "Get the lights on. Can you do that? Or find somebody who can?"

Kirk nodded.

"I'll find the electrician," he said. "It'll save time."

Kirk moved rapidly. But he saved very little time. The electrician was absent; shouts did not bring him. In the end, it was Kirk himself who pulled at switches a little gingerly, and pulled finally at enough of them to flood the theatre with light. Then the electrician appeared, from a comfortable smoke in the alley outside. He disapproved of Kirk's action with a frown; inspected the switches and, apparently to his surprise, found them undamaged. He shook his head gloomily and pushed irritably at a switch already closed.

Weigand, as the lights came up, scattered his men.

"Find her," he ordered. "If she's in the theatre, find her!"

The detectives scattered — back-stage, below stage, in the dressing-rooms. One climbed unhappily up ladders to the dim regions of the loft above the stage, and moved gingerly along catwalks. In the basement, where the light was always dim, flashlights stabbed it. In the lounge downstairs, sofas were hauled from against walls; in the orchestra, lights darted among the ranked seats. It was, Humphrey Kirk thought as he watched, as he saw detectives, working up, climb the stairs to the mezzanine, odd how, from the places they looked, one could tell that they expected to find a body.

They don't, Kirk thought, look first in the places a living woman might be. They look behind things, and under things. They are looking for death.

And perhaps, Kirk thought, although he doubted it, they are right. Another death might well be on the cards, unless somebody moved rapidly. And, thinking of Berta, his heart spun over.

I've got to find Berta, he thought. I've got to get her out of this — before — before. He did not finish the thought even to himself, because his mind shrank away from the logic that would finish it. If what he thought true was true, things were bad for Berta — any way you took it, things were bad for her. And if — But then a new thought came to the mind of Humpty Kirk. Murder might turn senseless, hysterical. If it did — if death moved wantonly as, if he were right, it might move — then Berta might be in its path. Nobody was safe when death became wanton.

Kirk whirled and faced the stage, scanning it anxiously for the girl. He did not see her for a moment, and he started to call loudly — for her, for Weigand, for help from somewhere. Then, as he realized his mood and overcame it, she spoke beside him. She had come down the aisle behind; now she stood at his side, her fingers on his arm. Her voice was very low, strained, tight.

"We've got to get out of here, Humpty," she said. "You've got to come with me. I need you. I can't do it alone."

He looked at her steadily for a moment, and then she nodded slowly, with a kind of finality.

"We've got to do it, Humpty," she said. "We've got to do it ourselves. How can we get out?"

Humpty knew the answer to that one, with the detectives scattered through the theatre; with only uniformed men guarding the doors. He guided the girl, holding her arm and talking as if they were conferring over something in the play, until they were near a fire exit — never locked from within. They stood there for a moment, still talking as if idly, while Humpty Kirk pressed down on the bar which held the door's catch. It was

288

down, without sound, and the door gave to his inquiring pressure.

"Now!" Humpty said. She moved instantly to his pressure. No one, Humpty thought in the alley outside, had seen them go. Now if they could make his car without being seen! It was a good thing the alley was so dark, the street on which it gave emptied so by night. The car was against the curb and they walked toward it boldly, once they were in the light.

Mrs. North hesitated when they came to the car, and for a moment the sense of unreality gave way to a coldness which seemed to start around her heart. If I get in the car it will be too late, she thought. We'll leave everybody behind. Then, desperately, she tried to call with her mind. "Jerry!" her mind called. "Jerry! Help me!" The weapon, unobtrusively against her side now, pressed as if the person who held it had heard her cry. The pistol pressed with a kind of warning.

"Get in, Mrs. North," the voice said. "Under the wheel. I want you to drive."

Mrs. North's mind fought to stay, but her body entered the car. That's how it is, Mrs. North thought, it's your body makes you. I always wondered about that, and why people went for "a ride" to be killed when they just made it easier for the murderers, and could refuse and die where they were, but it's their bodies makes them. The body doesn't ever give up. It grabs for minutes. And —

"Start the car, Mrs. North," the voice said. "I'll tell you where to go."

Mrs. North started the car.

"I'm going to take you home with me, Mrs. North," the voice said. It was level and quite reasonable. "Because I don't want them to find you too soon, and I can't waste too much time finding a place where they wouldn't find you. And because they will never expect me to take you there, even if they do suspect."

It amazed, and somehow heartened, Mrs. North to find that she could answer.

"But they will," she said. "And when they do, they'll know. But now they all think as I do — I mean as I did. They don't think it's you."

The voice was silent. Then it said: "Turn right, here." They turned uptown. "Go faster," the voice said. "But don't try to attract attention, or have a traffic man stop us. I want to see if there's anybody behind."

Mrs. North drove north, not too fast. The city was strange and empty at this hour.

People on the sidewalks seemed detached and distant. Only the traffic lights, switching now to red, seemed methodical with the method of daytime. But now, guarding an almost empty street, they seemed to mock themselves. Mrs. North brought the car to a stop, waiting for the light to change. She mustn't drive through it, because there might be a policeman in the shadows somewhere, and he might try to give them a ticket. And then the revolver would smash death into her side.

I must wait quietly for the light, Mrs. North thought, so that after a while I can die where it will be convenient. And then, mercifully, the sense of unreality came back. Something will happen, Mrs. North said. Jerry will come or —

"If you let me go now," Mrs. North said, "and I didn't go back, but hid somewhere until you got away —"

The sound beside her was almost a laugh.

"Why should you do that?" the voice said. "Whatever you promised, what difference would it make? You'd be a fool not to tell them."

It would be foolish to deny that, Mrs. North thought.

"Turn right again," the voice said. Mrs. North swung right, through a crosstown street. There were taxis parking halfway along the block, and one driver leaned into a window of another's cab, talking. If I could run into that cab, Mrs. North thought, and scream, then there wouldn't be time —

"No, Mrs. North," the voice said, uncannily. "Don't try it."

I must have swerved the car a little, Mrs. North thought. I must have given it away. She drove on. The lights were green at Broadway, where glaring lights illuminated emptiness and more idly waiting taxicabs. Mrs. North drove across.

"And now," the voice said, as if it were taking up a casual conversation, "if I did it now, I'd have to use the gun, which would be noisy. The other way was better — the first way. There was no noise at all, only it stuck a little. Then I hit it with my hand and it went in, with a smooth feeling. I got a doctor to show me where, you know. I told him a friend of mine, a writer, wanted to know. It is easy to fool people. It was easy to fool me, once."

And now the cold feeling came back, creeping over the sense of unreality. Because in the cold, conversational note of the voice there was madness, and only madness. But it was a madness calculated and cunning, and with a kind of horrible reason under it.

"After I kill you," the voice said, "I'll hide your body somewhere and nobody will find it for a long time. And then I'll go away." There was a pause. "I think the knife in the kitchen table drawer will be sharp enough."

It might have sounded absurd, had the voice been different. But to Mrs. North, driving across Sixth Avenue with the lights — and with the hard point pressing her side — it was only, and now finally and horrifyingly, real. Because now, in her mind, Mrs. North could see the knife, lying in the kitchen drawer, with a fork beside it and some spoons and — yes, a spatula. There would be a spatula in a kitchen drawer. It was not a long knife, as Mrs. North saw it, but it had a shining blade. You would use it to pare potatoes with, probably.

Mr. Tilford was glad to be away from the theatre. He was tired and it had been a long day, but now it was almost over. Thinking back over it, as he was inclined to when a day was finished, he decided that he had made no mistakes, although some of the things he had done he would have preferred not to do, if he could have chosen freely. However —

"You turn right, here," Mr. Tilford said,

leaning a little forward as he spoke.

It was a long time before they missed Pamela North. One by one the detectives came back, worried and apologetic, from the search for Mary Fowler. And then, while the last was explaining, Weigand suddenly broke in.

"Where's Kirk?" he demanded. "And the girl?"

And that started things again, but after a moment Weigand shrugged his shoulders.

"All right," he said. "It was always on the cards some of them would get away if they wanted to — I banked that they wouldn't. Now — let them all go." He looked at Detective Stein, who was staring at him, surprised.

"It's over here, anyway," he said. "Perhaps they're safer scattered out. Tell them we'll see them — tomorrow. Tell them they can get some sleep."

Stein told them — those of them there were. There were not as many, he thought, running tired eyes over them, as there had been.

"All right," Weigand said to Mullins. "It's a day. Tell the Norths —"

And it was only then, when Mr. North and Dorian joined Weigand and Mullins, that they discovered there was no Mrs. North. They were not worried for a moment, and called to her, their voices reverberating through the empty spaces of the theatre. And then, when she did not come, and when Dorian had looked in places she might be, and the comfortable belief that she was surely somewhere around was whittled away to nothing — then the color left Mr. North's face, and he called once more, his voice high and excited: "Pam! Pam — where are you?!"

Then Bill Weigand took Jerry North's shoulder, and said, "All right, Jerry. We'll find her." But Weigand's voice was tight and anxious, and when he met Dorian's frightened eyes his own went blank for an instant to hide an answer he did not want them to give.

"She'll be all right, Jerry," he said. He wished he believed it.

XVI
WEDNESDAY
1:35 A.M. TO 2:05 A.M.

It had been, Mary Fowler thought, an exhausting day; far more exhausting than she had thought it would be when she awakened that morning. It had not been a physically exhausting day, exactly; bodily she was less tired than often after a day at the theatre, with the inevitable demands on her patience, the endless adjustments which her relationships with the actresses she dressed made necessary, with the necessity always to meet the so often divergent demands of actors, directors, stage designers. But she had had, listening to the questions of the detectives, answering and listening to others answer, always a great many things to keep ordered in her mind. It was a strain, admittedly, and she was tired from it. But so far as she could remember, she had kept everything straight.

There would never be another day like it, she thought, remembering everything. First

296

Carney, and then poor Ellen, and Evans. She had not expected that; the discovery of Evans in the closet downstairs still amazed her. Poor Evans, she thought — that had been so needless. Because, if you could believe the detectives, Evans had not seen enough to make him dangerous to anyone. She hoped he would be all right and smiled inwardly to think that she must still have a hidden fondness for little Evans, although in the old days he had been more annoying than anything else.

Well, she thought, it's been a long day, but it's almost over now. I'll be glad to rest.

"You turn right here," Mary Fowler said, leaning a little forward as she spoke.

If it were only over! Alberta James thought, sitting in the car, with the fingers of her left hand clenched. If it were only over! If only those last dreadful moments were over like all the rest — dead like Carney and poor Ellen. I don't want to do it, she thought desperately. I don't want it to be this way; oh, I never dreamed it would be this way. But it had to be this way. Humpty was right; it was something they had to do, something she, because of everything, had to do. Because if the lieutenant didn't know now, at any moment he might know.

He finds out things, Alberta James thought — sooner or later he finds out things. Please God, she thought, give me time — just a little time, God . . . only long enough . . . make him not know yet, God. She awakened to her surroundings as the car slowed.

"You turn right here," she said.

"She was in the office," Jerry North said, his voice dull, lifeless. "She was behind me and I told her to come. She said, 'Coming, Jerry,' or something like that, and I thought she was right behind me. And then — oh, I thought she was with one of you . . . with you, Dor."

It was, Jerry said in answer to Bill Weigand's gentle questions, just after Mullins had come to tell them that Mary Fowler was missing. They had all gone out of the office, then, and Pam was last. But Jerry was sure that she had started to come, and had been not far behind him when he started down the stairs.

"Did you hear her, Jerry?" Bill asked. Mr. North shook his head slowly.

"I didn't hear her," he said. "I don't think I *heard* her. But I knew she was there — I — I always know when Pam is around, somehow."

He made no apology for the statement,

and to neither of the others did it need either explanation or apology. But in the moment, Bill Weigand's hand went out toward Dorian, standing beside him, and her hand was there to meet it. And neither of them could have told, in words, how the hands were at that precise watch-tick where they were. But Bill knew that he had, without thinking, sought in the realness of physical contact a reassurance that, although Dorian was tangible a foot from him, he had still needed. Their hands touched and reassurance was conveyed, and they did not even in that moment stop thinking of Pam.

"We've got to look," Jerry North said desperately. "We've got to look — everywhere!"

"Yes," Bill said. "We'll look — again, Jerry. Because we've just looked, you know . . . for Miss Fowler. . . . And we'd have found Pam if — if she'd been around anywhere. But we'll look again."

Mullins needed no instructions then. He was calling hoarsely in the theatre, summoning men to repeat the search they had just finished. And he was joining the search when Weigand, who had stood for a moment silently, called him back.

"Never mind, Mullins," he said. "Get the rest at it, that is, but I need you here. Let me have your notebook."

Mullins handed it over. While Weigand flipped the pages, Mullins stared at Jerry North, his face somber.

"Jeez, fella," Mullins said. "We'll get her all right." He shook his head, with an evident effort to make the shake convincing. "Nothing's gonna happen to Mrs. North, fella," he said. "She's — hell, nothing's gonna happen to *her*!"

Mr. North managed, somehow, to smile at Mullins.

"Right, Sergeant," he said. "Sure."

Then Weigand found what he wanted in the notebook, let it snap shut in his hand and looked at Dorian and Jerry and Mullins a moment. Then he spoke, and his voice was curt, final.

"We've got to take a chance," he said. "If I'm right — well, we've got to take a chance. Come on!"

The others followed him, almost running, through the lobby. Then they stopped, because the doors were locked. Mullins looked to the lieutenant for instructions and got them with a nod.

"Right," Weigand said. Mullins raised a heavy foot and brought it down hard where two of the doors met. There was a snap as the tongue of the lock tore loose from its socket. They were running as they crossed the sidewalk to Weigand's Buick, and Weigand, climbing the curb to swing on the far sidewalk, had the car facing east before Mullins was quite seated beside him. Dorian and Jerry, instinctively clutching, were hurled to the rear seat. Then the siren started and the red lights which signal emergency went on in front. They crossed Broadway in a roar.

At Sixth Avenue, the Buick skidded in a right turn and headed downtown. The siren screamed ahead of them through the night.

Weigand went fast, and Mullins looked at him. The Loot was in a hurry, all right. It had been a long time since he had seen the Loot in such a hurry.

"You turn right here," the voice said. They were below Fourth Street on Sixth Avenue — several blocks below. Mrs. North slowed the car — Sixth Avenue was broad and lighted; the little street which opened to the right was narrow and dark. All the broad, bright world I'm leaving, Mrs. North thought — all the beautiful world. I never knew Sixth Avenue was beautiful.

"Turn right," the voice repeated, harder now. The hard point against Mrs. North's side pressed, warningly, calling attention to the alternative. Mrs. North swung the car right. "Stop at the fourth house down," the voice said. "This is it."

Mrs. North stopped the car against the curb. Her hands fell from the wheel. This was the end of it. Blackness closed in around her; she felt herself in a narrowing circle of light with darkness pushing in. I'm fainting, Mrs. North thought — this is it — this is it — !

"Sit up, Mrs. North," the voice said. "You've got to get out here." A hand was on her shoulder, pulling her up. The blackness began to recede, leaving a kind of hopelessness. Dully, automatically, Mrs. North reached for the handle which would unlatch the door. And as she felt it, a new hope came through the dullness.

When she got out, Mrs. North realized, the car would be between her and the other, who would get out of the car on the opposite side. And then she would have a moment — a moment to scream — or to run. There were shadows among buildings, and doorways, and for an instant or two the car itself would be a barricade between her and the revolver. It was a desperate chance, but it was a chance.

"No," the voice said. "Do you think I'm a fool, Mrs. North? Slide this way!"

It would have been too easy; murderers don't let you have it that easy. A kind of numbness crept back as Mrs. North slid, still obedient to the command of the revolver, across the seat to the righthand door. The other backed out, keeping the weapon trained — Mrs. North could see it now, in the faint light from the instrument panel. It was short and dark and ugly.

Mrs. North stood on the sidewalk, with the other close against her, with the hard nose of the revolver boring into her side. She heard the tinkle of keys on a ring; the door they faced swung open into a dark hall. There were no words, now; the cold silence of the weapon was command enough. Mrs. North went ahead into the dark corridor. At the right a stairway rose — rose to somewhere that men and women slept innocently and secure.

The hall ended in another door and again the two stood side by side, with the revolver unwavering against Pam North's side. This other door swung inward in turn and Mrs. North went on at the gun's command. The room was dimly lighted from the end — beyond the far end of the room there was faint light shining in. And then there was a click behind her and she was stepping slowly into a low, spreading room, lighted now by lamps on tables and beside a chair. Mrs. North looked at the room and thought: I am looking at the room I'm going to die in.

But perhaps it was not this room. In the end of the room opposite that into which light had seeped, there was a door and the opening of an inner hall. Somewhere down that hall — or behind that door? — was the kitchen, and the table and in the drawer of the table such a knife as one might use to pare potatoes. The kitchen would be the room — the last room. She would walk through that door — or down that hall? — and still walk because she was alive and the revolver commanded. And then . . . But now the revolver did not command, and Mrs. North, with the other behind her, stood for a moment. Mrs. North stared down the room.

She was staring, almost unseeingly, at French doors which opened onto a garden. They were closed, but beyond them, now that the light fell from the room outward, she could see the green of bushes. It's late for green, Mrs. North thought; they must be evergreen. She looked on green things for the last time, she thought, and waited — only it was as if some one else were waiting in her place — for the command to go toward the little knife.

"Turn around, Mrs. North!" the voice behind her, and a little to the right, said suddenly, harshly. Mrs. North started to turn and, as her eyes swung faster, saw the hand go up with the revolver, held by the barrel now, in it. And now the revolver was coming down, like a club, aimed at the right temple which Mrs. North's half-turn had brought within reach. And then, miraculously, the numbness vanished. There was no sound, except of her breath coming in a little sob, as Mrs. North twisted and threw herself away from the clubbing hand. The weapon grazed her shoulder.

But now Mrs. North was running — with no plan and no hope, but running. She was running down the room toward the French doors and the garden beyond them; toward French doors that would be locked against her, and hold her while . . . Mrs. North did not check her flight when she came to the doors. Desperately she threw herself at them. They slapped at her and then it was a miracle. The doors parted, opening outward. Mrs. North, half falling, half on her feet, was in the garden. She was running with twigs of evergreen tearing harshly at her clothes. And running still with no hope beyond the next sobbingly drawn breath, because now it would be a bullet coming after her, mocking her speed with its own.

But instead of the revolver, Mrs. North, as she herself ran desperately toward the shadowy world outside, heard heavy running steps behind her. And hope surged up, brightly, blindingly. It wasn't to be the revolver then — because of the noise. The noise couldn't be chanced. And then, darting through a narrow aperture between bushes, Mrs. North saw why. The doors which had opened so miraculously as she rushed against them opened onto a small, hedged garden. But beyond there was a much larger garden, walled by four-story buildings, filled with trees and benches and paved paths. Running to her right along one of the paths, with the sound of running feet behind her, Mrs. North saw what it was.

Property owners with houses fronting on four streets had thrown the back yards together, creating a long, rectangular garden space, which had been developed as a unit. The buildings enclosed a small, green park, around the sides of which ground floor tenants had tiny, individual gardens, hedged off, like booths.

It was another miracle. Running from death in the low, spreading room, Pam North had run the only way there was to run. She had run toward what would have been, a thousand times to one, a boarded cul-de-sac — a tight, paved yard, made safe for privacy by twelve-foot fences. But this was that other time. She had run into a park. She could keep on running.

Her breath was coming fast, now. She couldn't run around and round the rectangle. She must find a way out. Perhaps there's a passage somewhere, she thought — perhaps —

The garden was dimly lighted. There was faint moonlight, from half a moon; there were four lights on tall poles, masked to throw light only inward, away from the houses. But behind squat evergreens, among ornamental shrubs, the shadows were black. And as she saw that, Pam North threw herself sideways from the path, and into the darkest of the nearby shadows. Once there, and seeing more shadow ahead, she started desperately to crawl on hands and knees.

Thank God my dress is dark, Pam thought, burrowing like some frightened animal into shadow. Off to her right she heard the pursuing steps. But now they slowed to a walk.

It will be easy to tell about where I am, Pam thought. But about isn't good enough — maybe it isn't good enough. She crept more slowly, now, trying to make no noise, trying to find the darkest place.

The police Buick shot down Sixth Avenue, the siren screaming at the almost empty street. It passed Fourteenth Street and, to Mr. North, fled through scenes suddenly, almost unearthly poignant with memories — there was Charles, where he and Pam ate so often; there the stores and little shops they had been going in and out of for almost a dozen years. Just there, once, he had walked by Pam, who was walking the other way, without seeing her, and was startled and embarrassed and very glad when he heard "Hey, you!" in a familiar voice and turned to find her smiling at him — laughing, almost, and very amused. It was right there, he thought — there by the subway station below Eighth Street. Looking out of the car, racing south, he could almost feel that he saw her standing there.

And then, a little way below Fourth Street, Weigand whirled the Buick toward the curb, braking hard and speaking tersely back over his shoulder.

"Kent Street," he said, demandingly. "Twenty-two Kent Street. It's here somewhere — hereabouts. Where, Jerry?"

It was Jerry North's part of town — Kent Street. Kent Street. It was a name he knew;

people he knew had lived on Kent Street. But in the maze of little streets which cross preposterously and dwindle and go out, and then in some other place as unexpectedly resume, and lie below Fourteenth Street and west of Sixth Avenue few residents are always certain. And now, desperately searching his mind, Jerry was not sure.

"Kent Street, Jerry!" Weigand repeated, as if by effort of will he could snap directions out of his friend. "Is it farther down? Have we passed it? Mullins?"

"Another block," Mullins said. "Or — maybe we've passed it. I don't know, Loot."

Mullins fumbled with the door.

"Ask somebody," he said. "I'll find —"

He looked at the dark storefronts, at the deserted sidewalks.

"It's on down, I think," Jerry said. "Beyond Charlton — oh, damn it to hell!"

It was futile, preposterous; something they might laugh about some day. But now, with a desperate urgency driving them, they were lost on the outskirts of a maze — a maze in which they might wander for an hour, and in which speed would only defeat them.

There was nothing for it, Weigand told them.

"We'll have to find somebody who knows."

He leaned from the car and stared up the

avenue. Then, as Mullins slammed the door shut again, Weigand whirled the car in Sixth Avenue and raced it back toward Eighth Street. It was agonizing to turn their backs. But it was better than groping through criss-crossing streets. And on the Jefferson Market courthouse tower the illuminated clock mocked at them.

Weigand swooped down on a taxicab standing at the curb just beyond Eighth Street. It was empty. But Mullins, knowing the ways of cab drivers, was out of the car before it stopped and running heavily up Eighth Street, running toward the lighted windows of an all-night lunch room. The hack driver was there, his elbows on the counter, a mug of yellow-brown coffee in his two hands. He looked up as Mullins banged the door behind him.

"Yeh," the hack driver said. "Sure — I —"

He was astonished to be jerked from his seat, to find himself running with Mullins back toward the corner. He was relieved to see red lights on the front of the throbbing Buick. So it was the cops! Well, they didn't have anything on him — or nothing he could think of, off hand. Kent Street, now — let's see. That was the little one off to the right, a couple or three blocks down. That was —

He was astonished to find himself in the police car, swooping dizzily in a u-turn. Kent Street — sure, he knew it. Jeez, he thought, I'd better know it.

The steps had slowed to a walk now. Pamela North crouched motionless in the deepest shadows. The steps were on the walk a dozen feet away — no, now they had stopped! Pam twisted her head to look back — now there was a moving shadow. It was coming toward her, slowly.

The tumult of the hunted filled Pam North's mind, and the frantic indecision. If she stayed — if, crouched thus, she were overtaken — she would have no chance. And search could not miss her for long — at most, hiding here, she had a breathing spell, but the end was certain.

It was a nightmare after that, for how long Pam North never knew — a strange, grotesque nightmare of dimly lighted walks and feet running on them; of shadows sought for safety and abandoned; of constant, despairing search for the way out that must be somewhere — somewhere! Once she crouched beside a stone bench, with the stiff twigs of a hedge tearing at her clothes, scratching harshly through thin silk. Then she was running straight along one of the walks, trying to scream, with the other running after her.

She could not understand why she could not scream, except that it is hard to run and scream, and it was not for a long time that she realized she had been wise. Because only silence gave her respite. That was tacit in the nightmare. If she screamed it was all over — if she screamed the gun screamed, because then there would be no longer a reason for silence. And so, bewildered, caught but not quite caught in a walled, rectangular prison, Pam North ran and hid, and ran again. But the other was tireless.

And then during one of the times she crouched in the shadows, and listened for the stalking steps, and was about to run again because she could not hear them, which meant the pursuing feet were falling quietly on grass — and that meant the feet were coming nearer — she saw the light!

There had been, in all the nightmare, only one light showing in any of the apartments which made a wall around the garden. And that was an evil light, shining from the room out of which Pam had fled, with her pursuer running heavily after her. And now, also in a ground level apartment, there was another light. Pam's breath caught in her throat as she saw there were two lights. Some one had come home late, or got up in the night, or heard the running feet — somebody had turned on another light, and it was a light which marked a haven. If she could reach it —

Slowly, as much in the shadow as possible, Pam stood up. There were two lights, and one meant safety and one meant death and — and then the numbness caught again at Pam's throat.

"I don't know which is which," Pam said to herself. "I don't know which is which!"

Each light was near the end of a long row of houses; one, as Pam stood in the shadows near the center of the garden, and faced one narrow end of the rectangle, at a distance up the long side and on her left; the other almost as far behind her and on her right.

"I don't know," Pam said. "Oh — I don't *know*!"

It's tossing a coin, Pam thought — it's fifty-fifty. She tried to find some tree or shrub or bench by which she could orientate herself. But the neat, matching regularity of the design defeated her. And then Pam, crouched again in the shadow, mentally tossed the coin. And as she tossed it she was running again, now with a destination — the lighted doorway up the side of the rectangle on her left.

There was no point in concealment now — she was right or she was wrong. And if she was right, a bullet might stop her before she reached the door. Pam fled along the path, with the moonlight on her, and her flesh winced away from the bullet that was coming — and did not come.

She had her hand on the knob before she knew, finally, what that meant. She knew then that she had lost the toss before the voice behind her spoke again with satisfaction and hard irony in the tone.

"So you came back, Mrs. North," the voice said. "That was — considerate of you."

That ended it, Pam thought. Her hand was at her throat as, inside the room, she turned.

Her voice was ragged, panting, but she stood as straight as she could.

"All right," Pam said. "Do it! Damn you — do it!"

The revolver came up again and fell again. And this time, although at the last moment Pam twisted away from it, there was an explosion against her head, and blackness came up around her. It was curious that, in the blackness, a bell was ringing.

It's funny they should bury me standing up, Pam thought, almost before she thought:

"Why, you do live after you die!" Because beyond question she was standing up. Although, she thought, maybe things don't feel the same after you're dead, and I'm really not standing up at all. And with mothballs, she thought disconnectedly, because the coffin certainly smelled of mothballs. It was very strange to smell mothballs after you were dead. Inappropriate, Pam thought, and moved her right hand. The fingers touched cloth rough to the feel. I thought always satin linings, Pam thought, and then it came over her that perhaps she was not dead at all.

Because really, she thought, I seem to be standing up in a very narrow closet with an old coat with mothballs in it. And my head hurts.

Then, without the formality of realizing she was alive, and had only been banged on the head and put in storage for reasons not yet clear, Pam began to listen to the voices. They were clear, and must be in the room just beyond the thin door of the closet. Pam knew all the voices. Two of them were women's voices.

"I had to see that you got the chance," one of the voices said. "Because — oh, why did you? Why?"

The other woman's voice sounded tired

and dead.

"You know why," it said. "You ought to know why — because of what he was going to do. What he did to me."

The other voice said "Oh!" It was the sound of someone hurt.

"And so," the other voice said, "you can't give me away, can you? Nobody could do that, when somebody else killed for them. You can't do that, you know."

"No," the man's voice said, sharply, coldly. "But I can. You forget that. You can't lay it on her. Because I'm here."

There was a strange, new note in the tired voice — an ironic note. It was the note Pam had heard, and thought the last thing she would ever hear.

"Are you, Humpty?" the voice said. "I wouldn't be too sure that —"

And then the voices stopped, except that one of them screamed, and there was a sound of movement and a chair fell before the revolver sounded. It roared in the room, and through the thin door of the closet in which Pamela North was locked. It roared twice, and then there was a sudden silence. In the silence Pam heard Humpty's voice, low and desperate.

"Berta!" Humpty was saying. "Berta! Darling — *why did you* — ?"

Then Pamela North began to pound on the door to be let out. Either she was making an unexpected amount of noise, she thought, or somebody else was pounding somewhere. And then she heard running feet and familiar voices and finally she managed to scream.

"Jerry!" she screamed. *"Jerry! Get me out of here!"*

Then the door opened and she fell out into Jerry's arms and stared down at Humpty Kirk kneeling beside Berta James, and talking incoherently to her. To Pam he seemed to be saying over and over: "Why did you, Berta? Why did you?"

It was a dreadful mistake, Pam saw, and wriggled in Jerry's arms until she could see Bill Weigand, who was kneeling beside some one else a few feet away.

"He's wrong, Bill," Pam said, anxiously. "We were all wrong! She didn't, Bill — it wasn't Berta at all. We were all wrong!"

Bill looked around at her, and then stood up and looked down for a moment at the woman beside whom he had been kneeling. Then he looked at Pam, and he spoke gently.

"Of course not, Pam," he said. "Only — I never thought it was. The dress threw you off, Pam — but that fitted just as well. Mary

Fowler was a dressmaker, Pam, in a way —
didn't you see that?"

Pam looked down at Mary Fowler lying
on the floor, and nodded.

"But not soon enough," Pam said. "I
thought all along — but what does Mr. Kirk
mean, then?"

Kirk, still kneeling beside Berta James,
and holding one of her hands in his, looked
up.

"She — when Mary tried to shoot me,"
he said. "Berta jumped in between us."

He said it quietly, and looked at the girl
whose long hair made a patch of color on
the floor as if he would never stop looking
at her. Then Pam heard Mullins through
the open door which led into another room
talking curtly into a telephone.

"Ambulance," Weigand explained. He
knelt beside Berta James, who managed to
smile at him. "Let me look," he said. Gently,
he tore the shattered silk which had covered
one of the girl's shoulders. There was blood
under it, but Berta was trying to smile. Weigand smiled back at her.

"Nothing a doctor can't fix," he promised
her. She closed her eyes, but the smile
loitered around her lips. Across her, Humphrey Kirk looked at Weigand, his eyes
demanding an answer. Weigand nodded at

him, and smiled faintly.

"Right," he said. "Nothing a doctor can't fix."

Kirk looked beyond Weigand, and Weigand answered another question which was not spoken.

"That's over too," he said. "She aimed well, that time. She'll never have to explain it."

"Somehow," Pam North said, using the fingers of her free hand to feel the bandage across her temple, "somebody always gets banged up. I suppose it's always a mistake to bump into a murderer."

They were back in the Norths' apartment — Bill and Dorian, Pam and Jerry — and properly equipped with tall glasses. Mullins was taking statements from Alberta James at the hospital, or would be as soon as the doctors permitted, and from Humpty Kirk, who couldn't somehow seem really to believe, in spite of everybody's assurance, that the first bullet from Mary Fowler's revolver had only grazed Berta's shoulder. Jerry sat beside Pam and held on to her, and Dorian sat on the floor beside Bill's chair, apparently where she could stop him if he tried to get away. But he seemed to have no intention of getting away.

"And by the way," Bill Weigand said, "why

320

did you, Pam? Bump into the murderer, I mean? What started her after you?"

Pam North hesitated and then looked at Jerry and said she was sorry.

"You always tell me not to," she said, "but I never remember. Talking out loud, Jerry." She told them about it. "In a way," she added, thoughtfully, "the joke was really on her, because up to then I thought the James girl." She looked at Bill Weigand. "Because of the dress," she said. "Didn't you?"

Weigand shook his head.

"Only that it was a woman," he said. "I couldn't see a man doing it. But Mary Fowler was always just as possible."

"Why did she?" Pam said. "It was an awful giveaway, even if it didn't give away the right one. Because of course Ellen hadn't hung it up, because she didn't hang things up. And no man would have. Did she just go in and find Ellen's dress on the floor and hang it up neatly and then go on and kill Ellen?"

Pam sounded puzzled. Weigand said he doubted it.

"I suppose it was after the murder," he said, "and in a sense automatic. She was looking around the room, probably, to see if she had left anything which would be suspicious, and instinctively picked up the dress

321

and hung it up. Because she, in her profession, must have had a special feeling for clothes — and because she may have been excited and not known what she was doing, or almost not known. As an orderly person may straighten things on a table, without realizing what he is doing — while carrying on a conversation. But she came out of it before she hung up the negligee, I suppose."

Mrs. North shook her head at that.

"Negligees are different," she explained. "They're *supposed* to sprawl. She wouldn't feel the same."

Weigand said he wouldn't know about that, but probably Mrs. North was right.

"And," he said, "it did point to Miss James, particularly since she had worked in a shop. But it wouldn't have been the habit with her it was with her aunt, because she was so much younger — the habit wouldn't have been fixed. And it already looked like being Mary Fowler, in any case."

Mr. North's voice sounded as if he had been waiting a long time.

"Why?" he said. "And how? Because she was supposed not to be in the theatre."

Weigand would, he said, start with the how, because that was simplest. He told them to remember how close the door which led to the basement was to the stage door. Mr. North and Dorian nodded, and after a moment Mrs. North nodded too.

That, Weigand told them, made it simple. Miss Fowler came to the theatre a little late, when it was probable that all the others would already have returned from lunch and joined Kirk in the conference he habitually held on stage before each rehearsal. She went directly to the stage door and went in, not trying to hide herself. And then, if nobody was looking, she simply opened the door to the basement and went down the stairs. That was the first step. He saw Mrs. North shaking her head at him, and smiled.

"I know," he said. "Suppose somebody had been there. Well, in that case, she would simply have put the whole thing off, because one day was as good as another. She might have done it tomorrow — today, that is. She might have done it day before yesterday. She could do it any time the conditions were right — and that's the reason she was habitually late to afternoon rehearsals. She'd been, we can suppose, waiting her chance for a couple of weeks."

About that they couldn't, of course, tell, Weigand reminded them. She may, equally, have tried to kill Dr. Bolton only that day, and been lucky at the first cast. Because, he said, nobody had seen her. She had got unobserved from the stage door through the basement door. Then she went under the auditorium, up through the lounge, and to the rear of the orchestra seats. From there she could spot Bolton, and again if he were talking with somebody or too far down front, she could let him live another day. Because, so far, she had taken no risks, done nothing which she couldn't easily explain; nothing which really needed explanation.

"Remember," Weigand said, "I'm guessing at some of this, some details may be wrong and we may never know. She made things hard to prove — the simplicity and the flexibility of her method helped her." He paused, for a moment. "In a sense," he said, "her method had the advantages, to the perpetrator, of a purely impromptu murder. It was a little, as far as timing went, as if she had merely waited until she happened to meet Bolton on a dark street and hit him with a club and walked away. Except that, obviously, she could be pretty sure in the theatre that the chance would come reasonably soon. But that kind of murder is always hard to break."

In any case, Bolton was sitting alone, and in the shadows. Then Mary Fowler committed herself. Any excuse to speak to him would do; apparently she pretended she wanted his opinion on the color of the material Berta James wanted in her dress. She showed the material to Bolton and, probably while he was holding it to get the light from the stage on it, stabbed him. She had to chance that he wouldn't have time to cry out. And he didn't have. He merely slumped.

"Then," Weigand continued, "she went back to the lounge, planning to go back through the basement. And there she ran into Evans — who had been her husband, incidentally, although it turns out not to be important. Now, of course, she was committed and had to try and smash whatever got in her way. She smashed Evans by pushing him down the stairs — in her hurry, and in the semi-darkness, she probably took him for dead. She got him out of sight, dragging him to the closet. Then she went on through the basement and up on the other side, and out through the stage door. This time she had to trust to luck that she wasn't seen — and probably she thought her luck held. She didn't, I think, know that Ellen Grady saw her and wondered about it — not then she didn't."

Out in the stage-door alley, Weigand told them, Mary Fowler probably breathed a sigh of relief. She went on up the alley to the front of the theatre, and then to the front entrance. Once she was there, it didn't matter whether she got in that way or not — *so long as somebody saw her trying to get in.* She could always make certain that she was noticed, even if it meant creating a minor disturbance. Fortunately for her, this wasn't necessary; all she needed to do was to impress her presence on the memory of the mounted traffic man. She did that. Then, pretending to be annoyed, she went around to the stage door again, went in openly and sat down in one of the orchestra chairs.

"And after that," Weigand pointed out, "she made every effort to be in somebody's company, or in plain sight, until the body was found. In that way, no matter when we finally decided Bolton had been killed, her time was accounted for — she either wasn't in the theatre at all, or she was with somebody. That we were able to guess pretty accurately as to the time of the murder, and it appeared to be before she was around at all, helped her. But it wasn't necessary."

And then, Weigand said, Ellen Grady threw her bombshell — *Ellen had seen her!* Why Ellen told her instead of the police they would never know. Perhaps she merely gave Mary a chance to explain before she went to the police; perhaps there had been some other, less innocent, plan in the back of her head. "Possibly," Weigand suggested, "she may have thought she saw a chance to raise money to put into the show; perhaps she thought the money she would put up for Ahlberg would come from Mary Fowler. We'll never know — but we know what she did get."

Weigand paused, because Pam was shaking her head doubtfully.

"I don't think Ellen knew the importance of what she'd seen," Pam said. "Like me, I mean — not knowing what she knew. Because if she were going to blackmail a murderer she wouldn't be taking a bath. Silly. I think that Mary Fowler just *thought* Ellen knew, the way she thought *I* knew. And Mary arranged to come around, maybe pretending it was something about costumes. And then she just killed Ellen, without asking her anything. I think that's much more likely."

Weigand nodded and after a moment said perhaps it was. There was another pause.

"Anyway, that's what Mary Fowler did, or about what she did," Weigand went on. "I don't think, incidentally, that she had had any intention of running when we missed her, just before she heard Pam talking to herself. She didn't think she had any reason to run. I think she had just come up here to the mezzanine to rest in a comfortable chair. We were all pretty tired — and she, being older, was probably more tired than the rest of us. She probably thought it was all finished business. And then she heard Pam telling herself she knew who had done it."

"Well," Mr. North said, "wasn't she safe?"

Weigand shook his head.

"I was pretty sure," he said. "I was looking for proof. Because she couldn't have seen Evans in the lobby, as she said she did. And I was looking for one lie, even an apparently senseless one."

"Why couldn't she, Bill?" Dorian asked, looking up at him. "I know why really, of course. Because she had already pushed him. But you didn't know *when* she pushed him, did you?"

Weigand shook his head at her. It was simpler than that, he said. Once you assumed, as he had found no reason not to assume, that Max Ahlberg was telling the truth. It was, he said, a matter of times.

"Ahlberg went through the lobby immediately before Miss Fowler started to knock," he pointed out. "And then Evans wasn't there. To get there, Evans would have had to come through from the theatre, and he would have had to pass Ahlberg to get where she said he was at the time we know she was there. It's a long lobby, remember — and Evans according to his own version, had poked around the only time he was in the lobby. That was, of course, before he was pushed. To get down to the front of the lobby, starting after Ahlberg was out of the way, he would have had to run. I couldn't see him running."

"But then why — ?" Mrs. North began.

"Because," Weigand explained before she finished, "she wanted us to believe that he was alive just before she came in. Because she was afraid she had killed him. If he was up and around when she knocked at the lobby doors, and she was in sight afterward — as she was — she couldn't have been the one who knocked him out. It jiggled things up, which was what she wanted."

Weigand stopped and took a long drink, and stared into his glass. Mr. North relinquished Pam long enough, but not without a warning glance, to fill it up again.

"And so," Weigand said, "that seems to be all."

Mr. North, who had just sat down again, put his own glass firmly on the coffee table in front of him.

"That," he said, "is not all. That's only

How. Where's the Why?"

Weigand looked faintly surprised, and as he took in the expressions on the faces of Pam and Dorian he looked a little more surprised. He said that he had thought, of course, that they had got that.

"Specifically," he said, "to keep Bolton from performing a sinus operation of Berta. Because that was what happened to Mary herself — or, perhaps it would be better to say, what she thought had happened . . . to make her eyes protrude."

Everybody stared at him. He nodded.

"That," he said, "was one of the first things I guessed. That Bolton had performed a sinus operation on Mary some time when they were living together and that the operation made her eyes hideous. Or, as I say, she thought that it did. I don't know whether it did or not; probably nobody does, or ever will. Probably Bolton himself didn't, although I suppose he denied it. But any doctor will tell you that such operations are ticklish things, that they sometimes have unexpected results. I asked Dr. Francis about it and he — well, he's a doctor and he was talking about another doctor, so he hedged. But finally he said, yes, he had known of a case or two when the eyes had behaved oddly after an operation, although nobody knew whether the operation had actually caused their odd behavior. And then he said: 'But if it were me, I wouldn't let anybody poke around in there. I'd rather go to Florida.' Coming from Francis, that was plenty.

"In any case, Mary Fowler was convinced that the operation Bolton performed had changed her eyes, and ended her career — had changed her from a beautiful woman into a woman people tried not to look at. She had told Berta that, and Berta told Kirk when they were driving down to — well, to tell Mary that they knew, and give her a chance to run for it before they told the police. Remember, Berta had lived most of her life with her aunt and — oh, well, it was natural."

Weigand paused, staring at nothing. Then he spoke again.

"We'll never reconstruct all of it," he said slowly. "What people did, or about what they did — yes, perhaps. But about what they felt — then we're always guessing. All we can say is, 'Perhaps it was something like this.' Perhaps, with Mary Fowler, after she had lost everything else, her whole life came to center on Alberta, so that Alberta was everything and she felt toward her all that desperate protectiveness that a mother may feel toward a child. If we assume that it explains a good deal. Say she felt that way and then, whether she was right or not — and probably she was partly right and partly wrong — she saw the girl going along precisely the tragic road she had gone along herself. She saw the girl turning emotionally to Bolton, as she had turned; caught as she had been by the charm he must have had for women, and by their knowledge of what he could do for them — and in the end by his ruthlessness. She saw it all starting over, and saw for Alberta all the betrayal and anguish she had lived through. And she saw the end the same, down to the same physical disfigurement, with all that it meant to any woman and, most of all, to any actress."

Weigand hesitated a moment.

"I don't suppose she was right in all this," he said. "About the disfigurement, for example, she was almost certainly wrong. That, even if the operation Bolton performed caused it, was an ugly accident, and accidents don't often repeat themselves in the same pattern. And there's no certainty that even the other thing — the emotional involvement with Bolton — would have happened again. But I think that Mary Fowler believed utterly that it would *all* happen again. I think that — for her — it was *already* happening again. And so . . ."

There was a pause.

"And," Mrs. North said, "I think she was a little mad."

Weigand's face was thoughtful. Finally he said that, in a certain sense, all murderers are a little mad — all murderers who premeditate, at any rate.

"So perhaps Mary Fowler was," he said. His voice sounded tired. "She had, when you come to think of it, almost enough to make her so — she had been lovely and famous, and lost it all; Bolton had pretended to love her, and had injured her and then because she wasn't beautiful any longer, had no more use for her. And staying in the theatre, as she had, seeing him going on, untouched — unhurt — well, I suppose bitterness lasted longer than it might have otherwise. What she felt about him made it — well, say easy — to decide that the only way to protect Alberta was to kill Bolton."

He paused and drank slowly.

"That's the madness of murder, Pam," he said. "The madness of not seeing any other way out."

He put down his glass and for a while nobody said anything. But now the silence, for the first time in many hours, was relaxed

333

and peaceful. Looking at Pamela North, Bill thought she might go to sleep at any moment, and gently he pulled at Dorian's hair, so convenient to his hand.

"Sleepy, Dor?" he asked.

She looked up at him, and smiled gently and shook her head. Bill looked down at her a moment.

"We might take a ride somewhere," he said. "Upstate somewhere, perhaps?" His voice was questioning.

Dorian continued to look up at him, smiling faintly. When she spoke her voice was low.

"I think that would be very nice," she said, a little like a child.

Bill and Dorian looked across at the Norths, and Mrs. North was really asleep. Her head had fallen on Jerry's shoulder, and her hand was tight in his. Bill and Dorian stood up quietly, while Jerry North watched them, and then, with their lips only they made the movements of "Goodnight."

Jerry looked down at Pam for a moment and then at the others with lifted eyebrows, which did for a shrug. Dorian and Bill Weigand went out very quietly.

In the car, Bill's fingers automatically switched on the radio with the ignition, and a voice began raspingly: "Car Number —"

But before the voice went any further, Dorian reached across and twisted the radio knob until it clicked. The voice, baffled, disappeared.

"Right," Bill Weigand said, in a very low, soft voice. Then they drove away.

ABOUT THE AUTHORS

Frances and Richard Lockridge were two of the most popular names in mystery during the forties and fifties. Inspired by Richard's series of non-mystery stories for *The New Yorker* about a publisher and his wife, Mr. and Mrs. North, the Lockridge husband-and-wife duo collaborated successfully to write twenty-six mystery novels about the couple, which, in turn, became the subject of a Broadway play, a movie (starring Gracie Allen), and series for both radio and television. After Frances's death in 1963, Richard discontinued the Mr. and Mrs. North series but continued to write until his own death in 1982.

Otto Penzler, the creator of American Mystery Classics, is also the founder of the Mysterious Press (1975), a literary crime imprint now associated with Grove/Atlantic; MysteriousPress.com (2011), an electronic-book publishing company; and New York City's Mysterious Bookshop (1979). He has won a Raven, the Ellery Queen Award, two Edgars (for the *Encyclopedia of Mystery and Detection,* 1977, and *The Lineup,* 2010), and lifetime achievement awards from NoirCon and *The Strand Magazine.* He has edited more than 70 anthologies and written extensively about mystery fiction.